The Offering

Lisa Frieden

This book is a work of fiction. Names, characters, places, and incidents are products of the author's imagination or are used fictitiously and are not to be construed as real. Any resemblance to actual events, locales, organizations, or persons, living or dead, is entirely coincidental.

Copyright © 2015 Frieden Press, www.friedenpress.com

Cover Art by Nicole Spence, www.covershotcreations.com

ISBN: 978-0-9969409-2-4

All rights reserved. No part of this book may be used or reproduced in any manner whatsoever without written permission from the publisher/author, except in the case of brief quotations in reviews.

DEDICATION

For you, my lovely Reader, and for *Buffy* and *Alias* fans
everywhere

CHAPTER 1

How the hell am I going to get out of this? Carla peered into the black pit that yawned beneath her.

The ropes dug relentlessly into her forearms and ankles. Rage, not fear, made her grit her teeth against the musty gag. Helplessness was not her forte. She preferred being in control, but tonight she hung helpless, bound spread-eagle to a large steel wheel suspended by chains from the ceiling above what appeared to be a bottomless pit.

What the hell is a pit doing in a farmhouse, anyway? She glanced around at the weirdly decorated room.

Black velvet drapes shrouded the windows of the abandoned farmhouse. Strange occult symbols in red and white covered the exposed walls and the floor around the pit. Flaming torches were mounted on several walls.

Peering through the curtain of her long black hair, Carla studied her captors. She squinted green eyes to see better in the darkness. Nine men in dark, blood red cloaks stood in a circle around the pit, their hands and faces hidden in shadow.

The leader chanted in a strange language she didn't immediately recognize. He stood on a dais beside the pit, his arms upraised. In his left hand, he held a black dagger shaped like a long, twisting snake. His face was hidden behind a black mask. Carla caught a glint of his eyes as he chanted.

Were they silver gray? Was he the same man who'd stopped the others from beating her unconscious before they brought her into the farmhouse?

"In the name of Abaddon, Sonneillon, and Lucifer, we make to you, our Lord, this Offering." The chanted words penetrated her consciousness, their meaning abruptly becoming clear.

The leader was speaking Latin. Her knowledge of the language was rudimentary, but the man's repetition of the words helped. His voice grew louder. The other men joined in. They began circling the pit in slow, measured steps. The leader turned to light black candles on the altar beside him.

What a bunch of crazies, Carla thought. Her neck ached from twisting it to watch them. She unkinked it for a moment and glanced down into the gaping pit.

Something was down there, something evil, deep in that black hole. She couldn't see it, but she felt it was there. Somehow, with a strange, inexplicable intuition, she knew it was rising, approaching the surface, and that when it appeared, it would claim her for its own.

Don't be ridiculous, she told herself. *Monsters don't exist.*

She peered into the fathomless depth, trying to discern what lurked in the darkness. If only she could see it, she'd feel better. She'd have a visual cue, something real, something tangible to attach to what she felt lurking in that black void. But there was only darkness. She shuddered, fear slithering through her, despite her attempts at control.

"In the name of Abaddon, Sonneillon, and Lucifer, we make to you, our Lord, this Offering." The chanting grew louder. The men circled faster.

Carla forced herself to focus on loosening the ropes and ignore the hair standing up on the back of her neck.

Sweat beaded her forehead as she struggled furiously with the ropes. The silver-eyed man had tied her to the wheel, but he hadn't done a very thorough job. He'd focused on tightening the rope binding her right hand, but she was left handed. Except for the loose ropes around her ankles, her feet had a decent range of motion because he'd removed her shoes and socks before tying her to the wheel.

She managed to wriggle her left hand and her feet free. Using all her fingers and toes, she gripped the edges of the ropes dangling in loops from the wheel's spokes. Tensing her muscles to the breaking point, she was just able to remain spread eagled under the steel wheel. Her right hand was still tightly bound.

The leader's chant suddenly altered. The other men fell silent. They stopped circling the pit and turned toward the leader.

Carla twisted her neck sideways to see him. The black candles smoked heavily beside him on the altar. The room grew darker. She couldn't understand the more esoteric Latin words, but the man's meaning was clear.

"We now submit to you, oh Lord, the Offering. We beseech you to accept our gift and all the magical connections allied with her. We humbly beg that you shed a measure of your power upon us, upon the Illuminati. Our power is your power. May the light within reflect the light outside."

It was obvious the ritual was coming to some kind of horrible climax. It didn't take a rocket scientist to know it wouldn't be good for her health. She took a long, calming breath and forced herself not to think about what would happen if she fell into the pit.

Then, she sprang into action.

Kicking her feet from the ropes, she pulled herself up and grabbed a spoke of the steel wheel with her left hand. Using her bound hand for leverage, she twisted her body hard to the side and swung herself around in a wide arc.

Like a bowling ball striking pins, she easily over three men.

"Stop her!" The leader shouted in plain English. He leapt from the dais and gestured wildly at her with the dagger.

"Abaddon!" One of the men yelled to the leader, but he was too late.

Carla kicked the dagger from Abaddon and caught it with her free hand. She immediately began sawing through the rope binding her right hand.

One man tried to reach her by leaning over the pit. She clenched her powerful abs to lift her legs upward. Scissoring them, she pulled the man into the pit. His cries echoed as he disappeared.

She hooked one leg over a spoke in the wheel to keep from falling and, with a final slice to the rope, cut her right hand free. She dropped the dagger and the ropes into the void. Grabbing the spokes of the wheel above, she swung her body like a pendulum and sprang nimbly clear of the pit, landing beside the altar.

She squared off against her remaining opponents. Seven were left, though only six remained standing. In the melee, she'd lost track of Abaddon. They all looked alike in their crimson cloaks. The six advanced on her.

Two men attacked from the left. Exercising a quick chop and kick, she knocked one to the ground and catapulted the other into the pit. His disintegrating scream was drowned out by the angry shouts of the four men as they rushed her.

She raised her fists, ready for battle. The white robe her captors had dressed her in gave her some protection. Many of the men's blows landed on empty material. At the same time, their hoods and masks restricted their visibility. She used this handicap to her advantage, blindsiding two men with disabling kicks to the head, then delivering a paralyzing blow to another man's neck when he was momentarily blinded by his hood.

The fight had taken all of two minutes, and she wasn't

even breathing hard. Six men had fallen into the pit. Four more lay scattered around the room.

Only one man remained standing, her final adversary. Their eyes met. His were a remarkable shade of silver gray. She noted his height. He was the silver eyed man who'd tied her to the steel wheel, she was sure of it.

"Bet you wish you'd tied those ropes tighter, huh?" She grinned at the man, confident she could take down a single opponent.

The man said nothing, his expression unreadable behind the black mask.

One of the men lying on the floor groaned. She had to escape before the others regained consciousness. The silver eyed man stood between her and the one door out of the room. She had to take him down, now.

Striking with her right foot, she delivered a lightening quick windmill kick to his left ear.

What the hell? Her green eyes widened in amazement. Her foot didn't connect. He'd deftly moved aside and used his right arm to block the kick.

She resumed fighting stance, her knees slightly bent, her fists raised at chest level. She knew she was fast, but he'd moved faster.

Out of the corner of her eye, she noticed one of the men sitting up, pushing his hood back into place over his bald head. There wasn't time to trade punches with this guy, especially since she might have underestimated his fighting ability.

It had been years since she'd had to use what she'd learned from legendary Henry Lee and his Green Dragon school of martial arts, but there was no time to lose. Time to engage Green Dragon fighting technique and make her getaway.

She shrugged off the white robe. Dressed only in her black cat suit, her body was now free to move at will.

She led her next assault with one of her favorite Green Dragon moves. Lunging forward and feigning a blow with her right fist, she quickly shifted her weight onto the ball of her right foot so that she could swing a surprise kick at the man's belly with her left foot.

"What the—?" she exclaimed.

The man anticipated the feint. He moved aside from the swinging impact of her leg and grabbed it above the ankle, twisting her leg around behind her and yanking her back against him.

"You've got lethal legs, lady. I don't want this free to do any more damage." The man spoke low, his voice husky in her ear. He slid his grip up her leg toward her knee and secured her in the precarious position against him. With his free hand, he pinioned her arms against her chest.

"Let go of me, or you'll be sorry," Carla growled.

"Really?" The man sounded amused. His steely strength encompassed her. One large hand imprisoned both of hers against her chest and the other forced her bent leg back and around him.

Adrenaline swept through her, her heart beating wildly. Fighting to stay calm, she took a deep breath. She inhaled the distinctive scent of expensive cologne mixed with man sweat. Shocked, she realized he smelled good.

His heart beat hard and fast through his robe where his chest pressed against her shoulder blades. All along her backside she felt his heated strength. His breath teased her neck and a shiver rippled down her body. Sensual awareness flashed through her.

Her contorted knee twinged. The pain snapped her out of her momentary daze. She twisted sinuously in his arms, using the flexibility from her yoga training, and faced him.

Oh Carla, that wasn't such a good idea, she silently chided herself.

The man now stood intimately between her thighs. She couldn't stop a small gasp of surprise. Was that a gun under his robe?

Her eyes darted to his masked, hooded face. His distinctive, silver-blue eyes stared intently down at her. A hint of a smile touched his lips. Well shaped, masculine lips. Kissable lips. Carla frowned.

It's just a gun, right? She looked up at him, thinking fast.

But maybe it wasn't. Maybe she could use it to her advantage. She'd never been much good at playing the femme fatale—cross-dressing was more her style—but it was worth a try.

She sighed and relaxed into him, letting her breasts press fully against his broad chest. She dropped her head back so she could glance up at him through her eyelashes. She parted her lips. Trying her best to look seductive, she teased the edge of her lips with the tip of her tongue.

I hope this works, she thought, but was dismayed to discover how good it felt being held by him.

It'd been over a year since her last attempt at a romantic date. Maybe that was it, maybe she was sex starved. But he was the enemy, for goodness sake!

She forced herself to ignore her body's response to the man and surreptitiously gauged his reaction. Her seduction seemed to be working. His eyes had darkened almost black and he was staring at her mouth.

His focus had blurred, and with his concentration divided, he'd loosened his grip on her hands, which still rested between them, directly below his chin. She squeezed her hands together hard. Refusing to think of the consequences, she rammed her clamped hands hard to the side and upward with a mighty thrust toward his nose.

The man's head snapped backward from the impact. He dropped her knee and both his hands shot up to cup his face.

She was free!

No time to worry about the damage she'd inflicted. It was time to get the hell out of there. She sprinted past the pit to the door. Luckily, it was unlocked. She flung it open and felt the cool night air waft in from outside. She cast one last glance over her shoulder.

The image would haunt her for days. Through the dim light, she saw her final adversary braced against the wall on the far side of the room. His head was in his hands. He was probably trying to stanch the blood flow from his injured nose. Several other men lay motionless on the floor. The man who'd been slowly regaining his bearings stood up and looked down into the pit. He staggered backwards, uttering a horrible scream that caused Carla's heart to leap violently in her chest. She followed his terrified stare.

Something was rising from the pit, something huge and black. Formless, shapeless, it was like a cloud of smoke, but utterly opaque. Devoid of any color, it was the blackest black she'd ever seen. It was as if the thing, whatever it was, sucked into it every last shred of light.

The logical part of her mind whispered that there must be a reasonable explanation for what she was seeing, but she couldn't hear it over the irrational terror seizing her. The fear obliterated any thought but to flee. She tore from the room and into the night.

Her long legs flew down the road away from the farmhouse, her black hair streaming behind her, her bare feet skimming the ground. She didn't feel the cold or the small stones pebbling the road. Her mind was still on that darkness. Men she could fight and defeat. That nameless black thing was something else entirely. She kept running at full speed, despite the moonless night.

As she put distance between herself and the farmhouse, she slowed her stride and became aware of the Virginia countryside around her, illuminated dimly by the starry night. Bare-leafed elms and maples formed skeletal silhouettes on one side of the road. On the other spread a grassy field lying fallow. Except for the sound of her breathing and the dull thud of her running feet, the night was utterly silent.

Whatever that black thing was, it certainly wasn't a monster, she told herself. There had to be a more reasonable, a more logical explanation.

When the man screamed, she must have fallen prey to the power of suggestion. The occult context of the setting and the mysterious, ritualistic behavior of the cloaked men must have led her to irrationally assign a supernatural aspect to what she saw, right?

By the time she saw the van in the distance, she'd persuaded herself that her imagination had played tricks on her. By the time she pulled open the passenger-side door, she'd convinced herself that she hadn't actually seen anything at all. She swung herself up into the passenger seat.

"Thank God you're here, Carla!"

Her partner and friend Tate McCormick fired up the engine and gunned the gas. Until they were a safe distance from the farm, she left the headlights off. The van surged forward into the darkness.

"I was getting worried." Tate glanced quickly in Carla's direction, pushing her short mop of curly blond hair from her eyes. "You told me three hours tops, but it's been four and half. You've never been off by more than fifteen minutes on an assignment with me, not in five years. What the hell happened? You know sunrise is just an hour away. I was going to give you five more minutes before I called in help."

Carla snapped her seat buckle in and held on as Tate maneuvered the van around a tight corner.

"Thank goodness you didn't," she said once they were headed safely straight again on the dark road.

If any of her colleagues had seen her tied helplessly to that wheel, she never would've been able to live down the embarrassment. After all, she prided herself as a hotshot operative. She wanted to keep her reputation intact. It would never do for them to see her helpless, no matter how momentarily.

"I appreciate your concern, Tate, but I had the

situation under control."

She had no intention of telling her friend the specifics. If Tate knew how dangerous things had gotten, she'd have certainly pulled in outside help, which would have meant alerting their superiors to what was going on.

No way was Carla going to let that happen. It wasn't CIA business. From the very beginning, there had been something disturbingly personal about the way she'd been targeted. Whoever the Illuminati were, they were after her. She had every intention of solving this mystery on her own.

"I hadn't expected there to be eleven members of the Illuminati," she said. "Based on our intelligence, I thought the magic number was five, so things got a little hairy there toward the end of the ritual. But you know me, always ready for a challenge." She grinned at her friend, teeth flashing white in the dark.

Tate frowned, focusing on the new intelligence. "That's what they call themselves, 'the Illuminati'? It doesn't sound very original. I swear I've heard that name before."

"Yeah, I was thinking the same thing. I'm pretty sure this group is assigning some kind of special significance to the word, something about 'the light within reflecting the light outside.'"

"Weird. What's that supposed to mean?"

"I have no clue. The man leading the ceremony used those words. At least, I think he did. He spoke in Latin."

"Latin? Really?"

"It surprised me, too. It was a good thing he chanted the same words over and over again, because at first I had no idea what he was saying. Then I recognized 'lux' and a couple of the verbs he used. Remarkable, considering we never learned to speak it in high school."

"Father Roberts had enough trouble getting us to read it!"

They laughed, remembering how their high school

Latin teacher had looked old enough to have been born in ancient Rome.

Carla leaned back into the van's bucket seat. With the adrenaline wearing off, she felt the little aches and pains of her ordeal. The edge of her left foot throbbed, injured probably when she kicked the one man in the neck before he fell into the pit. The barefoot run across a half-mile of rock-studded dirt hadn't helped, either.

"The guy leading the ritual called himself Abaddon," she said, absently rubbing a raw spot on her wrist.

"You think he was the same guy who sent you those threatening emails?"

"I don't know. He was obviously in charge of the ritual. The other men were following his lead."

She didn't mention the silver eyed man, or how he'd helped her. Why had he? What did he stand to gain? She remembered how he'd held her against him. That was something else she was glad none of her colleagues had seen.

But thinking of him brought back other memories, like when he'd whispered in that low sexy voice, his breath warm against her neck, his lips grazing her ear as he spoke, his body pressed intimately against her.

She shifted in the bucket seat, trying to squelch the memory and focus on the next plan of action, but it was hard to think. The adrenaline had worn off, leaving her exhausted.

"You keep mentioning a ritual. What exactly were they doing? What part were you supposed to play?"

They approached a small town off the main highway. Tate turned on the van's headlights and slowed the vehicle to the lawful speed limit.

Carla looked out the window at the darkened streets, stalling for time and quickly thinking through how she could answer her friend about the Offering without revealing her particular role in the peculiar ritual.

Just past the town, they cruised onto the highway and

picked up speed, heading for D.C. The predawn glow lightened sky. Tate clicked on the van's cruise control and turned to Carla.

"So, are you going to tell me, or what?"

"You know what I think about the occult, Tate. It's all just smoke and mirrors, a bunch of tricks used to fool people gullible enough to believe in magic. The Illuminati is nothing different. Believe me, I should know. They had all the usual paraphernalia to put on a good show, the fancy red robes, masks, black candles, ritual daggers."

"Don't you think you're being too simplistic?"

"What do you mean?"

"Your mom believed in magic, and your sister does, too."

"A lot of good it did my mom, locked up in a loony bin, and you know it's just a matter of time before Gwen lands herself in hot water." Carla tried but failed to keep the bitterness from her voice.

Thinking about her mother and her sister's obsession with witchcraft bummed her out, especially now that Gwen was being initiated into a coven. It didn't help that Circe was the same coven her mother had led as High Priestess, before going nuts.

Couldn't they see how dangerous believing in magic was? It was much better to be realistic. Empirical evidence, logic, and reason, these were real things, testable, deducible. They didn't rely on nebulous belief but on physical fact.

"The Illuminati is just another bunch of crazies." She yawned.

"But what about Abaddon? If he were just some harmless guy, how was he able to break through the Agency's email security to get to you? And you still haven't explained how they captured you and what role you were supposed to play in the ritual. Were you the offering he mentioned in those emails?"

Damn, Tate had a good memory! Sometimes she

wished her friend weren't quite so smart, but then Tate wouldn't have been a top agent, and she wouldn't have wanted her as backup.

"Yeah, I was supposed to be their offering." She shook her head dismissively. "But that's not what's important. What matters is that we now have names and connections to work with, which will make our job tracing them much easier."

"But why are they after you?"

Carla couldn't answer that. For a moment, the vision of that rising black formlessness crept back into her mind. A shiver ran down her spine. She ignored it.

The best defense is a strong offense, she reminded herself.

"Why is irrelevant," she said. "What matters is that I will track them down and find them and stop them from whatever it is they plan to do."

Tate pulled the van into a parking spot across the street from Carla's apartment. The sun was just peaking over the eastern horizon. Carla climbed down from the van and moved to the driver side. Tate rolled down the window. Carla leaned against the door and said goodbye to her friend.

"Overall, I think it was a successful mission." She tried to put a positive spin on the night's adventure.

"Except that it took you an hour and a half longer than it should have." Tate frowned, concern darkening her light blue eyes.

"Yeah, yeah, I know, but I got out. And now we know there are eleven members in the organization and that they call themselves the Illuminati. We also now know for sure that Abaddon is connected with them and that he's their leader. The one thing I would've liked would've been to get a good look at their faces, but they wore masks and cloaks. In fact, it was very 'cloak and dagger.'" She laughed, trying to lighten Tate's expression. She pulled her keys from the secret pocket of her cat suit.

"I think we've both had enough cloak and dagger for

one night," Tate replied. "Let's get some sleep. I'll see you at HQ later."

"Sure thing, Tate. Good night." Carla bounded up the steps to her apartment, ready for a few hours of shut-eye.

CHAPTER 2

"You've got to be joking!" Carla exclaimed five hours later, when she saw the directive in her email inbox. She shoved her chair back from the desk and angrily charged down the hall to Tate's office. Not bothering to knock, she threw open the door, ready to hurl accusations at her friend.

"I told you I could handle it, Tate. There was no need to tell Frank!" she blurted out, before she saw the other person in the room. He stood by the window across from Tate's desk. Frank Carson, their boss, turned away from the view of the river.

"Oh, excuse me, Mr. Carson. I didn't see you, sir." She pulled the door closed behind her as she entered the room.

Dressed in the ubiquitous charcoal-gray suit of an Agency manager, Frank Carson's eyes were sharp and piercing behind thick, black-framed glasses. He left the window and strode toward Carla. His deeply lined face creased even further as he frowned at her.

"It's no longer just about you, DeVille," he said. "McCormick has given me the salient details of your little adventure last night. She tells me that you made contact with the Illuminati. I hear you've uncovered some useful information." He gave a brief nod, acknowledging her achievement. "But there are things you don't know about the group, things that could dangerously jeopardize not just our national security but potentially global peace."

Carla and Tate focused on Carson. He was not someone prone to making melodramatic pronouncements. If he said something was dangerous, he meant it.

"Care to elaborate?" Tate asked tentatively, knowing that most likely their boss would not.

"The most I can tell you at this point is that the Illuminati has links to international terrorism."

"Really? From what I've seen, the group seems more like some kind of lunatic occult sect," Carla interjected.

"That's obsessed with Carla," Tate added.

"We're not sure how you factor in." Carson rubbed his jaw and looked at Carla, scowling. "We've learned that the leader, Abaddon, has an interest in nuclear bombs. I'm sure you both realize that religious fanaticism and nuclear weaponry make for a dangerous mix."

They nodded and he continued.

"You'll work tag-team on this. McCormick, you'll work as liaison here at headquarters. DeVille, we'll use Abaddon's fixation on you to our advantage. You will go undercover to Santa Barbara and follow up on a lead we've gotten. Use your family ties there as a front to pursue the investigation. McCormick, I'll expect regular updates on your progress." He moved to the door and opened it.

"Be careful," he said to Carla. The door clicked behind him.

"I'm jealous," Tate smiled at Carla. "It looks like you get a trip home, while I'm stuck here at the office. I hope you get the chance to check in with the gang. Did you know Kristi's expecting again?"

Carla wasn't going to let Tate distract her from what Tate had done.

"Tate, I don't appreciate you going directly to Frank without consulting me." She didn't bother reminding Tate that it was thanks to her own hard work that they now had as much information about the Illuminati as they did.

"You know you're like a sister to me and I don't want you to get hurt." Tate came around the desk and faced her. "After last night, it seemed to me like things were getting out of hand. I know you think you're a hotshot, Carla. Hell, you *are* a hotshot." Tate ran a hand through her short blond hair. "You know as well as I do, though, that there are times you can't do it all yourself."

"I guess." Carla relented, feeling a little sheepish. "What can I say? You've always been the brainiest of our bunch." She sat on the edge of Tate's desk and changed the subject. "So, Kristi's pregnant again?"

"Yep. Things are crazy busy for her, what with her two boys and running her business. You know she started her own detective agency, Eye Spy Private Eye? Anyway, it looks like this time around she's having twins. She's due in a couple months but the doctor told her to stay off her feet as much as possible. Brian's doing the best he can to help, but he's so busy at his law firm."

While Tate prattled on about the details of her sister's pregnancy and other bits of McCormick family gossip, Carla thought about going home again.

During the troubled years growing up in Santa Barbara, she and her sister Gwen had spent as much time as possible with the three McCormick sisters, Kristi, Izzy and Tate. The five girls had called themselves the Cota Club, since they all lived on Cota Street, but unlike Carla and Gwen, the McCormick girls had come from a happy, loving family. Kristi was the oldest of the gang and the only one married.

Carla made it a policy to never ask Tate about Santa Barbara. She tried not to think about the past. It was so much easier and relevant to her present day life that they only discuss CIA business and their lives in D.C. Now it looked like things were going to change. Going home again was going to force her to face the past and all those demons she had tried to escape. She didn't relish the idea.

"You know, you could help Kristi with Eye Spy. It would be the perfect cover," Tate said.

"That's a great idea. Would you mind feeding Larry for me while I'm gone?"

"Okay, but I think I should just adopt him and be done with it. At the rate you're never home, that poor fish is going to die of starvation." Tate laughed.

"Hey, can I help it if I've got such a busy schedule solving mysteries and kicking ass?" Carla smiled cheekily. "I'll make sure to say 'hi' to the gang for you." She pivoted on her stilettos and left the room.

An hour later, she kicked off her shoes as she entered her small apartment in downtown D.C. and tossed the mail on the kitchen counter. She squished her toes through the thick carpet and breathed a sigh of relief. She was glad that no more mysterious symbols had appeared on her door.

Two days over the past week someone had drawn symbols in blood on her apartment door. The CIA lab had determined it was goat blood. Tate had sketched the images and sent them to one of her connections in the CIA's cryptography department to see if he could decipher the meaning of the symbols. They were still waiting for his results, but they were similar to those she'd seen on the walls of the farmhouse. She was sure someone from the Illuminati had drawn them, though she still had no idea what they were supposed to mean.

She pulled an unopened bottle of wine from the refrigerator and a wineglass from the cupboard and set them on the counter. Cracking the bottle, she took a sip of the chilled white and gave Larry a few fish food pellets. Wine was a luxury she didn't usually allow herself, but she needed fortitude. She had to call her sister and make arrangements to fly back to Santa Barbara.

For years her work had consumed her, keeping the past at bay, most of the time. Though she checked in with

Gwen every few months between assignments, she'd made it a point to avoid going home unless absolutely necessary. Like now.

She took another gulp of wine and sank down onto the cushy carpet of her living room floor. After five years, she still hadn't gotten around to buying furniture for the place, so much of her time was spent undercover.

She stared up at the blank white ceiling, picturing the occult store her family had run on Cota Street since her childhood. They had lived in the rooms above the shop even after their mom had been taken away. She picked up her cell.

"Magic Shop, may I help you?" Gwen answered on the first ring.

"Hey Sis, it's me, Carla."

"Carla? Oh my Goddess! How good to hear from you! You must be psychic because I was planning to call you. How are you doing?"

"Great. Hey, I'm coming to Santa Barbara."

"Really? When? How long can you stay?"

"Easy there, girl. I didn't know you missed me so much!" Carla laughed.

"You have no idea, Carly. Things are getting pretty scary. You're being here would really help."

Gwen hadn't used the pet name since high school, since those days long ago when it seemed Carla was forever rescuing her impetuous little sister from trouble. And like those days long ago, she reverted to her typical big-sister behavior. Taking charge of the situation, she came to her sister's defense.

"What the hell's going on?" she demanded.

"Someone's using bad magic against Circe. You remember the coven I'm being initiated into?"

"Of course, Gwen, how could I forget?" She drained the glass of wine. "You of all people know how dangerous believing in that stuff is. Didn't you learn anything from what happened to mom?" She impatiently combed her fingers through her long black hair, pulling at it as she spoke. "There is no such thing as magic. It's all just the power of suggestion created by crafty human minds to manipulate others. If I uncover who's been targeting Circe, I'm sure I'll eliminate whatever mystery there is. "

"But—"

"No buts." She cut Gwen off, the wine making her more impatient than ever with her sister's fascination with the occult. "Listen, I'm flying out today and you can tell me everything that's going on then. My plan is to help Kristi run Eye Spy while she finishes up her pregnancy." She got to her feet and headed toward the bedroom. "Would it be OK if I stay at the Magic Shop?"

"Of course," Gwen said. "But I think you should know that Mark Lyons just started working for Kristi."

"Mark Lyons?" Carla cursed under her breath. "You're kidding, right?"

Mark had been her high school nemesis, her passion and her poison. She hadn't seen him since that fateful night ten years ago, when her dreams had come crashing down. Most days, she managed not to think of him. Nights he still haunted her.

"No, I'm not," Gwen continued. "But it's been so long, you're over him, right?"

"Sure," she laughed, and lied. "I've got to pack. I'll see you tonight, OK?"

She hung up with her sister. Yanking her carry-on from the closet, she threw it on the bed.

Damn! It was bad enough having to go home and face the demons of her family's past. Going back and facing Mark would be ten times worse.

The wine had lowered her inhibitions and dulled her mind. Distracted, she didn't notice she was forgetting to pack as neatly as she usually did. She tossed clothes haphazardly into the carry-on, wondering. Why on earth would one of Santa Barbara's elite, a man from one of the town's richest families lower himself to work for Kristi's agency?

#

Carla's cell rang the instant she stepped off the plane in Los Angeles. She stepped aside from the people deplaning and moved to a more private location near the airport windows.

"Good, I'm glad you picked up right away," Tate said, her voice businesslike. "Before you head to Santa Barbara, we've got a lead on a company in LA. Our sources indicate it might be fronting money to the Illuminati."

"That was fast! What's the name? You got an address? If I can get access to their files, I bet I can trace their revenue stream, and I bet if I can do that we'll be a whole lot closer to cracking the Illuminati." Carla's green eyes glinted with the challenge.

"Easy, girl," Tate laughed. "Before you rush over there with guns blazing, let me give you a word of warning. I checked with Dan Moreno at the LA office and got their specs on the layout of the building. After what happened to you at that farmhouse in Virginia, I want as much information as possible before you waltz in there."

"I know you're worried, Tate, but come on, I'm sure it's just some office building with maybe a few hired security goons hanging around. I can handle that scenario in my sleep."

"I'm sure you can," Tate agreed, but then a note of concern crept into her voice. "Listen, I've got a bad feeling about this Illuminati thing. I know you prefer logic and reason over such things as gut instinct, but I don't know... Something tells me we should approach this case carefully." Tate paused for a moment, thinking, and then continued. "The company is called LSA Enterprises. I'm emailing you what Dan gave me as we speak."

"Good," Carla said. "Do we have a building layout?"

"It's a ten story office building on a major boulevard and commercial strip. Besides a retail optometry shop and a bank on the first floor, the rest of it belongs to LSA

Enterprises, which appears to be some kind of financial holding company. Your target is the executive suites on the top floor. Our intelligence indicates that there are surveillance cameras on each floor and there's the standard security guard at the reception desk on the ground floor."

"OK."

"That's the limit of our intelligence on the interior of the building, but I bet you won't have much trouble getting in," Tate said, knowing how good her friend was with locks. "Now, for the escape plan: the rear exit to the building consists of a loading dock, and the garbage for the complex is stored at the back of the building in dumpsters. The building sits on a busy street, but behind the commercial strip is a maze of alleys. Any of them would make a good exit route."

"It all sounds pretty cut and dried to me," Carla said, excited. Undercover work was such a rush. Her heart beat faster in anticipation.

#

"*City of Light, City of Night...*" The Doors' tune filled Carla's head as she cruised Santa Monica Boulevard in the generic sedan she'd rented at LAX, admiring the polished surfaces, smooth faces and perfect bodies of LA. The traffic was just as bad as she remembered, back when she'd spent her first year after CIA training working with Dan Moreno at the LA office. The city had continued to grow by leaps and bounds. More steel and glass high rises stabbed the sky.

By the time she completed a drive-by of LSA Enterprises, Santa Monica Boulevard was packed with late afternoon traffic. She smiled. The more people, the more distractions. Her getaway should be a cinch. She parked five blocks to the west on a side street.

Grabbing her black duffel bag from the back seat, she pulled out a worn, baggy blue jumpsuit. Rather than remove her black jeans and tank top, she pulled the jumpsuit up over the clothing. It was a bit of a squeeze behind the steering wheel, but not too difficult. She donned a baseball cap with gray-haired fringe. Pulling off the adhesive backing, she pushed a thick gray moustache against her upper lip. A fake goatee completed the facial hair. She added a little charcoal to smudge her visible skin and slid on a pair of thick-framed glasses to complete her sex change.

She found her lock pick kit at the bottom of the duffel bag next to her Colt Defender. With luck, there would be no need to use her favorite lightweight handgun, but just in case, she stuck it along with the lock pick in the deep jumpsuit pocket.

Adjusting her gait and hunching her shoulders slightly, she looked every bit like an old male janitor as she shuffled toward the office building. The building was nestled between high-rise apartments on the one side and a hotel on the other. At the last moment, she ducked into the alley between the hotel and the office building. Dan's information was accurate. A string of dumpsters sat alongside a loading dock next to the rear entrance.

A surveillance camera was focused on the loading dock, so she pulled the cap a little lower on her head as she walked up the ramp. A woman came out of the building, undoubtedly headed home after work. Carla caught the door as the woman passed, and entered the building.

She'd have preferred taking the stairs, but instead, she walked into the service elevator, acting just as if she were a janitor going on duty. Her adrenaline started to pump. At any moment, someone might enter the elevator. Beeping at each floor, the elevator seemed to take forever as it brought her closer to her quarry. Her heart beat faster.

She let out a deep breath when she finally made it to the top floor without incident. Tate had told her there were utility closets on every floor, handily located near the service elevator and stairwell. She headed straight for the utility closet, noting that the cameras on this floor were trained solely on the entrance of the executive suite rather than the rest of the hallway. She tried the door to the utility closet, but it was locked.

Pretending to fumble with her keys, she used her lock pick to quickly open it. Inside was a room containing mops, brooms and other assorted cleaning supplies, plus a large pushcart with a full-sized garbage can placed on it. She shoved one of the dusting rags into a back pocket of her jumpsuit and wheeled the pushcart into the hall. Tate had told her the cleaning staff typically began its shift at 7 p.m. It was now 6 p.m. If everything worked as planned, she'd be in and out before they arrived.

She wheeled the cart to the door of the executive suite. Using the cart to block the camera's view of the door handle, she quickly went to work on the lock with her picks. This lock was not as simple as the utility room lock, but it was not a multi-point high security locking system, either.

They must not think a financial holding company would be a target, she thought to herself as she wiggled the lock with the pick.

Just then, the door to the suite burst open, causing her to drop the pick. The door slammed against the cleaning cart and a dark-haired man in a navy business suit cursed at her.

"Watch yourself, old man!" he barked.

In his hurry to leave, the businessman rushed past Carla without so much as a backward glance and headed to the elevator.

She propped the door open with the rag and knelt to retrieve her lock pick, the cleaning cart still shielding her from the security camera. Surreptitiously, she watched the man as he jabbed repeatedly at the elevator button. He looked vaguely familiar, but she couldn't place him. He wore a charcoal gray Armani suit and carried an alligator leather briefcase in one hand. With the other, he impatiently checked the time on his flashy Rolex.

I wonder what's got that bee in his bonnet, she thought. He could be late for a date, or eager to get home. Just because her intentions were nefarious didn't mean his were. But why did he look familiar? She'd have to run his description by Tate.

When she stood up again, she ducked her head away from the camera to maximize the camouflage provided by the janitor cap. She pushed the cart through the door.

The executive suite of LSA Enterprises looked much like any other well-to-do financial company. Expensive mahogany and cherry wood office furniture, sedate blue carpeting, tasteful prints and office decor filled the spacious rooms.

Carla eyed the walls and ceiling for surveillance equipment, but none caught her eye. Listening for a moment, she heard no one, so she boldly pushed the cleaning cart down the hall to the corner office. The office door stood open. Her eyes immediately went to the jumble of files littering the desk and side table. The computer docking station was empty.

Damn. It looked like someone had gotten there before her. Had it been that man she saw? He certainly seemed eager to get out of there.

After a few moments of rifling through the useless files on the desk, she headed for the filing cabinet against the wall. It was locked, but she could see where someone had taken a letter opener and tried to pry the lock open. The silver letter opener lay on the thick blue carpet.

A smile tilted her lips. The rank amateur hadn't been able to open it. She timed herself. In under a minute, she had the cabinet open and started speedily sifting through files.

At the very back of the bottom drawer, she hit pay dirt, a folder labeled "Ilumine Corp."

She checked her watch. Ten minutes to get out of there before the real cleaning staff came on shift. Clearing a space on the mahogany desk, she spread out the contents of the first file and quickly scanned through the spreadsheets, correspondence, and invoices. She noticed something interesting. Thousands, perhaps millions, of dollars had flowed through LSA Enterprises to the Illumine Corporation, which was listed as a Swiss company.

The only name she recognized in the file was Charles Harrington. She pulled her Agency-issued camera from her coveralls. In order to better photograph the documents, she took off the thick-rimmed glasses of her disguise and set them on the desk. She quickly began snapping pictures of the pages that looked most important.

What are they doing with all that money? And what does Charles Harrington have to do with it, she wondered.

Harrington was a Santa Barbara politician who'd long been active in local politics. He'd recently made the jump onto the national scene and been elected to Congress.

Abruptly, she realized the man she'd just seen was Charles Harrington. Had he been the one trying to get into these files?

She grabbed the next file. It was much more cryptic. She couldn't decipher the first several pages, which were written in a foreign language. She knew enough German to recognize it as the language used in the documents, but she didn't know enough to translate. Judging by the formulas sprinkled liberally across the page, she guessed the document contained some kind of scientific information. She snapped more photos, finished that file, and opened the next. To her surprise, it contained several pages of text she recognized as Latin.

What on earth? Forgetting to photograph the page as she studied it, she tried to remember the meager amount of Latin she'd learned in high school.

"What the hell are you doing?" A deep male voice demanded, startling her.

"Disculpa," she muttered. Relying on her training as a CIA operative, she smoothly slipped the camera back into her pocket and quickly replaced the fake glasses onto her nose before turning to the man.

But all her training wasn't enough to prepare her for who she saw standing there. He was the last man she'd ever expect to run into in LA, much less in the executive suite of her assigned target.

Mark Lyons, her high school nemesis!

Ten years had passed since she'd last seen him, ten years to grow up and mature. Sure, he was older, filled out, more manly. He'd grown another inch or so, too. The loose golden curls he'd worn in high school were now cut shorter, and she'd never seen him in a business suit.

But ten years made no difference. She'd have recognized those intense silver gray eyes, the clean cut of his chin, the feline grace of his body, anywhere. If anything, he'd become more delicious with age.

Like fine wine, she thought, slightly hysterically. Her already racing heart broke into triple time.

Oh man, she couldn't stop staring at him, drinking in his masculine perfection, remembering everything she'd tried so hard to forget, and noticing all the intriguing ways he'd grown up.

She stared a moment too long. A strange expression passed fleetingly across his face. Had he seen through her disguise? Her heart skipped a beat.

There's no way he can recognize me, she assured herself.

But then what on earth was he doing here? Was he connected to the Illuminati? Or maybe he just happened to work legitimately for LSA Enterprises and this was all some kind of bizarre coincidence?

He stepped closer.

She had to make her escape, but her body refused to budge.

"Mark, what are you doing here?" Another man entered the room. It was Mark's younger brother, Paul.

Carla fought to keep her face neutral. She hadn't known him as well as Mark, but the family resemblance was undeniable. He had Mark's gold coloring, but his eyes were light blue. He was also a good deal shorter, only several inches taller than Carla.

"I meant to call you and let you know I was coming by, but I forgot," Mark addressed his brother.

Carla ignored the frantic surge of adrenaline pumping through her body at the sound of his voice. It was deeper than she remembered, huskier, and dangerously compelling. She had to get away.

She moved past the two men and picked up the office garbage can by the door, emptied it into the bin on her cart, set it back down, and forced herself to calmly leave the room. Once in the hall, she abandoned her reserve and raced for the front door of the executive suite, pushing the cleaning cart ahead of her.

Outside LSA Enterprises, she forced herself to move sedately down the hall past the security camera, despite the fact that every bone in her body told her to run. At any second, Mark or his brother might come after her. She headed for the service elevator.

Just then, an enormous hulking man flung open the stairwell door at the opposite end of the hallway. He looked like trouble. She knew it as soon as she saw his beady black eyes, his crew cut, and his massive, muscular body squeezed into a black business suit. She saw it in how he came charging down the hall toward her.

She ducked her head, trying to look inconspicuous and praying the cap and wig would keep her gender a secret. He briefly slowed as he passed her. She nodded in what she hoped was a manly gesture. As soon as he disappeared into the executive suite, she jammed her thumb frantically on the service elevator down button.

When it arrived, she heard voices inside. Relying on instinct, she jumped into the garbage can on the cleaning cart and covered herself with paper debris and the musty cloth she found at the bottom of it.

"Hey, Jerry. What the hell you doin' leavin' this here cart out in the hall?" An authoritative male voice demanded.

Carla squeezed as low as she could in the garbage can, difficult in the tight space. She wanted to hold her gun, but she didn't dare move.

"I didn't leave it out, Mr. Amano. I swear. I just got on shift. You know, I bet it was that no-good Sam. You should fire his ass." The second voice was higher-pitched, deferential.

"Well, if you don't empty that garbage and get back up here in record time, you're gonna be fired, too."

"What?"

"You heard me, get crackin'. The elevator's here, so get goin'."

Carla felt the cart jostle across the metal grate and into the service elevator. So far, so good, she thought, as the elevator began to descend. Seven, six, five. With each beep, she breathed a little freer. Just a few more floors and she'd be home free. Suddenly, the elevator stopped. They had only reached the second floor. The door opened.

"Old man, you the janitor for the tenth floor?" A guttural, menacing voice demanded.

"Nah. That's Sam, but I ain't seen him tonight. Hey, why you lookin' for him?"

Oh crud, Carla thought. Why did the poor old janitor have to start asking questions? She felt the elevator dip slightly under the man's massive weight.

Logic told her it must be the hulk she'd seen on the tenth floor. Fear made her breath catch in her throat. With the abrupt intake of air, dust lodged in her nose and she felt a desperate need to sneeze. *No way*. She squeezed her eyes together. Tears ran down her face as she struggled to stifle the urge.

"You don't mind if I ride the elevator with you," the Hulk said. It was not a question.

"Nah. But, you didn't answer me," Jerry persisted. "Why you lookin' for Sam?"

The elevator beeped as it reached the ground floor.

Carla felt the cart being propelled outside and onto the loading dock at the back of the building.

"What the—?"

Jerry's last words ended in a loud snap, followed by a deadly silence. A shiver ran down Carla's spine. She suspected the Hulk had quickly and efficiently just broken Jerry's neck.

The janitor's body landed with a heavy thud in one of the dumpsters. She knew without a doubt that if the Hulk caught her, her own death would be neither so clean nor so simple.

Would he think to look in the garbage can? Her hand crept to the gun in her pocket. She'd use it if she had to, but she'd rather not. It was much better to come and go silently, invisibly, like the spook she was.

Just then, footsteps approached at a fast clip.

"We've checked the other floors," another man said. "There's no sign of that janitor."

The Hulk uttered a violent oath before replying. "Let's check with the others out front. If he's escaped, the Master will not be happy."

Carla listened intently as the footsteps receded. Except for the sound of traffic and a jet passing overhead, all was now quiet. Heart pumping, she pulled the dusty rag off and climbed from the garbage can. Not taking time to right the skewed janitor cap and wig, she jumped down from the loading dock and sped toward the alley.

Once in the privacy of the alley, she yanked off the cap, her long black hair tumbling down her back. She blew the dust from her nose and looked up. The sun was sinking through thick smog and the sky looked like it was smeared with blood. She ran toward the setting sun.

CHAPTER 3

The stretch of Highway 101 along the Rincon was dark, the Pacific Ocean a black vastness to the west, broken only occasionally by the brilliant twinkling of offshore oil wells. When Carla was little, her mother had told her they were Christmas trees. Now, she barely registered them as she accelerated up the climb to Carpinteria.

She had to get to Santa Barbara. Gwen was in real trouble. While she was playing janitor at LSA Enterprises, Gwen had called her. She replayed Gwen's message once more.

"Carly, where are you? There's a man downstairs, someone evil. I can feel his negative energy." Gwen's voice was a mere whisper. Carla's fear for her sister's well-being kept her from rolling her eyes at Gwen's New Age references. "Oh no! He's breaking things. I've gotta go."

The message broke off abruptly. What the hell had happened?

When Carla tried to call her back, not even the Magic Shop's answering machine had picked up. During their last conversation, she'd casually dismissed Gwen's fears as melodramatic, but now it looked like she'd been wrong.

To distract herself, she dialed Tate's cell but wasn't

surprised to get voicemail. After all, it was pushing midnight in D.C. She briefly updated her friend on her detective work in LA and promised to email the digital photos of the mysterious documents as soon as she could.

Her thoughts strayed to Mark Lyons. What had he been doing at LSA Enterprises? If he was supposed to be working for Kristi at Eye Spy in Santa Barbara, why was he in LA? Were he and his brother involved with the Illuminati, or was it all just some kind of weird coincidence? She didn't share her sister's belief in fate and destiny. She did not believe in synchronicity.

Frowning, she gripped the steering wheel tighter, her eyes on the dark road ahead. In the darkness, distant memories welled up, of strong arms folding her against a muscled chest, of a warm male body pressed against her on a chill Santa Barbara summer night.

Mark Lyons was the last thing she needed right now. With her sister in trouble and threats being made against her, she couldn't afford to be thrown off guard, let alone distracted. Lord knows, he'd succeeded brilliantly in doing just that, all those years ago at Henry Lee's Green Dragon School of Martial Arts.

At eighteen, she'd prided herself at being independent and in control of her life. She'd been totally unprepared for Mark. He'd been rich, arrogant, and a snob, but he had also been talented, smart, and wickedly gorgeous. She'd never met anyone like him. In three months, he'd destroyed everything she believed true about herself—or had her own weakness done that?

Whatever the reason, she despised the needy, dependent girl she'd become. She had spent years trying to erase the memories.

She exited the freeway onto Laguna Street, her emerald eyes glinting in the dark. It would be a cold day in hell before she let him get under her skin again.

No light came from the Magic Shop. She pulled on a pair of black leather gloves before trying the door. It was unlocked and swung open into an eerie silence.

She'd only returned home a few of times during the rare and brief breaks she'd had between assignments. Now, like the other times, memories of her mother haunted her. As she entered the Magic Shop, she fleetingly remembered those distant, happier times, before her mother had been taken away and before she'd had to take over running the family business until Gwen was old enough.

She pulled the Colt from her handbag and tucked it in the back of her waistband. The cold, hard feel of it against her spine was reassuring. It would have been even more reassuring if she could have kept the gun in her hand, but it was safer this way. She could grab it at a moment's notice, and this way she didn't risk shooting the wrong person in the dark.

She used her flashlight to navigate through the disorderly room, not risking turning on the light. Broken glass crunched under her boots and she had to be careful not to trip over the overturned display cases.

Fury over the wanton destruction of the shop fought with her fear for Gwen. Not taking time to examine the mess for clues, she hurried upstairs to her sister's room. It appeared in order, the bed neatly made and a little altar with fresh flowers placed on a table by the window.

She touched one of the daisies, thinking of Gwen, who like their mother aspired to magic and secret knowledge, to witchcraft and supernatural power.

Dangerous, crazy stuff, she thought, turning to open the closet door. Much better to trust logic and reason.

"What the—" Her voice was abruptly cut off by a large leather-gloved hand clamping over her mouth. She dropped the flashlight as she was lifted off her feet and into the arms of a tall man.

"Who are you?" The man's lips brushed her ear as he spoke. His voice was deep, soft, and familiar.

She grit her teeth in frustration.

Mark! She tried to fight her way out of his embrace, but he was too strong.

"Let go of me!" she demanded the instant he removed his hand from her mouth.

He released his hold on her and switched on the closet light.

"Mark Lyons, what the hell are you doing here?"

She stared at him, telling herself to stop noticing how his tanned biceps and chest filled the black T-shirt and how well his long legs fit the jeans.

He didn't immediately answer. Instead, he raked her body with his eyes, a slight smile touching those lips she couldn't forget. The arrogance was still there in the proud tilt of his head and the sensual curve of his mouth. She still hated how much he affected her.

"Carla. You're all grown up." He moved forward to brush a strand of jet black hair from her face.

"Don't touch me!" She jumped back, batting his hand away, her green eyes bright with anger and challenge.

"I'm sorry." He broke eye contact and turned away.

She couldn't help but drop her guard and gape at him. An apology? No way.

Not once had he apologized to her that summer in high school, not after he'd sprained her wrist in a sparring match, not after the kiss that'd changed her life, and not after his mother had made it perfectly clear that she wasn't good enough for her son, or even good enough to set foot on their estate. Why would a high and mighty Lyons from Montecito ever need to apologize to a mere orphan from the wrong side of town?

Stop it! she told herself, forcing her mind off distant memories and back to the present situation of Mark standing in her sister's room.

"You didn't answer my question, Mark. What are you doing here?"

"Look, there will be time to explain everything later." He moved back toward the closet. "The important thing right now is to find out what has happened to Gwen."

Carla kicked herself and cursed him for being there and for being so reasonable. How could she have forgotten her sister? Her emotions, her hormones, were clouding her judgment and distracting her from her mission.

"What do you make of this?" He stood in the doorway and pointed into the closet.

She squeezed by him, wishing he'd been polite enough to step back. Instead, she felt their bodies brush as she passed him. She inhaled the aroma of an expensive cologne mixed with his own unique scent. A shiver of familiarity ran through her and a startling suspicion raced through her mind.

Was he the man she'd fought at the farmhouse in Virginia?

Before she could think through the implications of this possibility, she saw what he was pointing to. Strange occult symbols covered the back walls and floor of the closet.

"That's blood, isn't it?" She shuddered. The symbols looked a lot like the ones that had been painted on the doorstep of her apartment in D.C. Those symbols had been goat blood. Were these, too?

"Either that or dark red paint," Mark said.

A disturbing thought crossed Carla's mind. What if this was Gwen's blood? No, it couldn't be. She refused to believe it, at least not until she had definite confirmation. Whoever's blood it was, the connection was clear: the Illuminati had abducted her sister and left these symbols as some kind of cryptic message or warning.

She spun around and stared at Mark. Had he been at that weird farmhouse? He definitely had been at LSA Enterprises this afternoon. He must have driven like a bat out of hell to get to the Magic Shop within minutes of her own arrival. Why? Was he a member of the Illuminati, and if so, what kind of game was he playing?

He stared back at her from the doorway, his eyes dark

and unfathomable.

"I think you'd better explain what you're doing here." She pushed passed him and out of the closet so as to put some distance between them. Hands on hips, she turned to confront him.

He leaned against the doorjamb, digging his hands into the front pockets of his jeans. The action drew her eyes downward. She had to fight from noticing how well he filled his jeans. Her eyes flew to his. He was watching her, but no smile played on his lips.

"I work for Kristi's detective agency, Eye Spy Private Eye."

She wanted to ask him why a Lyons would debase himself to work for a lowly detective agency, but she forced herself to curb the sarcasm.

"Go on."

"Gwen called Eye Spy and left a disturbing message. Kristi called me and told me to come and check on Gwen. So here I am. Now, why don't you tell me what you're doing here? Aren't you living on the East Coast or something? Did Gwen call you, too?"

He pushed away from the doorway and moved toward her, his silver eyes darkening to midnight blue. "You didn't seem very surprised by those weird symbols in the closet. Do you know what they mean? They have something to do with Gwen's disappearance, don't they?"

She stopped herself from backing away as he loomed closer. He was the one who should be answering questions, not she!

"My sister takes after our mother. You remember Madeline, don't you?" She shot him an angry glance. "You never missed an opportunity to tell me she was an insane witch, remember?"

She hadn't meant to bring up the old hurts, but she couldn't stop herself. She glared at him, blinking back tears and fighting to control the emotions that had always plagued her when they tangled.

"I'm sorry about that," he said.

She stared, shocked by the sincerity in his eyes.

"Two apologies in one night? That's got to be a record for a Lyons. You sure your pride can take it?" she said bitterly, dropping her gaze from the intensity in his eyes.

Before she could stop him, he moved close and with gentle hands cupped her face and brushed away an errant tear with his thumb.

The feel of him touching her shimmered through her. God, she'd fought so hard to forget him and the defenseless, emotional way he made her feel.

She had grown up, she reminded herself. She was a top notch CIA operative, a black belt in Green Dragon technique. She was rational, intelligent, and in control of her life.

But her hands refused to stop him from touching her and her legs refused to move her away from his warm heat. Instead, she gazed up helplessly, furiously, into his eyes.

"People change, Carla" he said, his expression serious. "I'm not the person you used to know."

That was obvious, but who was he now? Ally or foe?

His hands slowly caressed her face and combed through her hair. She tried to think, but her brain was powering down as her body took over. She remembered the last time, the only time, they'd ever kissed. Her body quivered with the memory.

She licked suddenly dry lips and saw his eyes catch the movement. Unreasonably, irrationally, she wanted him to kiss her like he had, all those years ago on that dark night in August. She wanted to dig her hands into his thick hair and pull his head down to her. She wanted to press her body against him and feel his mouth on her.

For a second, he leaned in and she thought he might actually kiss her. She held her breath, her eyes sweeping closed in anticipation. He exhaled sharply, deeply. She felt a cold draft as he moved away and toward the door of

Gwen's room.

"We've got to find your sister," he said. "You know as well as I do that those symbols in the closet are proof that her interest in the occult has gotten her into trouble."

Damn, it had happened again! Her emotions had distracted her from her mission.

She studied Mark for a moment, realizing that whatever his motivation, if he wanted to help find her sister, she may as well let him. At least then she could keep an eye on him.

He pulled out his phone and took several photos of the symbols. "Whoever abducted Gwen, assuming she was abducted, must have wanted to leave some kind of message. But making assumptions can be tricky. I'm going to Eye Spy and get on Kristi's database. Maybe I can dredge up something about these symbols."

"I want to check something." Carla hurried down the hall.

"What are you doing?"

"Gwen may not have been abducted." She peered out the window at the end of the hall. When they were kids, she and Gwen used the window to slip out of the shop to visit friends or climb up to the roof to enjoy the view.

"This window opens onto the fire escape. She could have climbed through here and escaped." She jiggled the window. It slid open.

But did that mean Gwen had escaped, or had she simply left the window unlocked? Carla bolted the latch.

"Do you think she got away?" Mark asked.

"I'd like to think so," Carla frowned.

"It's hard to know exactly what happened. Why don't you come with me to Eye Spy? Two minds are better than one." His lips quirked up in a grin and her heart stopped. He was gorgeous when he smiled.

"When you put it that way." She found herself smiling, too, despite her suspicions.

As he moved away, her eyes drifted down his body,

taking in the thick, bronze hair crowning his head and the wide expanse of shoulders tapering to a narrow waist. He'd definitely filled out in all the right places.

She scowled, forcing her eyes from him and thrusting her gun into her purse as she headed for the door. The last thing she needed was to be distracted by hormones gone wild.

They stepped out of the Magic Shop onto the dark, glistening street. The March night was cool and damp.

As they walked toward State Street and Eye Spy, Carla knew she had to call Tate even if it meant simply leaving a message, considering the late hour. At least Tate could get started on the new intel first thing in the morning.

"I want to check my messages," she told Mark. "I'll catch up with you."

"I'll wait at the corner," he said, moving on.

She waited until he was out of hearing range and dialed Tate, who answered on the second ring.

"Hey, what are you doing still up?" she asked, surprised.

Tate laughed. "Unlike you, Carla, I've been known to go on dates every now and then."

"Who was it? Was it fun? Isn't it a little early to be coming home from a date?"

"Whoa there, girl! It's still a weeknight, remember? I need to get my beauty sleep. Unlike you, I've gotta be at the office first thing in the morning or Frank will have a cow."

"So, cut to the chase. Who was it?"

"Hmm, maybe I shouldn't tell you. Besides, it was only a first date."

"You're seeing someone at HQ, aren't you? Let's see. Could it be Jim? Or how about Sam over in cryptography?" Carla rattled off several more names.

"You're impossible!" Tate laughed. "It was Sam, OK? Satisfied?"

"I hope you had a good time," Carla said sincerely. It

was good to know that at least one of them had the promise of a normal love life.

"Did you hook up with Gwen?" Tate got down to business.

"No." Carla clenched the phone against her ear. "It's possible the Illuminati has abducted her."

"What?"

"She's missing. I checked out the Magic Shop. Someone left blood symbols in her room. The symbols looked a lot like the ones at my apartment."

"Why on earth would the Illuminati want to abduct your sister?"

"And why me, huh?" Carla ran a distracted hand through her hair. "I don't know yet. Has Sam managed to decipher the meaning of those symbols left on my doorstep?"

"He's still working on it, but he has been able determine that they're a combination of alchemical and satanic symbols."

"The Satan stuff doesn't surprise me, but alchemy? That's interesting. It looks like our cult is better schooled than I thought."

While working at the Magic Shop in high school, she'd learned how little most people interested in the occult knew about alchemy.

"I'm not sure 'cult' is the right word to describe this group," Tate said.

"What makes you say that?"

"We were right that the name sounded familiar. The Illuminati or some version of the organization has been around since the 1700's in Europe, and to this day, there have been different groups claiming the name for their own. It looks like the one we're dealing with consists of both intelligent and well financed members."

"Speaking of that, while I was at LSA Enterprises, I came across several technically sophisticated, scientific-looking documents that may be connected with the

Illuminati. I'll email them to you as soon as I have a chance."

She glanced up to make sure Mark was still out of earshot and tried to keep her voice neutral.

"Did you get my message about Mark Lyons being at LSA Enterprises? Were you able to uncover anything about him?"

"I ran a quick background check on him. What a surprise! "

"What did you find?" Carla failed to keep the impatience from her voice.

"He graduated from Harvard with a degree in East Asian Studies."

"I could have predicted a Harvard degree, but East Asian Studies? That's a surprise. I'd have thought he'd major in business or economics or something else that would help the Lyons dynasty continue its efforts at world domination."

"Aren't you being a little overdramatic?" Tate laughed. "But seriously, judging from the information I was able to dig up, Mark's degree served him well, at least for a few years."

"How so?"

"After graduation, he went to Japan and worked for a US diplomat in the region. Then he spent a few more years in Hong Kong, then mainland China. He was involved in several Asia-U.S. business ventures. And get this, he was married for a year to a U.S. National."

"Really! But only a year? Did you find out what happened?" Carla's mind raced. Mark had been married! She'd give anything to know the story.

"No. The only records I could find were of a divorce on file." Tate paused.

"Yes?" Carla prompted.

"Well, then things get a little weird."

"How?"

"After that, he disappears, at least on paper. I couldn't

uncover any more information about him. In fact, if you hadn't told me he's now working at Kristi's agency, I wouldn't have known it. Kristi's either paying him cash or hasn't paid him yet. There's no record of his social security number being used recently. As far as the paper trail, he dropped off the face of the earth two years ago."

"That *is* weird."

Neither of them had to say what was instantly on each other's minds. Mark had gone undercover and had now resurfaced. Why?

"It sure does seem an unlikely coincidence that he'd turn up at LSA Enterprises," Tate said.

"There are no such things as coincidences in our line of work," Carla said with conviction. She didn't mention the possibility of Mark being at the farmhouse. And she wasn't ready to tell Tate that Mark was just up the street waiting for her.

"Can you run a deeper background check? I've got a hunch he's involved with the Illuminati. In the meantime, I'll keep my eye on him."

"I'm sure you will! Hey, is he still as gorgeous as ever?"

"What? I never knew you thought he was cute. You mean all these years you've been holding a candle for the guy?" Carla laughed, but the laugh died abruptly when she realized what she might've just revealed.

"Oh Carla, don't be silly. We've all known for years you were crazy about him."

"No way. I always hated him. He used to drive me crazy."

"As I said, you and he had a *passionate* relationship." Tate underscored the adjective, laughing. Before Carla could object, she continued. "You never did tell me what he looks like now. Are you avoiding the subject?"

"OK, OK, I give up. Geesh," Carla sighed. Tate was one smart cookie, or maybe she just knew Carla too well. "He's still hot, satisfied? His hair is darker now, and shorter, but it looks good. He looks good." Carla gave herself a figurative pat on the back for the understatement.

"Whatever you say, girlfriend," Tate laughed, but then her voice grew serious. "Be careful, Carla. I know you have a history with him, but that was a long time ago and things can change. People can change. Don't let your judgment become clouded."

"I won't," Carla snapped, trying not to be offended by Tate's assumptions. "You know me, Tate. I am first and foremost a professional. No man is going to distract me from my mission! Now, if you don't mind, I've got to get back to it." She hung up.

She felt bad snapping at her friend, but she couldn't help it. What Tate said hit too close to home. She closed the phone and started up the alley toward Mark.

Suddenly, huge arms seized her, trapping her, and a beefy hand clamped over her mouth. The cell phone clattered to the ground, breaking into pieces. She was hoisted off her feet and carried down the alley behind Cota Street and away from Mark.

Hell no! She flew into motion, slamming her head backward while simultaneously kicking viciously at the man's shins.

In surprised pain, the man relaxed his grip on her enough so that her feet touched the ground. Gaining leverage, she twisted her body in the man's massive arms and rammed a knee into his groin. As the huge man groveled on the sidewalk, she recognized him. He was the Hulk, the ruthless murderer she'd encountered at LSA Enterprises.

"Who are you? What do you want with me?" she demanded, knowing she could outrun him if she had to.

The Hulk slowly rose to his feet. He stood well over six feet and seemed as wide as he was tall. He wore the same black business suit she'd seen him in earlier. His beady black eyes peered at her, but his face was strangely impassive. His lips moved as if he were in some kind of trance.

She strained to hear what he was mumbling. At first, the words were indistinct, jumbled. Then she heard him say, "The Offering," and abruptly realized he was speaking in Latin.

She listened intently, trying to translate. The chant sounded very much like the one the leader of the Illuminati had uttered at the farmhouse, something about "Abaddon," "the Illuminati," and "the Offering." There was something almost hypnotic about the low stream of words. She stood transfixed, listening to the man's words as he pushed himself to his feet and lurched towards her. Maybe if she listened long enough, she could figure out what he was saying.

"What the hell is going on here?" A loud male voice broke the spell.

There was a flurry of movement, the hollow thud of a big body slamming against concrete, footsteps running away, and the next thing she knew, she was in Mark's arms again.

CHAPTER 4

"Mark!" Carla exclaimed, looking up into his concerned face, feeling his hard heat and male scent envelop her.

Her senses were already heightened from the fight with the Hulk and now in Mark's arms they kicked into overdrive. She stared up at him, his concerned expression, the firm cut of his jaw line, those kissable lips. The years slipped away. Memories threatened to overload her. His gaze slipped to her mouth. Was he going to kiss her?

She had to get away!

Wrenching herself free, she put some distance between them and tried to clear her mind. Damn. Things were moving too fast. She needed time to think.

"Are you OK?" He touched her arm, concern filling his voice.

"I'm fine," she lied, brushing past him.

She let out a deep breath and told herself to pull it together. Stalling for time, she walked back to retrieve her cell phone. It lay in pieces at the entrance to the alley. Damn, contacting Tate securely would be virtually impossible, at least until she could get another Agency phone.

"Hey, wait up." Mark came after her. "Who was that

man? What was he saying to you?" His concern sounded sincere, but she couldn't be sure.

"Don't worry about it. I'm fine." She pocketed the pieces of the phone and looked up into his fathomless silver eyes, thinking fast.

Why hadn't the Hulk put up a fight? Did the two men know each other? Her thoughts flashed to LSA Enterprises. Both men had been there. Had Mark seen through her disguise? There'd been that moment when their eyes had held an instant too long. Had he recognized her? If so, then he'd know she'd already met the Hulk. But maybe not. After all, it'd been over ten years since they'd last seen each other. Still, her instincts told her to be careful.

"You're not acting fine," he said. "Why don't you tell me what's going on? You weren't exactly fighting that guy off, were you? Do you know him?"

She had the same questions he did, but she couldn't very well tell him about her investigation of the Illuminati, not when he might be one of its members.

She looked up into his hypnotic silver eyes, surprised at his perception and angry she was even considering confiding in him.

He'd always held too much power over her. As a teenager, she'd found him intriguing, fascinating, compelling. Now she grew irritated. It wasn't as if she hadn't spent the last ten years of her life fending for herself. She prided herself at being independent and in control of her life and her feelings.

"Nothing I can't handle. " She shrugged dismissively.

"Really," he said, crossing his arms against his chest and cocking his head to one side as he looked at her. "From what I could see, you didn't seem to be handling much of anything. "

She fought the urge to slap him, or reach up and smooth one of his curls that had fallen across his brow. She squelched both urges.

"Thanks for coming to my rescue, Mark. You're my knight in shining armor." Her voice dripped sarcasm.

"At your service." He grinned wickedly.

"Don't let it go to your head." She scowled, feeling the attraction pulsing between them.

Hadn't she learned anything from the past? The arrogant words Mark's mother had spoken to her years ago still rang in her ears. Barbara Lyons had made it perfectly clear that a lowly deVille from the wrong side of town would never be good enough for a Lyons.

She broke eye contact with him and picked her purse up from the ground, vowing silently to herself that she would *not* repeat the errors of the past!

"That man was probably after my purse." She hitched it over her shoulder.

"No, I don't think so," Mark said. "Something else was going on. He was saying something to you, and you were listening. What was he saying?"

"I don't know, but he was obviously mentally disturbed or something. Let's get out of here." She started walking toward State Street and the Eye Spy offices.

"Not that way." He took her arm. "That guy might come after us. Come on." He guided her back down the alley to a sleek, black Porsche. That must have been how he'd gotten from LSA Enterprises to the Magic Shop so fast.

"Here, get in." He unlocked and opened the door.

She quickly checked the locking mechanism on the door before climbing in, then breathed a sigh of relief. At least the lock wasn't booby-trapped. If he was Illuminati, at least she'd be able to leap out of the car if necessary.

Surreptitiously, she watched Mark start the car. She had to admit she was glad to no longer be a walking target on the dark Santa Barbara streets. The murderous Hulk was out there somewhere.

Was Mark after her, too? She felt the reassuring weight of the Colt in her handbag resting on her lap. He must have felt it against her back when he'd grabbed her in Gwen's room. If he knew what was good for him, he wouldn't mess with her.

"You're going the wrong way." Tensing, she noticed he'd turned off State Street, away from the Eye Spy offices, and was heading for the Riviera, the hill above town.

"I want to make sure no one's following us." He glanced in the rear view mirror.

She turned and looked over her shoulder. "I don't see anyone. "

"Doesn't hurt to make sure." He turned the car back toward State Street. "So, why are you in town?"

"It was time for a visit." She looked out the window and tried to distract herself from the intensity she felt radiating between them. The dark intimacy of the small sports car just made things worse. She needed to get away from him and think.

"I'm feeling pretty tired, what with the time zone shift. Maybe we can connect later. Would you mind dropping me at Kristi's?"

"Of course."   He turned the Porsche around and headed west toward the Mesa, the raised strip of land across from the Riviera on the opposite side of town.

"I forgot how beautiful it is here," she sighed, turning her attention away from him and drinking in the vivid contrasts, the bright lights of the city, the black Pacific, the oil wells twinkling on the black velvet of the ocean. Her sister was out there somewhere. Was she OK?

"When was the last time you were in town?"

She felt his eyes on her in the close darkness of the car but she couldn't read their expression. Should she tell him why she'd come back those few times, to check up on Gwen and her crazy witch mother, locked away at the mental hospital? She decided to keep it simple.

"Not in a while." Her stomach grumbled. The last food she'd eaten had been the airplane snack on her flight out from DC. With all the excitement, she'd forgotten about food.

"What's going on, Carla?" His deep voice interrupted her thoughts. "First, your family shop is trashed and your sister disappears, and then, not more than an hour later, some guy attacks you. It can't be a coincidence."

"Why not? Weirder things have happened." Like running into your high school nemesis for the first time in ten years while cross-dressing as an elderly janitor. She smiled. She didn't believe in coincidences, but for the moment, it'd be easier to pretend she did.

He let her comment slide as he pulled the Porsche up to the curb outside Kristi's, but then he turned, his silver eyes intent as he studied her face.

"Get a good night's sleep and let's meet up at Eye Spy tomorrow, OK? We can go over everything then. But, Carla, just remember, assumptions can be dangerous. Don't assume what's going on is coincidental."

"Don't want to make an ass out of you or me, right? Good night, Mark." She laughed and swung the car door shut.

As she walked up the front steps to Kristi's house, his words echoed in her head. The smile died from her lips. Was he warning her about the Hulk, or himself?

#

The delicious warmth of the sun on her face woke Carla the next morning. Excited young voices clambered down the hall and the front door slammed. She stretched under the soft comforter in Kristi's guest bedroom and had to admit that it felt good to be back in Santa Barbara. Today she'd find Gwen, she was sure of it.

She took a quick shower and pulled on last night's jeans. At some point, she'd have to get her stuff from the rental car parked near the Magic Shop. Maybe Kristi would have a clue about her sister. At least today she'd be able to touch bases with Tate again. She found Kristi in the kitchen washing dishes.

"Carla! How wonderful to see you!" Kristi wrapped her in a tight hug. "Brian told me you got in late last night. He took the kids to the park, so we could have a little quiet time and catch up."

"You look great." Carla returned the hug with affection. Maternity definitely agreed with Kristi, who glowed with good health, her complexion pink under a head of frizzy blond hair.

"So do you. What has it been, two years?"

Carla nodded. "You were pregnant with Danny the last time. But I must admit, you weren't nearly as huge."

"That's what twins will do," Kristi smiled. "You want some coffee? There's still some left over from Brian's pot this morning."

"Sure, but let me get it. Why don't you sit down and take a load off?"

"Don't be ridiculous. I may be on 'couch rest', as the doctor likes to call it, and banished from Eye Spy for a while, but I can still walk around my own kitchen." Kristi poured her a cup of coffee and led her out to the patio.

Carla inhaled the scent of jasmine and orange blossoms. The morning was cool, but sunny and dry. Last night's rain had left the air clean and fresh smelling.

"I always forget how nice it is here." She took a sip of the hot coffee.

"A little slice of paradise, if you're lucky enough to afford it," Kristi said.

Carla nodded and changed the subject. "Gwen's missing." She turned from admiring the small walled garden to look at her friend.

"What?" Kristi's smile dropped away. "She left me a message last night while I was putting the boys to bed. She didn't sound right, so I had Mark go over to the Magic Shop and make sure she was OK. I assumed everything was fine, because I didn't hear back."

"He probably didn't want to worry you." Carla took another sip of coffee and looked at her friend. Best not to worry Kristi. She kept it simple. "When I got to the Magic Shop last night, Gwen was gone."

"She didn't leave a message or anything?"

"No." Carla didn't elaborate.

"Maybe she's over at Izzy's." Kristi got up, stretched out her back, and then turned, a glint in her sky blue eyes. "Brian says Mark dropped you off late last night, so you two must have hooked up."

Carla heard the innuendo in Kristi's voice. Her friend had always been a sucker for gossip.

"Brian was kind enough to heat up some leftovers for me. You make a mean tuna casserole," she said.

"You're changing the subject." Kristi laughed. "What aren't you telling me?"

"Nothing about Mark, that's for sure." Carla rolled her eyes. She wanted to know more about why Mark was working for Kristi, but that could wait. "How has Gwen been doing lately? Do you know anything about that coven she's been hanging out with?"

Kristi frowned, her blue eyes sharp as she looked at Carla. "Circe?"

Carla nodded. "You knew she was being initiated?"

"Yes. I hope Moon Ray is strong enough to keep the coven safe."

"Moon Ray?"

"That's the name the new coven leader goes by. I don't know her given name, but I do know she studied under your mom years ago when the original coven was still together. After what happened to Madeline, the coven disbanded and Moon Ray went to Europe. She came back a year ago and restarted the coven."

"Do you happen to know if she solicited Gwen to join, or did Gwen seek out the coven on her own?" The timing of Moon Ray's sudden reappearance after so many years sounded suspicious and coincided with the Illuminati's appearance in her own life.

"I don't know," Kristi said.

"Do you have any idea how I can get in touch with Moon Ray?"

"Actually, I do. I'm pretty sure I've got her phone number upstairs."

While Kristi went to get the information, Carla finished her coffee and thought about what she had learned.

Her mother hadn't been mentally strong enough to handle whatever had happened to the coven years ago. The facts around what had happened to Madeline deVille had been obscured by history and her mother's subsequent descent into madness. At least in the current situation, Carla was sure there were real live human beings threatening herself and her sister. Magic had nothing to do with it.

With Kristi still upstairs, Carla borrowed the house phone and gave Tate a quick call.

She answered on the first ring. "Carla, what are you doing at Kristi's? Did you find Gwen? I tried to call you this morning but your cell wasn't on."

"Gwen's still missing and my phone broke."

"What?"

"It's a long story and I don't want to bore you. Can you just get the Agency to send me a new one?"

"What aren't you telling me?"

"Look, we don't have much time. Kristi's upstairs getting me the contact info for Circe's coven leader but she'll be back any moment. Can you get me a new phone?"

"OK, OK, I'll pick one up for you. Where should I send it?"

"The Magic Shop, better yet, just send it here."

"We're still keeping Kristi out of the loop, right?"

"I think it's safer that way, don't you?"

"Definitely. Do you have any new clues to throw my way?"

"I'm going to Eye Spy this morning and will have Internet access. I'll send you the pictures I took from LSA

Enterprises first thing. Oh, Kristi's coming."

"I'll keep an eye peeled for the files. And Carla, I know you're not telling me everything." Tate paused. "Be careful."

"I will," Carla said and handed the phone to Kristi. "It's your Sis."

"Hi Tate, hang on a second," Kristi said. "Here's Moon Ray's number." She gave Carla a slip of paper.

"Thanks. I'm off to Eye Spy." Carla folded the paper and stuck it in her pocket.

"You want Brian to give you a ride? He'll be back shortly."

"Thanks for the offer, but I don't want to wait." Carla headed for the front door. "I'll take the bus."

#

It was a ten minute bus ride to downtown. As the bus twisted down the hill from the Mesa onto the flat western part of town, Carla noticed how upscale the area had become. It had been practically a slum when she was growing up. Now, colorful bougainvillea graced the arches and private courtyards of opulent townhouses. Santa Barbara had become a playground for the rich. The thought reminded her of Mark. Maybe today she'd find out what had really led one of Santa Barbara's elite to work for a detective agency.

The bus dropped her off on State Street. Before heading to Eye Spy, she walked the few blocks back to the Magic Shop. Daylight might yield clues she'd missed last night. She was surprised to see the "Open" sign hanging in the window. She entered and found a young, red-haired woman cleaning up the mess.

"Hello," Carla said. "Who are you?"

The woman hurried to stand up, a slender white hand pressed to her chest. "My, you startled me." She spoke with a slight Southern lilt. "I'm Sally. I work for Gwen. You must be Carla. You look just like her, but you're a heap taller."

"Yeah, I've heard that before." Carla scanned the room for clues. Nothing jumped out at her.

"Do you know where Gwen is?" Sally continued. "I just got here a little while ago, but she's not here. And this place—" She gestured at the merchandise and display cases littering the floor. "Why would someone do this? I'm taking inventory, but so far it doesn't look like anything was stolen. Do you think I should call the police?"

"I'll take care of that. Can you run the store by yourself for a few days?"

"Sure, but is Gwen OK? Where is she?"

"Don't worry about her. She's fine," Carla lied. She had no intention of publicizing Gwen's disappearance, at least not until she had more answers.

"Do you know when she'll be back?"

"I'm not sure, but thanks for helping out while she's gone. I really appreciate it. If you'll excuse me, I'm in a bit of a hurry and I've got to go upstairs for a moment." She hurried past Sally.

At the top of the stairs, she scanned the hall once again for any sign of a struggle. Nothing. She checked the window at the end of the hall. Still locked. She entered Gwen's room. The closet door was closed. Weird. She'd left it open last night.

She opened it and turned on the light. Nothing. The closet walls were bare. There was no trace of the blood symbols. Damn. Now there would be no way to verify if they had been made of goat blood, or if, God forbid, they had been Gwen's own blood.

She retraced her steps through the room, examining everything once again, slowly, carefully, with a laser eye for details, but the place had been swept clean.

Frowning, she turned on her heel and checked the other rooms upstairs: her old room, her mother's, and the little kitchenette. There was no longer any evidence of foul play.

She hurried downstairs. "You weren't upstairs this morning, were you?" she asked Sally, who was still cleaning up the mess.

"I never go upstairs. Is everything OK up there?"

"It's fine. I've gotta go." She hurried out the door.

Nothing in the mess could be attributed to anything more than possible petty theft or a prank. Damn it! It didn't make any sense. Why would the Illuminati go to such effort to leave the elaborate signs and then get rid of them? Unless they were for her eyes alone. But what about Mark?

As she stalked back to State Street, only one thought filled her mind. Mark. He had been in LA. He'd shown up so conveniently when she'd gone to the Magic Shop last night. He had interfered when the Hulk approached her in the alley. Had he been the one to wipe the evidence after he dropped her off at Kristi's last night?

She stopped at the bakery in the storefront downstairs from Eye Spy and picked up a chocolate croissant plus more coffee, then headed upstairs. She grasped the cool glass doorknob of the agency and entered.

In her visits home, she'd never visited Kristi's company, so she looked around with interest. Her first thought was that her assumptions had been off about the PI agency. Apparently, Kristi had well-heeled clients.

The main reception area was fashionably decorated in blue and white. High quality prints hung on the walls. The waiting area was comfortably furnished with plush chairs and a small sofa placed around a glass coffee table covered in glossy magazines. Several offices opened off the main room. Directly in front of her, a petite blond sat at the reception desk behind a computer.

"May I help you?" the receptionist asked, pushing fashionable, frameless glasses back up her nose.

"I'm here to see Mark Lyons. I'm Carla deVille."

"Oh yes, Mark is expecting you. He's in the second office." The receptionist gestured to a partially closed door as the phone on her desk rang. "Excuse me." She answered the phone and began hastily typing a note.

Carla approached Mark's office. She heard his voice through the partially open door. It sounded like he was on the phone. Surreptitiously, she glanced over her shoulder to make sure the receptionist wasn't watching. The woman was still on the phone. She never wasted a good opportunity to eavesdrop and she was burning to know what he was up to.

"No, it's nothing to worry about, at least not at this point," he said. Silence followed as she listened, then he said, "Don't worry. I've got her where I want her. Just a minute—" He broke off when a buzzer sounded. Carla heard the sound of buttons being pressed. "Yes Mandy, I'll see her now," he said into the intercom. His voice dropped. "I've got to go."

When she heard the phone drop into its cradle, she knocked on the door.

"Come in," Mark called.

She opened the door. Had he been talking about her?

"Good to see you again," he said.

Dressed in khakis and a white sport shirt, all tanned skin and muscle, he rose from behind the desk and gestured for her to take a seat across from him. Tall and lean, he radiated power, privilege, and authority, just as he always had.

Damn, she'd forgotten once again just how much he attracted her. Her mouth went dry and her legs refused to budge.

Lightening sparked between them. For a moment, it felt like the very first time they met, that day years ago at the Green Dragon School. His silver eyes probed deep into her, as if bridging the gap between their souls. She stood silent, spellbound in the doorway.

Get a grip! She told herself, clenching her hands at her sides. The pain of her nails squeezing mercilessly into her palms broke the spell. Her green eyes narrowed as she searched his face. Was that what he was doing, weaving some kind of spell with his seductive gaze? Well, it wasn't going to work. She tore her eyes from him and walked over and sat down in the large, remarkably comfortable leather armchair on the other side of the desk.

"I hope you had a good night's rest." He took a seat and acted as if nothing had just happened.

"Yes, I did, thank you." She wanted to cut the polite crap and get down to business, but instead she said, "Kristi is an excellent hostess. I had a chance to catch up with her this morning."

"Did she have anything else to add about Gwen's whereabouts?"

"Not really." She didn't plan on telling him about Moon Ray, not if she didn't have to. "I think what I found this morning at the Magic Shop is much more important."

"What do you mean?" he said, one dusky blond brow rose.

She gave him a meaningful stare, but he seemed blind to the innuendo, his silver eyes blank as he listened to her.

"The place is clean," she said.

"What do you mean?"

"Just that. Someone came in after you and I left last night and removed the blood symbols. Gwen's closet is immaculate."

"Really?"

"Yeah, what do you make of that?" She couldn't help the challenging tone in her voice.

"I'm not sure. Do you have any ideas?" He continued to act innocent. Maybe he was. Maybe he wasn't.

"I don't know. Yet," she exhaled in frustration and then changed the subject. "You mentioned checking for leads in Kristi's database. Did you find anything?"

"Not yet. I got tied up with something else, but I was just about to start."

I'll bet, she thought, remembering the phone conversation she'd overheard. Wiping the Magic Shop would have taken some time last night, too, assuming he'd done it.

"Do you mind if I use one of the Eye Spy computers?"

"Not at all. Kristi said you have some experience with detective work."

"You'd be surprised what insurance agents sometimes have to do when investigating claims." She smiled.

Besides her sister and Tate, Carla had kept her work at the CIA secret from most everyone, including Kristi. Her cover was that she worked for an insurance agency in DC. She and Tate had been careful to keep their partnership at the CIA a secret, which had come in handy on more than one occasion.

"Use the computer in Kristi's office." Mark paused a moment, his silver eyes catching hers. "I realize your search for your sister takes top priority, but what with Kristi being out and Eye Spy's business booming right now, maybe you could spare some time to help me with a case I'm working on? Do you think you might be able to help out, if you get the chance?"

She tried to fathom his expression. What was he up to? Was this an innocent request or some kind of tactic to distract her from hunting down the Illuminati? His face was impossible to read, except for that sensual awareness that kept her heart pumping a little too fast.

"If I get the chance," she said noncommittally.

"Don't worry," he said, noticing her hesitation. "All I'll really need you to do is a little Internet research on the parties involved. You won't need to do any real detective work."

"OK." If he only knew the kind of detective work she could do!

"Great, I really appreciate it," he said. "Here are the quick nuts and bolts of the case. It involves several of Santa Barbara's prominent families."

"Don't tell me someone in your family has gotten into trouble." She couldn't resist the jab.

His mouth tightened. "Can't you ever see past your prejudice? My family's rich, but we're not crooks, Carla."

She dropped her eyes from his, feeling contrite. Maybe she had gone a bit too far.

"I'm sorry," she said.

Apologizing to him grated. He was the one who should apologize! Remembering how his family had treated her still sent a stab of pain through her heart. She squashed the feeling and replaced it with the cool numbness she had cultivated over the years. At least the numbness allowed her to remain level-headed and rational. That's what she needed now more than ever, cool-headed logic. But it was difficult when looking at Mark brought the past flooding back.

"What is the case about?" She leaned back in the comfortable chair and met his gaze again.

He nodded, his mouth relaxing, apology apparently accepted. "It's the eternal tale of greed and coveting what one doesn't have. You're probably familiar with some of the names. Sebastian Dupree used to be in Hollywood. He ran unsuccessfully a while back for Mayor. His wife Marie is big around town in charity events. The couple historically has been close friends with the Jacksons. Have you heard of them?"

When she shook her head no, he continued. "Well, Martin Jackson originally made his millions as a Texas oilman before he retired and moved to Santa Barbara. He was a widower when he arrived, but within months of moving here, he met and married DeeDee Castillo, a local Santa Barbara woman and at least twenty years his junior. He now has political aspirations and is running for the state legislature. Until recently, the two couples were pretty close."

"What happened?"

"It's complicated, but to make a long story short, Sebastian Dupree has hired Eye Spy to investigate the whereabouts of his most prized art work, which has turned up missing. He believes Jackson stole the piece. But that's not the end of it. The latest twist is that Sebastian just heard yesterday from a mutual friend that his wife was spotted last week with Jackson, if you know what I mean." He shot her a suggestive look.

"I get the picture," she nodded. "It's the old story of infidelity and betrayal." Her work in CIA covert operations rarely dwelt with such domestic cases, but this seemed pretty straightforward.

"So, you interested in finding some lost art and spying on an illicit couple?" He leaned back and clasped his hands behind his head, waiting for her reply.

She forced her eyes off the broad expanse of his chest, which was emphasized by how he was sitting. "Sure, when I'm not busy looking for Gwen."

"Great." He stood up and she followed suit. "Let me show you to Kristi's office."

Unlike his office, which had been bare and impersonal, Kristi's was warmly welcoming. Photos of her family lined the desk and walls, and comfortable furniture in feminine ivory and blush tones adorned the room. The office had an excellent view of the Santa Ynez Mountains, looming austerely behind Santa Barbara.

"I'll let you get settled. If you have any questions, please don't hesitate to let me know, OK?"

Carla nodded but didn't notice when he left the room. Her attention was riveted on one of the framed photos. Picking it up from the desk, she studied it, a rush of conflicted emotions sweeping through her as she remembered the day the picture had been taken. It had been both Tate and her seventeenth birthday.

The photo pictured the Cota Club, the five best friends with their arms slung across each other's shoulders mugging for the camera. Tate and she stood in the center with Kristi, Gwen and Izzy on the sides. They were decked out in their nicest outfits. They'd saved for weeks to afford the celebration. When the day came, they went for lunch at the Montecito Country Club. It had been one of her best memories, but what had followed had been one of the worst.

She and Gwen had come home, laughing and excited to tell their mother about their experiences at the fancy country club, but strange men were in the Magic Shop taking Madeleine away. They said she'd become a danger to herself and others. When Carla and Gwen begged her to tell them what was going on, she said nothing, just stared blankly at them as if they were unrecognizable.

The day that had begun in loving camaraderie had ended in screams, tears and an aching emptiness. Nothing had ever been the same since, and now Gwen was missing.

I'll find you, I swear, she vowed, tracing her sister's smiling face in the picture with her finger.

She carefully placed the framed photograph back on the desk and switched on Kristi's computer. She pulled the tiny digital camera from her purse. First thing to do was send the photos she'd taken of the documents at LSA Enterprises to Tate. With the CIA's resources at her fingertips, Tate would be able to decipher them. Just as she clicked "Send," the intercom buzzed.

"Carla, you've got a visitor," the receptionist said.

"Really?" That was surprising, considering she'd only been at Eye Spy for under an hour.

"A woman named Emily Trent."

The name didn't ring any bells.

"OK, send her in," she said.

She slipped the camera back in her purse and pulled up an innocuous search site on the computer. Whoever Emily Trent was, she wasn't taking any chances.

CHAPTER 5

A petite woman dressed in a jean jacket and a long flowered skirt opened the door. Judging by her short gray hair, Carla guessed the woman was pushing sixty. The woman carefully closed the door.

"But you look just like your mother!" the woman exclaimed. A radiant smile lit up twinkling brown eyes as she took Carla's hand in a delicate grip. "How wonderful to meet you. I am Moon Ray." She spoke with a slightly foreign accent. The way she purred the "r" in "Ray" led Carla to suspect that she might be French.

"What happened to 'Emily Trent'?" Carla took a seat and gestured to the chair across the desk from her.

The older woman sat, her eyes widening in surprise. "As Madeline's daughter, you must know that witches have two names, their given name and their magickal name, yes?"

"Of course." Carla didn't tell her that she'd done everything she could to forget what her mom had taught her of the occult. She needed this woman as an ally if she hoped to find Gwen.

"My given name is Emily Trent, you see. That is the name I use in public and which I gave to your receptionist, but I would be honored if you would call me Moon Ray." Her voice dropped and she leaned forward, placing her small hands on the desk. She wore pale silver fingernail polish on her long, well-manicured nails. "Kristi told me I would find you here this morning. I would have preferred to meet you in a less public place, but time is of the essence. Your sister's life is in grave danger."

"What kind of danger? Do you know where she is?"

"I am sorry it has come to this." Moon Ray straightened in her chair, the lines of her face grave. "It is a long story and I am not sure what you already know."

"How about you start at the beginning?" Carla crossed her arms over her chest and fought to keep her expression neutral. She was trying to keep an open mind, but she couldn't help thinking this woman had been a bad influence on Gwen and had encouraged her sister to pursue dangerously irrational interests, interests that had now gotten her into terrible trouble.

Moon Ray cleared her throat. A look of indecision flitted across her face.

"What I am going to tell you must be kept confidential," she said. "You will keep what I say secret, yes?"

Carla nodded.

Moon Ray studied her intently for a moment. Apparently satisfied, she continued. "Years ago, when you were still a child, your mother was High Priestess of Circe and your father was High Priest."

"What?" Carla interrupted. "You knew my father?" She stared at Moon Ray in shock.

Her mother had always refused to tell her anything about her father. She and Gwen had given up asking questions, but she'd always assumed he'd abandoned the family immediately after Gwen was born. She had never seen a picture of him and didn't even know his name.

"Oh dear, I thought you knew that." Moon Ray looked unhappy.

"Do you know his name? Do you know where he is now?" She was getting off topic, but she couldn't help it. This woman might hold the key to finding her long lost father.

"No, *ma belle*. I am sorry I never learned his given name. He disappeared a while before the coven disbanded and..." A pained expression crossed her face.

"And my mom was sent away," Carla finished for her. "Look, Mom would never talk about my dad. Is there anything you can tell me about him? What was he like? What did he look like?"

"She must have had her reasons. Maybe I should not say anything." Moon Ray looked undecided.

"Please. It would mean a lot to me." She couldn't help pushing.

"You poor girl. Your family is in pieces and now your sister is missing. You are all alone in the world." The older woman's brown eyes moistened and then closed for a moment. As if remembering, she said, "Your father was very handsome. He was tall and he had dark hair. He was very strong, very powerful." Her expression altered, darkened, and a shuttered look fell across her eyes. "That is all I can say," she broke off.

"What aren't you telling me?" Now was not the time for Moon Ray to stop her reminiscences, not when Carla was about to get some answers.

"Pardon, *ma belle*, but I must not say more. It is too dangerous. What I can tell you is that, how shall I say—" Moon Ray broke off for a moment, her expression thoughtful. "The forces of the universe work in balance. With great power comes great responsibility, and great danger."

Carla stared at the older woman. What was that supposed to mean? Just when she needed real answers, she got supernatural mumbo jumbo. She gritted her teeth, wanting to push for more but realizing she couldn't risk alienating Moon Ray.

"OK, whatever." She changed the subject, hoping to get back on track. "What about Gwen? You say she's in grave danger, what do you mean?"

"There are forces moving against Circe that are of the same kind as before."

"What do you mean?"

"Do you know why Circe originally disbanded?"

"My mom had a mental breakdown."

"That was, as one might say, the final straw. For months before that terrible day, we had been fighting against a malevolent force. I was still in training so Madeline did not reveal all the details to me, but my intuition tells me that the force succeeded in overthrowing Circe. You know," she paused, looking at Carla with inscrutable, birdlike eyes, "I suspect your mother never actually had a mental breakdown. It is my belief that her mind was stolen. I believe she is being held captive in some kind of spell, perhaps a curse."

"Wait just a minute." Carla fought to keep from rolling her eyes. Her mother had had a mental breakdown from believing just this sort of irrational superstition. "It's quite a stretch to connect what happened to my mom to what's going on now, and intuition and beliefs aren't going to help me find Gwen, either. You've got to give me something real, something tangible I can work with."

"I am sorry," Moon Ray sighed. "I wish I could be specific in the way that you want, but the magical world does not work like that. What happened to your mother, to Circe, has haunted me like an unquiet ghost. I hoped that by starting Circe anew I might be able to make peace with the past. When Gwen asked me if she might become an Initiate, it pleased me to think I might help her find peace, as well." Moon Ray looked sad. "It is ironic, I suppose, that where I had hoped to perhaps ease the curse against your mother, I have instead resurrected old ghosts, old demons." She frowned. "Within a month of Gwen joining Circe, forces began to move against us."

"Like what? Can't you be more specific?"

Moon Ray shrugged. "I assume you mean physical manifestations?"

"That would be a start."

"Gwen found strange symbols drawn on the doorstep of the Magic Shop."

Carla's heartbeat kicked up. She narrowed green eyes at the woman.

"Really? Did they look anything like this?" Grabbing a pen off the desk, she sketched the one symbol she clearly remembered on the back of a business envelope. Someone had drawn it both in Gwen's room and on her own doorstep. It looked like an eye with the numbers five and thirteen inscribed along the eyelids.

"Oh heavens!" Moon Ray exclaimed. "How did you know?"

"I saw it and several other symbols in Gwen's room last night." She wasn't prepared to reveal that she, too, had had similar symbols painted on her doorstep, at least not until she had more answers about who was after Gwen - and her.

"Were they made with blood?" Moon Ray asked.

"It looked like blood," Carla nodded.

"Oh dear Goddess." Moon Ray shook her head, clucking her tongue and dropping her eyes to her hands where they lay clenched tightly together in her lap. "It is worse than I thought."

Carla felt her stomach drop. "What do you mean? Was it Gwen's blood? Has my sister been killed? "

"Pardon, *ma belle*, but I do not know. I suspect that she is safe at the moment, but there is not much time." Moon Ray jumped to her feet. "I must go now, immediately, and call a meeting of Circe. There is much to be done to ensure her safety." The older woman pushed the chair back and walked toward the door.

"One more thing," Carla said, stopping Moon Ray in her tracks. It was a worth a shot and she didn't think it would give too much away. "Does the word 'Illuminati' mean anything to you?"

Moon Ray spun around with a gasp and stared at Carla, her dark eyes piercing. "What do you know of the Illuminati?"

"Not so fast." Carla stood up. "I asked you first. What do you know?"

"No!" Moon Ray shook her head vigorously. "We are wasting time that might mean your sister's life. I must go."

Carla raced around the desk and caught the woman by the arm. Moon Ray knew something. This was the closest she'd come to getting a real lead and she wasn't about to let the moment slip away.

"Please, something. Anything." She shook Moon Ray's forearm slightly. "What you know could be the key to finding Gwen."

"Ask your mother." Moon Ray's inscrutable eyes peered up into Carla's for an instant, and then with a twist, she freed her arm from Carla's grasp and bolted from the room.

Carla stood rooted to the spot. A strange feeling of dread shuddered through her. Her mother? What would her mother know of the Illuminati? There was only one way to answer that question. She'd have to pay a visit to the mental hospital in Atascadero.

#

The two hour drive to Atascadero passed by in a blur. The beauty of the rolling, oak-covered hills and miles of vineyards were nothing to Carla as she mulled over the events of the last couple of days. Her sister was missing. A man she hadn't seen in ten years had suddenly shown up and kept showing up in the most unlikely places. And now she was about to see her mother, whom she'd last seen five years ago when she and Gwen had moved her from the state hospital in San Bernardino to the private clinic in Atascadero. Things were definitely not looking up.

After her meeting with Moon Ray, she'd discovered that Mark had left Eye Spy on business related to the Dupree case. She told the receptionist she'd be out the rest of the afternoon. She didn't say where she was going.

She arrived in Atascadero at 1 p.m. As she exited the freeway, her stomach grumbled. She was in no rush to see her mother, so she took a detour to her favorite fast food place. Fortified with a cheeseburger and chocolate shake, she felt as ready as she ever would to face what was left of her mom.

Driving up the winding road to the clinic, she noticed the neat flower beds and manicured lawns. Funny how mental hospitals presented such an external appearance of order. It was as if they were trying to compensate for the internal disorder of their patients. This place was a step up from the state mental hospital, where her mother had been treated little better than an animal in a cage. Carla shuddered at the memory.

"I'm Carla deVille, here to see my mother, Madeline," she told the receptionist at the front desk.

For a moment, the meticulously dressed woman stared at her through large, gold-rimmed glasses. The receptionist wore a lot of gold, on her fingers, wrists, gold hoop earrings and a big gold necklace. Even the woman's gray hair had been touched up with gold highlights.

"Is there a problem—" Carla read the woman's nametag, "Sarah?"

"No, it's just that you look a lot like your sister."

"Gwen? Has she been to visit Madeline recently?"

"Yes, she has."

"When? How long ago?" Carla tried to keep her voice calm.

"Let me see." Sarah swiveled her chair so she could look at her computer. Tapping a few gold-painted fingers expertly on the keys, she pulled up a screen. "Why, it was just yesterday. Seemed like longer ago. Guess I must be ready for the weekend." She hid a yawn behind her shiny-nailed hand.

"Does Gwen visit often? I've been traveling a lot and gotten out of touch." That was one way to put her self-distancing from her mom's madness.

Sarah queried her computer, scrolling through several months of dates, and then shook her head. "No. Before yesterday, your mother has only had one other visitor this year."

Interesting. Why would Gwen come to visit Madeline now?

"Who was the other visitor?"

"That information is confidential."

"Don't be ridiculous." Carla was getting impatient. "You just told me my sister was in yesterday. I have a right to know who's been visiting my mom."

"You have a point." Sarah frowned, small pearly white teeth gnawing her lower lip and marring the meticulously applied lipstick. Then, as if making up her mind, she consulted the computer again. "It was a woman, an Emily Trent."

Carla's brows rose, her green eyes narrowing. Moon Ray hadn't mentioned that she'd been to visit Madeline.

"You're being very helpful, Sarah, and I appreciate it. Can you tell me when Emily was last here?" She smiled broadly, hoping the compliment would work. It did.

"Sure," Sarah smiled back. "It was last Friday."

Maybe the visit had been simply to check in on an old friend. Maybe. But the timing seemed too coincidental. Coincidence? Not likely.

Over the years, she'd learned that what seemed like coincidence was actually just a lack of information. Maybe her mother could explain why she'd suddenly become so popular. Carla frowned. The last time she'd visited, her mother had made no sense at all.

And now? There was only one way to find out.

She followed the attendant, a tall black woman named Janelle, down the hall. Janelle was dressed in the white uniform of the clinic attendants.

As they walked, Carla noticed the hallway was tastefully decorated with nature prints on the walls, but the photos only marginally softened the blinding white linoleum and didn't succeed in distracting visitors from seeing the locks on each of the patient's doors. A few windows looked out across the rolling lawn toward the hills of the coastal range. There were no bars on the windows. Carla glanced quickly at the glass. Probably crash-proof.

Janelle knocked on the door to a room.

"We like to observe manners as much as possible," she said to Carla. "Ms. DeVille?" she called through the door. "You available for a visitor?"

Carla heard a muffled voice answer in the affirmative.

Janelle extracted a large ring of keys from her pocket and quickly found the right one.

Carla held her breath as the door swung open. The last time, her mother had spent the entire visit huddled in a rocking chair by the window, her black hair streaked with gray, hanging long and messy down her back.

To Carla's surprise, Madeline stood by the door, her graying hair swept up in an orderly bun and her clothes neat.

"Carly, how wonderful!" Her voice came out low and husky, as though she hadn't used it for a very long time. She spread her arms wide to greet her daughter in a warm hug.

Carla went into her mother's arms without hesitation. For a moment, she forgot everything but the wonderful, comforting sensation of being held by her mom. But then she felt the frail boniness of Madeline's body. Her mom had aged.

She pulled out of Madeline's arms and looked at Janelle, who stood watching them.

"Would you mind giving us some privacy?" she asked.

"I'm sorry, but I gotta stay. It's company policy."

Carla shrugged and turned to her mother.

"Here, Mom." She led Madeline to the rocking chair by the window. "Have a seat."

As Madeline settled into the chair, Carla sat down beside her on the bed and looked about the small room. It was decorated simply. A narrow bed stood against one wall, covered neatly by a plain white duvet. A dresser stood adjacent to the closed closet door. Not one picture graced the bare white walls. The only unusual thing in the room was a spectacular throw rug spread on the floor in the middle of the room. Ornately woven in a wild splash of rainbow-colored fibers, the rug's primary image was a spiral that appeared to spin into the center of the rug. The pattern drew one's eyes hypnotically to it.

Madeline watched her look at the rug. "You like it?" She slowly rocked in the chair, her hazel eyes intent. A small smile played on her lips.

"I don't remember it. It's beautiful. Is it new?" Carla asked, both surprised and pleased that her mom was speaking to her. During her last visit, Madeline had simply rocked slowly in her chair, her face a closed mask. Maybe today her mother would be lucid enough to answer at least a few of her questions.

"Yes, it is new. It was a gift." Madeline said.

"Really? From who?"

Madeline didn't answer. Instead, her eyes darted from Carla to Janelle, who stood leaning against the door. When her eyes returned to Carla, they had lost some of their lucidity. A vacant smile played across her face.

If circumstances had been different, Carla would have sworn her mom didn't want the attendant to hear her answer. As it was, however, and knowing her mother was mentally unbalanced, she wondered if Madeline was simply being unresponsive.

Damn. She wanted to groan in frustration. If her mother wouldn't speak with the Janelle in the room and if Janelle refused to leave, there'd be no way to get the answers she needed.

She glanced out the window at the rolling hills. The clinic's lawns spread away toward the oak-covered hills in the distance. Clouds scudded out of the north and covered the sun. Another March rainstorm was headed toward central California. She had to think of a way to get the attendant out of the room.

"I'm really thirsty. Mom, would you like a glass of water?"

Madeline's eyes were blank. Her only response was the quiet creaking of her rocking chair as she rocked slowly back and forth.

"Janelle, would you mind getting my mom and me some water?" She turned toward the attendant. Janelle looked ready to protest, so Carla spoke quickly. "I ate a cheeseburger for lunch. You know how salty they are, right? I'm really thirsty. Would you mind?" She gestured to the glass pitcher that sat almost empty on the small bedside table. When Janelle continued to look unmoved, she pushed. "It won't take but a moment to fill this. Please?"

"OK. I'll be right back." Janelle pulled the big ring of keys from her pocket. "I'm sorry, Miss, but I'm gonna have to lock you in."

"I understand," Carla said.

As soon as she heard the lock click closed, she took her mother's hands in hers. They felt cool and bony. She looked down at them and realized with a pang how much her mom had aged. Remorse swept through her to think five years had passed since her last visit. Her heart felt heavy with sadness to think her mom might spend the rest of her life here. She looked up into her mother's eyes.

Madeline stared back, her hazel eyes instantly, sharply focused.

"Mom?" Carla whispered, afraid to hope.

"Carly, it's been so long."

"I know. I'm sorry, but the attendant will be back at any moment. I need your help."

Madeline nodded.

"Did Gwen come to visit you yesterday?"

Madeline nodded again.

"Why? Was it simply a social visit? What—?"

Her mother sprang from the rocking chair, her hands still gripping Carla's. She practically dragged Carla to the closet. Her grasp was surprisingly strong.

"In there." She pulled the door open and switched on the light.

Carla peered into the small, crowded closet. There were some clothes on hangers, some shoes on the floor, and a few boxes on the shelf above the clothes, but she didn't see anything out of the ordinary. Was her mom simply acting crazy?

"What? I don't see anything."

Madeline pushed past her and jerked the hanging clothes aside, exposing the closet wall behind.

Carla gasped. "What is it? What does it mean?"

Though drawn in blue crayon, the image on the back wall of the closet was obviously some kind of occult symbol. It looked nothing like those of the Illuminati, which had been angular, geometrical and numerical. This image formed a spiral that was interpenetrated by a group of concentric rings. As had happened with her mother's rug, Carla found her gaze drawn to the image. She didn't believe in magic or occult powers, but nonetheless she felt the hair on the back of her neck rise.

When her mother didn't respond, she asked, "Did you draw this?"

She forced her eyes away from the drawing to her mother, who stood crammed beside her in the tight confines of the closet doorway. Madeline stared back. Something else suddenly occurred to her.

"Did you show this to Gwen?"

"Yes. Gwen. Is she OK?" Madeline gripped Carla's forearms hard, pulling her closer.

Carla looked down into her mother's intense hazel

eyes. A shiver ran down her spine. Did her mother know something had happened to Gwen? Or was she simply asking out of courtesy?

The eerie drawing combined with the close confines of the closet and her mother's strange behavior all added to the odd sensations coursing through her body. One thing she did know was that at any moment Janelle would be back, and it was obvious her mother didn't want the attendant to see what she'd drawn.

"Let's go back and sit down, OK?"

Madeline needed no further urging. She shoved the clothes back over the drawing and rushed to her rocking chair. Carla closed the closet door and resumed her place on the bed just as the attendant returned with the pitcher.

"Here you are," Janelle said, pouring two glasses of water.

"Thanks," Carla said.

She wanted to ask her mother more questions, but she wasn't sure what Madeline would say with Janelle standing there. As she sipped the cool water, she stared down at the throw rug again, wondering what to do. The beautiful, rainbow-colored spiral pulled her gaze into it. Her brain lost focus and she forgot what she wanted to ask.

"Something happened, didn't it?" Madeline's question broke the spell, bringing her back to the present.

She tore her eyes from the rug and noticed her mother's furtive glance toward Janelle.

"Yes," she said.

Was Madeline's paranoia justified? Or was it simply a manifestation of her mental unbalance?

She wanted to tell her mom about the threats she'd received and about Gwen's disappearance, but there was too much at stake. The attendant was listening to every word they said. Better to keep things vague.

"She's missing."

As if she understood, Madeline simply asked, "When?"

"Last night."

When Madeline nodded, acting so much like the mother she loved and missed, Carla couldn't resist asking her what was foremost on her mind.

"Does the Illuminati mean anything to you?" She quietly mouthed the words, hoping Janelle wouldn't overhear.

Madeline's eyes drifted down to the throw rug. She stared at it and began to rock her chair, slowly and then more vigorously. Carla had to fight the temptation to follow her mom's gaze and look at the rug. Instead, she focused her eyes on her mom. Madeline's head began to jerk from side to side. Her small hands clenched the arms of the rocking chair. Her eyes swept shut and she began mumbling.

"Beware the light," she muttered.

Suddenly, she sprang from the chair and grabbed Carla's hands. She peered down into Carla's face, her eyes wide, pupils dilated. Carla fought the urge to pull back.

"Not all light is true. Beware the false light, for it is an agent of darkness." The voice that spoke was deep, guttural, as if someone or something had taken possession of Madeline and was speaking through her.

"That's enough, Ms. deVille. Don't overexcite yourself." The attendant pushed away from the door and moved toward them.

"She's OK." Carla waved Janelle back and wished for the thousandth time that she and her mother could have some real privacy.

She helped Madeline back into the rocking chair. The weird intensity and unusual strength had evaporated, leaving in its place the frail older woman that Carla recognized.

"I think it best you leave Ms. deVille to rest now," Janelle said.

Carla leaned over and kissed her mother goodbye. To her surprise, Madeline returned the embrace.

"Be careful, my dear," Madeline whispered. "They have

taken Gwen. They're after you. I'll do the best I can to stop them, but they are very powerful."

Who were "they", Carla wanted to ask, but Janelle now stood beside them.

"It'll be OK, Mom. I'll make sure of it." She moved to the door.

Madeline sat small and shrunken in her rocking chair. A slight smile played across her lips as she watched Carla leave. Her hazel eyes were vacant once again.

CHAPTER 6

Carla replayed the visit with her mother as she gunned the rental over La Cuesta grade. Had her mother been referring to the Illuminati when she'd warned, "Beware the false light"? Who had given Madeline that rug, because there was something distinctly peculiar about it? She may not believe in magic, but it was obvious the spiral design and the symbol in the closet were meant to convey some kind of occult meaning. It was also obvious that her mom was still involved in witchcraft. And what about Emily Trent and Gwen's recent visits? Coincidence? Both were members of the Circe coven. She needed to talk to Moon Ray again, and it was time for another powwow with Tate. She pulled up to Kristi's at sunset.

"Perfect timing," Kristi said as Carla went inside. "We're almost ready for dinner. Hungry?"

"Definitely. Thanks for offering to feed me." Carla smiled and followed Kristi into the living room.

Kristi's husband Brian and their two sons were sprawled across the off-white Berber carpet near the picture window and playing some kind of rowdy game that involved the two boys climbing onto their dad's back and him shaking them off.

"I'm the king of the mountain," crowed Danny, the

youngest, as he kneeled precariously on top of his dad's back.

"Not for long!" Geoff used Brian's feet as steps to climb up onto his back.

"Better get ready. An earthquake is about to strike," Brian laughed. He wriggled and began shaking his body about. The two boys screamed with fun as they clung to keep from falling off.

"OK, you guys. Enough rough housing! Carla's here and it's time to get dinner started," Kristi shouted over the din.

"Don't stop on my account," Carla laughed. It was hilarious to see such a big man on his hands and knees subdued by two youngsters. She sank down onto one of the oversized lounge chairs near the large picture window.

"Come on, you boys. Time to wash up for dinner. You too, buster." Kristi stopped her husband before he could take a seat on the couch across from Carla.

"Aye, aye, Captain." He gave Kristi a quick kiss before trooping after his two sons.

"Your family is such a treat," Carla said when she and Kristi were alone. "I can tell Brian's a great dad."

"Ain't he ever," Kristi beamed.

The phone rang and Kristi hurried down the hall to answer it. Carla looked out the window. The house faced east across Santa Barbara. Night had fallen and the lights of downtown twinkled merrily. Another swath of lights adorned the Riviera hillside. Behind it all, the Santa Ynez Mountain range loomed up, an inscrutable darkness. So much darkness up there, so little light. A chill crawled over her skin.

"It's for you." Kristi's voice broke into her thoughts.

"Really? Who?" She took the phone.

Kristi wiggled her eyebrows. "I've got to go finish getting dinner ready." She left the room.

"Hello?"

"Hey, it's me." Mark's low, gravelly voice filled her ear.

Another shiver swept through her, but this time with heat.

"What's up?" she asked.

"Have you found Gwen?"

"No, but I have a few leads." She wasn't about to tell him where she'd been. "How did your day go?"

"Were the leads solid? Do you know where she might be?" He ignored her effort to redirect the conversation, sounding tense.

"No, not yet, but—"

"Are you planning on spending the night at Kristi's?" He cut her off, his voice still low and urgent.

"Yes. What of it?"

"You can't."

"What did you say?" Who did he think he was, calling her up and telling her what to do?

"I said, you can't stay at Kristi's. It isn't safe."

"Come on, Mark. Aren't you overreacting?"

"No, I don't, not after what happened last night. A full day has gone by without any sign of your sister. You were accosted last night, too."

"That could have been a coincidence."

"It could have been, but I don't think so. Besides, have you thought about the danger you could be putting Kristi and her family in? Let's just assume that the people after Gwen are also after you. They probably know who your friends are. Wouldn't Kristi's house be one of the first places they'd look?"

"I could always go back and stay at the Magic Shop."

"Don't be ridiculous," he said impatiently. "You can't go back there. It's too risky. I'll bet that either the guy who attacked you or someone else has the place staked out. If you go back, you could be walking into a trap."

He was insisting on the connection between Gwen's disappearance and her later being attacked. Didn't he realize that this insistence indicate he knew too much about the situation? Apparently not, because he kept talking about how to keep her safe.

"Another option would be for you to stay at my family's townhouse, but that won't work either."

"What townhouse?" The only place she remembered the Lyons family owning nearby was their palatial estate in Montecito.

"My dad has some real estate investments in town. He bought a townhouse for general family use. I stay there sometimes when I have to work late at Eye Spy."

Images of Mark cozying up with her in a deluxe townhouse sprang to mind.

"Why won't that work?" she asked, clearing her throat.

"That guy in the alley got a good look at me. I may not be as well known around town as my folks, but I'm sure he's going to place me eventually. Then he'll know I'm involved with you. That leaves both the townhouse and my parents' place off limits."

Was his insistence that she leave Kristi's and not return to the Magic Shop a ploy to remove her from the safety of her friends?

"Carla, we have a lot to talk about, but right now, we've got to stay focused on getting you someplace safe." He spoke earnestly, his voice dropped lower.

Her toes curled inside her boots. The idea of phone sex suddenly made a lot of sense.

"OK." She let out a breath she hadn't even realized she'd been holding. If she worked with him, she could keep her eye on him.

"Good, I'm glad you agree. I've come up with a plan. Now, before you freak out, listen to my whole proposal, OK?"

"If you insist." Her eyebrows shot upward as he continued. "Married? What?"

"It'll work, I'm telling you," he insisted. "We'll pose as newlyweds on our honeymoon. We can stay down at the beach on the tourist strip and use assumed names. It's so crowded down there, we'll blend in just fine."

Before she could interrupt, he rushed on. "It's the perfect cover. Listen. We can use aliases and pay cash for the rooms. As newlyweds, our privacy will be respected, and in disguise as sightseers, I bet we'll be able to travel around town without anyone identifying us."

"Are you crazy?" Imagining them alone together in a townhouse had been bad enough, but in a hotel room dominated by a huge California king-sized bed?

"Don't worry," Mark laughed. "I'm sure the newlywed suites have couches, or I could always sleep on the floor."

"You've got to be kidding." She couldn't think of anything else to say.

She was still imagining them together in an intimate honeymoon suite. In high school, she'd been young enough, silly enough, to fantasize about them getting married. She grimaced. How naïve she'd been.

"I'm serious, Carla. I've thought through the options, and this makes the most sense. And like I said, I don't have any designs on your body." His words came smooth and fast, as though he'd practiced that little speech.

She scowled, pissed he thought she couldn't handle the situation. That his voice tempted her with deliciously erotic designs on his body pissed her off even more. She held her tongue. Better to let the subject of their bodies drop.

Instead, she considered his proposal and had to admit it had merit. Locals never paid attention to the tourists wandering around town. But how would she be able to talk to Tate and conduct CIA business with him breathing down her neck day and night?

Not that that would be all bad, she thought, remembering his breath on her neck when he showed up in Gwen's room. He may have come up with this plan as a way to keep tabs on her, but it could work both ways. A slow smile touched her lips as she thought of all the ways she could give him the slip if necessary.

"OK," she said. "But since I'm already here at Kristi's,

I'm going to stay for dinner. Then I'll get my stuff together."

"Excellent. Meet me at Cabrillo and Del Mar outside Farley's. I'll be driving a rental."

"You think we can get a suite there?" Farley's was one of the most exclusive resort hotels on the Santa Barbara beachfront and was always packed, either with tourists or conventioneers.

"Don't worry, it's taken care of."

"You're kidding."

Mark ignored her. "When can you get down there?"

"How about 10 p.m.?"

"See you then."

Dinner with Kristi and her family was a treat that ended all too quickly. Carla excused herself from spending the night by explaining that she had a lead she couldn't afford to pass up.

"But how is Mark involved?" Kristi wasn't stupid and guessed that his call had instigated her change of plans.

"He's offered to help with my case," Carla said. "But don't worry. I don't think he'll let any of Eye Spy's official cases slip."

"I'm not worried about that." Kristi bit her lip and looked carefully at her friend. "You be careful with him."

"Don't worry, Kristi. Whatever happened between Mark and me happened years ago." Carla spoke confidently. "A lot has happened since then. We're grown ups now." She slung the black duffel bag over her shoulder.

"Just be careful, OK?" Kristi wrapped her in a tight hug. Standing in the doorway, she watched Carla head down the walk to the street.

#

The ocean front along Cabrillo was fairly deserted by 10 p.m. Carla had no trouble spotting Mark. He was leaning against the side of a generic silver sedan. She drove slowly past and parked her rental half a block away.

No point taking unnecessary chances. She scanned the area before getting out of the car. No one nearby. She walked toward him, her heart pumping fast. The streetlights under the stately palm trees lining the boulevard radiated a subdued orange lighting.

He was wearing a black leather jacket and dark jeans. As she approached, she told herself to calm down. Just because her heartbeat kicked up and her palms were sweating didn't mean she'd let him know how much he affected her, but boy did he look good. The jeans emphasized the lean muscled length of his legs. His eyes practically glowed above the white turtleneck he wore under the jacket. He was watching her watch him.

"Hi there," he said when she reached him. He opened the passenger door. "I've got something for you."

"What?" She fought to keep her tone light.

"Your disguise." He didn't wait for her but moved around to the driver side and got in.

"So how'd you spend your day?" She asked, fastening her seat belt. Though curiosity and suspicion drove her question, she kept her face impassive and tried to look nonchalant.

"Working on the Dupree case." He rummaged around in the back and pulled a plastic bag onto his lap.

"Any new developments?"

"I think I've got a lead on the missing artwork." He pulled several items out of the bag.

"Really? Does that mean the case is almost wrapped up?"

"No, but don't worry. I don't need your help just yet. I know your finding Gwen takes top priority."

She didn't tell him about visiting her mom. There was some kind of connection between her mother and the Illuminati, and he, too, was involved with the Illuminati. Until she could figure out how these different relationships interconnected, she had to keep him in the dark.

If Mark knew where she spent the afternoon, he gave

no indication. Instead, he handed her a big blond wig.

"Where did you get this?" She held up the wig to get a better look at its bouffant style.

"Eye Spy. And here's a dress to go with it."

"You've got to be kidding," Carla cringed. Even in the dark interior of the car, the brilliant fuchsia and aquamarine floral pattern stood out.

"Come on, hon. Don't you like your presents?" He affected a Southern drawl as he pulled off his leather jacket. "I'll give you a moment's privacy while you slip into the dress." He climbed out of the car.

She kept an eye on him, but he stood decorously with his back turned.

What the hell, she thought, and quickly pulled off her jeans and T shirt and shimmied into the dress. Twisting her hair up into a knot, she donned the wig. Maybe he prefers blondes, she smirked, looking in the mirror.

"I didn't know Kristi was a mistress of disguise," she said as he slid back into the car. She laughed as she tucked the last strand of her ebony hair up into the platinum wig. Under other circumstances, she'd never be caught dead in such a loud dress.

"You'd be surprised what an enterprising sleuth has to do sometimes." Mark affixed a brown goatee to his chin and placed wire rim glasses on his nose.

Don't I know it, Carla smiled to herself.

"How's that, do I look suitably professorial?" He grinned at her.

In the close confines of the car, she looked at him. His disguise did nothing to hide his classic good looks. Maybe it was the darkness, or their proximity, or maybe the late hour, but the past juxtaposed itself with the present and she found herself staring at his lips - firm yet full, with an intriguingly curved upper lip. If anything, they had become even more kissable. The thought swept her back to those few precious moments when he'd kissed her in the gazebo and she believed her dreams had come true.

We know how that turned out, don't we, she told herself.

But then she realized he was staring back at her. Peering through the glasses of his disguise, his eyes were riveted on her mouth. Was he remembering, too?

Ridiculous. She had to stop acting like a romantic fool. He had, after all, been married and divorced since their time together in high school.

She forced her eyes away from his mouth and looked down at the tweed coat he was wearing and its elbow patches.

"The coat definitely screams professor," she said. "Where do you teach?"

"We're from Oklahoma, dear." He added a graceful lilt to his voice. "I teach at OSU, and you're my dearly beloved. We're John and Christine Fairchild, and we just got married."

He took her hand in his, sliding a massive rock on her finger, and she bit back a gasp. She barely registered the weight of the costume jewelry. His big warm hands burned her, lighting fires in hidden places deep inside. The sensation left her mouth dry and speechless.

"Now honey, you just wait here while I go check in." He raised her hand to his mouth and pressed a light kiss on the back of it.

Wasn't he taking this charade a bit far? With her hand tingling and a fine tremor running through her, she couldn't find the words to ask.

"I'll be back in a jiffy." He got out of the car.

She let out a deep breath and watched him cross the street and head toward the lobby of the Farley Hotel. Impatient with her overactive hormones, she rubbed the back of her hand on her thigh and reminded herself she needed to touch bases with Tate. As soon as Mark disappeared inside the hotel, she jumped from the car and hurried to a payphone she'd spotted near the corner.

10:30 p.m. in Santa Barbara meant 1:30 a.m. in DC. Tate's voicemail kicked on.

"Hi Tate, it's me again, calling from a payphone. Gwen's still missing. I went to visit my mom. She acted as if there's a connection between Circe and the Illuminati. Have you turned up anything more on Mark? I really need to know what I'm up against with him. Can you confirm if he's a member of the Illuminati? I'm going to pay a little visit to his family home tonight and see if I can find anything. The Lyons' estate is big enough to hide an army. Hopefully, I'll get the cell phone tomorrow, so we can connect."

Mark had arranged to keep her with him, ostensibly to keep her safe, but she wasn't naive. All of this could be a ploy to keep tabs on her for the Illuminati. As she hung up the phone and hurried back to the car, she vowed not to turn her back on him.

#

The hotel suite was more spacious than the intimate room Carla had imagined. In addition to the main bedroom, which had French doors opening out onto a patio with an ocean view, the suite also included a massive bathroom with a built-in tub, a walk-in closet, a kitchenette, and a couch. She immediately counted three ways out of the suite: the front door, the balcony doors and the huge window off the bathroom. Giving Mark the slip would be a cinch.

"This place must have cost you an arm and a leg!" She plunked her duffel bag on one of the suitcase stands in the large walk-in closet.

"Don't worry about it. For our alias to work, it has to look like the real deal."

But it wasn't the real deal. They weren't really newlyweds. She didn't know where to look, because her eyes kept moving to him. He stood in the center of the room, all muscled strength beneath the stark white turtleneck and dark jeans.

"Ready for bed?" He pulled off the tweed coat and ran his hands through his hair.

Desire arced between them in the charged silence.

"I'll change in the bathroom," she blurted, grabbing her duffel bag and rushing into away.

She closed the door, locked it, and yanked off the costume and wig. The closed door between them and the cool evening air from the bathroom window wafting over her body helped her shake off the sensual newlywed fantasy and brought cool, objective reality back into focus.

A long night lay ahead and her eyebrows knit in concentration as she thought through her plan. She pulled on the black cat suit, then covered it with one of the hotel robes. She'd be much too warm, but it wouldn't be for long. She left the duffel bag on the floor by the bathroom window.

When she came out of the bathroom, the suite was dark. In the dim moonlight filtering through the French doors, she could just make out the shape of Mark's body where he reclined on the couch. He wasn't wearing a shirt. His face was turned away from her, so she gave in to the temptation to feast her eyes on him. A comforter covered him to his waist, but above that, his muscled chest gleamed a subtle shade of silver in the moonlight. With the glint of curls crowning his head, he looked like a Greek statue, except for the slow rise and fall of his flat abdomen as he breathed. Better than a statue, she exhaled. He'd be warm to the touch, his skin smooth as heated steel. Her nails cut into her palms as she balled her fists.

Forcing herself to move to the bed, she lay down stiffly. Her body felt tight and all her senses were attuned to the man lying across the room. Listening intently, she could hear the distant sounds of the Pacific Ocean lapping against the white sands of Ledbetter Beach and the nearby sound of a car traveling along Cabrillo Boulevard. Faintly, she could hear the rhythmic sound of his breathing. Maybe, if he was half asleep, she could get some straight answers out of him.

"Mark?" she half-whispered.

"Huh?" He rolled to his side and looked toward her. The comforter fell lower across his waist. Was he naked?

Her eyes skittered away from the hard chest, the flat belly, the arrow of masculine hair disappearing below the comforter.

"Do you and your brothers still live at home?" She patted herself figuratively on the back for managing to ask the question casually. Whatever huskiness was in her voice she hoped, if he noticed, he'd attribute to her being tired.

"My older brother Nicholas moved out years ago."

"I never met him."

"He had already graduated from high school by the time I met you at the Green Dragon."

"Where does he live now? Is he still in town?" Besides trying to uncover clues about his connection to the Illuminati, she was curious to hear about his family. It was so much easier to talk with him about other family members than their own history.

"Yes, he still is. He lives down by the Marina. Dad put a lot of pressure on him growing up, probably because he was the first-born. Maybe that's why he decided he didn't want any of the Lyons money and the responsibilities that go with it." He chuckled. "But I guess success must be in our blood, because he now owns a successful eco-tourism company. They run boating and diving tours off the Channel Islands."

"Did he ever marry?" Imagining Mark an uncle was an intriguing idea.

"No. He' works too hard to have time for that sort of thing, although a couple of years ago he was voted Santa Barbara's most eligible bachelor. Ever since then, he's had to fight off hordes of women throwing themselves at him."

If he looks anything like you, they can't help themselves, Carla thought. Hell, she'd once thrown herself at him. She itched to ask about his own marriage. Why had it only lasted a year? What woman would be stupid enough to let him go? Realizing the direction of her thoughts, she moved the conversation toward her real quarry.

"What about Paul? Is he still in town?" She didn't ask if he was still as strange and brilliant as he'd been back in high school. Tate had told her he'd gotten a Ph.D., but she feigned ignorance of the fact.

He paused before responding, which set off warning bells in her brain. Why the hesitation? Was he thinking up a story? He leaned back against the couch and crossed his arms behind his head. His muscles rippled in the moonlight and she noticed the hair shadowing his armpits.

Damn. Did he have any idea how seductive he looked, spread out half-naked on the couch? She had to get control of herself! She forced her eyes up to the ceiling.

"Paul's done very well," he said finally. "He recently finished a Ph.D. in atomic physics at Princeton."

"Wow, that's quite an achievement. Is he still on the East Coast?" Atomic physics reminded her of Frank's intel linking the Illuminati with nuclear terrorism.

Again he paused. She twisted onto her side to look at him, but he had turned away from her and was looking out the window.

"No. He's back for a visit with my folks, figuring out the next stage of his career."

She figured what he'd told her so far was true, but there was so much she wanted to ask him about himself, like what had he been up to all these years, and what was his connection to the Illuminati?

"I know it's been a long time, Carla, and we've got a lot of catching up to do, but it's getting pretty late. How about we pick up in the morning?" He yawned and hunkered down on the couch, effectively putting an end to their conversation.

"Sure." She lay back against the pillows for a few minutes but then sat up and said softly, "I think I'll take a bath to unwind. I hope it won't disturb you."

"Not at all."

She felt his eyes on her as she slid from the bed, but then he rolled over and faced the window, pulling the covers up over his shoulders.

She tiptoed past him as she headed into the bathroom. Locking the door, she turned the bath on high and grabbed the duffel bag.

CHAPTER 7

She arrived in Montecito within twenty minutes of shucking the nightgown and climbing out the bathroom window. She couldn't remember the exact layout of the Lyons estate, not surprising since she'd only been there twice before, and that had been almost ten years ago. Mark had told her both Paul and he were currently residing at the estate, but all she really knew was that he and his brother were somehow involved with the Illuminati and that the Illuminati was somehow involved in her sister's disappearance. Her mission tonight was to uncover anything that might turn those "somehows" into something more definite.

She parked the rental car on the gravel shoulder of the winding mountainous road a few hundred yards from the front entrance of the estate. Climbing over a low stone wall, she moved through the avocado grove, her feet crunching the fallen leaves. Moonlight streamed through the trees and left stark patterns of black and white on the dirt beneath the grove.

The moonlit darkness reminded her of the last time she'd been here. How naive she'd been. When Mark's mother had discovered them together in the gazebo, that night of the Green Dragon fundraiser, Mark had smoothly, contemptuously, turned his back on her and returned to his mother and all that the Lyons stood for. What a little fool she'd been, to think their earth-shattering kiss would make him drop his pride and allegiance to his family to be with her.

The avocado grove ended abruptly at the edge of a large field, beyond which she could see the enormous bulk of the Lyons mansion and its gardens, including the white-framed gazebo. Not a single light shone from the boxy three-story mansion. Nevertheless, if she moved directly across the field, she'd be quite visible in the bright moonlight. It wasn't worth the risk.

Instead, she headed to the right and to a dirt road located alongside a line of eucalyptus trees. She soon arrived at a group of buildings, one of which was a stable. The smell of hay and horse filled the air and a horse whickered softly from one of the stalls.

Though her main goal was to investigate the house, she figured scoping out the stables wouldn't hurt. It certainly would be easy to do, unless of course there were any insomniac stable hands around. She listened carefully but heard nothing unusual, so she pulled open the stable door. Except for an initial screech of rusty hinges, her entrance was quiet.

She switched on her flashlight. Four of the six stall's Dutch doors were open. The first two held beautiful specimens of horseflesh. Only the best for the Lyons, she thought, as she admired the black Arabian mare and the Quarter horse. There had been a time when she'd desperately wanted to own a horse or at least ride one, but her mother had told her it was impossible. They didn't have the money. To make her daughter feel better, Madeline had bought her a black cat. Carla had loved Felix, but she'd always known he was a consolation prize. She ran a hand down the black mare's smooth neck. The horse nuzzled her hand.

"Sorry I don't have a carrot for you," she whispered.

The next two stalls were empty, just a few scraps of hay on the floor. The upper doors of the last two Dutch doors were closed. She tried the first door. It was unlocked. Inside, she found a tack room filled with the usual equipment. Nothing seemed out of the ordinary.

The second door was locked. She stood for a moment trying to decide if it was worth taking the time to break into the stall, since it would probably be a dead end. Looking at the lock, she decided what the hell. It was a simple two lever lock. She could open it in less than three minutes. She timed herself as she whipped out her slim lock pick set and set to work.

"Boy am I good," she muttered as she cracked the door open in two minutes flat.

The stall was pitch-black. Her flashlight cut through the inky darkness. She gasped.

A bedroll lay against one wall and on it were some ropes, a bottle of water, a roll of duct tape, and a rag that might have been used as a gag.

She rushed over and studied each item closely, looking for clues. Her heart rate shot up when she spotted several long strands of black hair stuck to the side of the roll of duct tape. She pulled one off and fingered it. Could this be her sister's hair? Had Gwen been held prisoner here? Or was it simply hair from the black Arabian? It looked too fine for horsehair, but she'd need a DNA test to confirm it was her sister's. She pulled the black strands loose from the roll and placed them carefully inside her lock pick case.

Closing the stall door and relocking it, she glanced at her watch. 3 a.m. She had at least two more hours before sunrise. She moved stealthily out of the stables and hurried up the dirt road toward the mansion. Avoiding the front entrance, she crept around to the vast granite terrace overlooking the garden. She frowned as she studied the lock on the back door. Damn. Unlike the stable door, this would be a challenge. She dug out her lock picks again. To better see, she clamped the flashlight between her teeth and trained it on the lock while she worked the double-ended slim line pick.

All her concentration was focused on the effort. Suddenly, a long arm wrapped around her waist and a big hand clamped over her mouth. The flashlight clattered to the granite terrace as she opened her mouth in surprise. It was all she could do to keep from dropping the picks.

"What do you think you're doing?" A familiar voice growled in her ear.

Mark! She inhaled deeply through her nose, smelling him, furious he'd followed her. With a swift stomp, she rammed her heel down hard onto his foot.

"Damn it, Carla!" he exclaimed softly through clenched teeth, his hands tightening their grip on her.

Her ploy hadn't worked. Instead of releasing her, he carried her off the large terrace and into the garden. She struggled violently and almost wriggled free.

"What the hell do you think you're doing here?" He let her go and gingerly took the weight off his injured foot, grimacing at her in the moonlight.

"Where do you get off man-handling me?" She needed to stall him long enough to come up with an alibi, quick.

"Didn't I just catch you attempting to break into my house?" His voice was a furious whisper.

How on earth could she explain her presence without revealing her suspicions? Her brain spun through possible excuses, but it was difficult to stay focused when he stood so close to her in the same garden where they'd once kissed. Remembering how that evening had ended years ago fueled her anger. Fortunately, with the anger, reason returned, but she still couldn't think of a plausible alibi. She tried a different tack.

"I'm a good insurance agent. I always check out my prospective clients. Lock picking has come in handy on occasion, OK?" She tried not to sound defensive.

"Yeah, right. But what the hell are you doing lock picking my house? Don't tell me you're planning to sell me insurance in the middle of the night." It wasn't a question. He stared at her in the moonlight, keeping the weight off his injured foot.

"I can't tell you." That kept it pretty close to the truth and utilized one of her favorite tactics for difficult situations: when in doubt, obfuscate.

She spun away from him and headed deeper into the garden. He followed, his footsteps crunching unevenly on the gravel behind her. She walked faster, dodging around one of the tall hedges, hoping to lose him. She rounded the corner and found herself face to face with the gazebo. The ornate Victorian filigree of the wooden structure rose above her, a ghostly white presence in the darkness. She stopped dead in her tracks. Time stopped. The present collapsed into the past.

Mark rounded the corner and collided into her. He grabbed her by the upper arms to keep from knocking her down. His warm body pressed against her. For a moment, she leaned into him. Her disobedient body willfully forgot the years that had passed since they'd last stood together in the garden.

"Carla," his breath traced her ear.

She turned to look up at him. He was staring down at her, his mouth sensually curved, his silver eyes piercingly intense. His hands tightened.

She wanted to ask him, did he remember that August night? Did he remember how it felt when they finally kissed? All the sparring, teasing, and torment they'd inflicted on each other had melted away when they kissed. In that magical instant, she'd really believed they'd spend the rest of their lives together.

Abruptly, she remembered he'd married someone else. She wrenched herself free of his grip and turned on him.

"Stop man-handling me!"

"OK, OK. I'm sorry." He held up his hands in

surrender.

She arched a single black brow at that. Another apology from a Lyons, how uncharacteristic.

"We've got to talk," he said. "Do you mind if we sit down?" He limped to the gazebo steps and sank down.

She reluctantly followed. The steps were narrow and it required some effort to keep her distance from him. She'd had enough of him touching her, especially since she couldn't trust her own body to behave. She watched him rub his foot again and felt a twinge of concern that she might have done real damage.

"I'm sorry. I didn't mean to stomp on you quite so hard."

"You've got lethal feet," he chuckled.

Those were the exact words the cloaked man had said that night in the Virginia farmhouse. Not only were the words the same, but the tone and timbre were identical as well. Mark had to be the same man. Remembering that night reminded her of his connection to the Illuminati. She tensed, all romantic thoughts gone.

"I'm sorry, what were you saying?" she asked. She'd been so deep in thought she'd missed his last words.

"I said, we've got to talk. I want to help you find your sister, but I can't do that if you don't tell me what's going on. Why do you think my family is involved in Gwen's disappearance? That's the real reason you snuck out here in the dead of night, right?"

"Oh, come on, Mark," she couldn't help a snort of laughter. He had caught her red-handed. It was too late to try and preserve her cover, so she said, "Do you really think I'd tell you if I knew something? For all I know, you could be involved, right?"

He didn't immediately answer, one way or the other. Instead, he stared out into the night. She wasn't sure it made her feel any better that he didn't try to defend himself.

"I think I'd better get going." She rose to her feet. "I'll

see you around."

"Wait, Carla." He stood up and caught her hand. "Things are complicated right now, really complicated."

"So, explain." She shook his hand free. It was easier to remain detached that way.

He ran a hand through his hair, his silver eyes glinting in the dark. "I can't, not right now. But I will, as soon as I can, I promise."

"Gee, that's helpful. I can really use that to find Gwen." He was involved, it was obvious, and his denial—or was it obfuscation—pissed her off. "Bye, Mark." She started walking away.

"But what about your safety? Are you going back to the hotel?" He followed her through the garden.

"I appreciate all your effort to set up our disguises and that hotel room, OK? But I think it's better we go our separate ways."

"You've got to be kidding! What about that man who attacked you, and what about whoever it was who trashed the Magic Shop? Gwen's missing and someone is after you. How are you going to stay safe on your own?"

"I can take care of myself."

"You're not going back to Kristi's, are you?"

"I'm not stupid."

At the edge of the garden, she hopped the wall and began heading down the dirt road.

"Carla, wait!" He grabbed her and spun her into his arms. "Where are you going to go?"

She looked up into his eyes and felt her disobedient body meld against the hard lines of his. His hand left her arm and strayed into her hair.. His other hand strayed to her waist. He stared down at her with what looked like real concern.

Concern for her safety, or concern he'd lose track of his quarry? She met his intense gaze, her heart revving to double time. Her mouth went dry as sand paper. She licked her lips and his eyes dropped to her mouth. His muscular chest was a solid wall against her breasts and his thighs pressed into hers. Was he going to kiss her? Her heart stopped. Emerald eyes met silver. She took a deep breath and reined herself in.

"Like I said," she spun away from him. "I can take care of myself."

Whirling on the ball of her foot, she took off down the dirt road at a sprint. With his injured foot, she doubted he'd give chase.

She checked her watch when she reached the rental car. 3:30 a.m. She got in, released the emergency brake, and gunned the sedan back toward Santa Barbara.

As she drove the winding mountain road, she rubbed her eyes. Many of her assignments required her keeping long hours, but she still looked forward to getting a few hours of shut-eye. Tate was sending the new Agency phone to Kristi's, so she'd have to get to Kristi's at some point soon. Mark was right, though. If she really was in danger, she didn't want to put Kristi and her family at risk by staying with them. Where else could she go?

There was always Henry Lee and his Green Dragon School. It had been a couple of years since she'd last paid him a visit, but she was sure he'd give her safe haven.

But was she actually in mortal danger? She only had Mark's word that she was, and his word was definitely suspect.

Screw it, she thought. *I'm going to go home and get some shut-eye.*

If the Illuminati or whoever else was after her tried something, all the better. She was itching for a confrontation. At least it would be something real, something tangible, and something she could sink her fists into. She parked several blocks over from the Magic Shop and her adrenaline started to pump.

"Bring it on!" she muttered to herself as she pocketed the rental car key.

She strode quickly toward the Magic Shop through the

deserted Santa Barbara streets, prepared to meet whoever might be waiting for her. Her eyes darted over the buildings and other landmarks along the street. No sign of the Hulk or anybody else. She almost felt disappointed, but then she saw the Magic Shop. A dim light flickered in its front window. Her green eyes narrowed. Someone was in there, and she'd bet good money it wasn't her sister.

Rather than rush in through the front door, she slipped around the side. The Magic Shop was one of three shops in the building. An alley ran behind the building with rear access into each of the storefronts. She paused a moment at the alley entrance, looking and listening for a sign that anyone had staked out the place. The orange, low-watt streetlights cast a surreal glow over everything. Besides several dumpsters and a pick-up truck parked further down, the alley appeared empty. She hurried to the back door of the Magic Shop. Retrieving her other set of keys from her pocket, she quietly opened the door.

It was almost pitch black. She ran her hand along the wall to orient herself as she crept forward. The soft sound of feminine voices chanting came from the front of the store. As she approached, a candle's light dimly flickered.

She edged into the main room of the Magic Shop. The chanting had stopped. A ring of eight women sat cross-legged on the floor, holding hands and swaying. The candle and a collection of assorted items had been placed at the center of the circle. The display cases that usually stood in the middle of the room had been moved to the side to make room for the circle.

She scanned the women's faces. Of those facing her, she immediately recognized Moon Ray. None of the others was familiar. They all had their eyes closed. She moved more fully into the room, and from the new vantage point, she recognized one other woman, Sally, Gwen's assistant shopkeeper.

Moon Ray spoke and the coven repeated the chant.

"With fire and water, with earth and with air, bring

power and protection to this circle of faithful."

Moon Ray opened her eyes. She removed her hands from her neighbors and picked up a stick that lay in front of her. "Let us close this ring with a blessing for Carla deVille, our dear friend."

Carla looked at Moon Ray in surprise. The witch must have seen her come in, but as far as she could tell, Moon Ray had not once looked in her direction.

"So let it be," the other women said in unison, then released each other's hands.

Carla moved forward as the women rose to their feet.

"Carla!" Sally exclaimed when she saw Carla. The young woman hurried over. "Have you found Gwen?"

"No, not yet." Carla moved past Sally to where Moon Ray stood by the front door.

"So this is Circe?" she asked the older woman, who was carefully placing the objects from the ring ritual into a large, purple velvet bag. "What are you doing here?" She didn't add that it was just passed 4 a.m. and that they were trespassing.

"Yes, *ma belle*. This is Circe." Moon Ray turned to the other women in the room, who were in the process of moving the display cases back. "Ladies, may I have your attention for a moment. Gwen's sister Carla is here."

The members of the coven came forward and murmured their greeting. Carla nodded at them in return.

"You still didn't answer my question." She looked pointedly at Moon Ray. "What are you doing here?"

"Is it not obvious, *ma belle?* We were working a protection spell to keep Gwen safe."

Carla gritted her teeth. A protection spell wasn't going to do her or her sister any good. What she needed was to get a good solid lead on the Illuminati. She suddenly remembered that when Moon Ray had come to see her at Eye Spy, the witch had not answered her questions about the Illuminati.

"You never told me what you know about the

Illuminati."

"Please, not at this moment." Moon Ray put a finger to her lips, her dark, birdlike eyes sharp as they looked at Carla and then glanced around the room. The other women had congregated by the front door. "I will speak with you in a moment," she said and then went to the other women.

"*Merci*, my ladies, for your hard work." She addressed the other witches. "Let us reconvene tomorrow night once more for a recharging of the protection spell. *Bonne nuit.*"

When the last of the women had left, she turned back to Carla, a worried expression creasing her brow.

"You must be careful, *ma belle*. I would advise you not to speak too casually of that which you mentioned. I do not want you to frighten my coven. They are already terrified as it is."

"Why? Simply because Gwen has disappeared?"

Moon Ray shot her a calculating look. "I am not sure how much I should tell you. I would hate to put you at risk."

"I'm already at risk, OK? I won't bore you with the details," she sighed, "but suffice it to say, I'm running out of leads of where to look for Gwen. You need to tell me everything you know. It's the only way I stand a chance of finding my sister. What do you know of the Illuminati?"

"Please, if we are to speak of this matter, you must speak more softly." The old woman's eyes darted fearfully about the room. "Walls can sometimes have ears."

"Follow me," Carla said.

She led the woman down the hall, using her flashlight to shine the way. Unlocking the storeroom door, she gestured Moon Ray inside and switched on the light.

"Don't worry. There are no windows. No one can see us from the outside," she said when she saw Moon Ray quickly glance about the room. "Now, what can you tell me about the Illuminati?"

"You speak of a powerful association, *ma belle*, an association of very powerful sorcerers."

Carla fought to keep her expression neutral. Sorcerers, indeed. More likely a bunch of dangerously loony men.

"And?" she urged, when the older woman fell silent.

"They are not good men." Moon Ray spoke reluctantly. "They are conjurers of the blackest darkness."

Memories of the dark pit in the Virginia farmhouse swept through her. What manner of thing had it been, that massive blackness, that eater of light, that rose from the pit? A chill passed through her. She shook it off with impatience. Irrational fear wouldn't help her find her sister. What she needed was to exert calm, rational thought. She remembered something else about that night in the farmhouse.

"Moon Ray, does the expression, 'May the light within reflect the light outside,' mean anything to you?"

The old woman's face blanched and she swayed on her feet.

"Are you OK?" Carla took hold of her arm.

"I must sit down."

"Here." Carla pulled the storeroom stool out from under a shelf.

Moon Ray sank onto it, running a hand distractedly through her short graying hair. "I grow too old for such things," she sighed.

"What things?" Carla crouched down to look the woman directly in the eye.

"The battle of good and evil, *ma belle*. I only pray that I am strong enough to keep Circe safe through this dangerous time."

"What about Gwen?" Carla couldn't help the accusation implicit in her question.

Moon Ray dropped her head into her hands. "I am so sorry for that. I thought she and the others were safe within the unbroken circle of Circe. I did not anticipate that they would single her out or that they would actually take her. I was unprepared for the lengths they would go. Believe me, my dear." Moon Ray looked up at Carla, her expression earnest. "I am doing all that I can now to keep her safe. With the help of the other coven members, my protective charm should be strong enough to keep her from harm."

"Do you know for sure that the Illuminati has abducted her?"

"Yes," Moon Ray nodded.

"OK, so who are they?"

"You do not know what you ask," Moon Ray frowned. "They are men of prestige and great influence within society. Their identities are kept secret, even from each other. I do not know any of their given names, or even their magical ones. All I know is that when they come together, they are able to practice a magic of tremendous power. Unfortunately for us all, they do not work to increase the true light."

With those final cryptic words, Moon Ray rose and walked slowly to the front of the Magic Shop. Carla accompanied her, but made sure to keep out of the light cast by the streetlamp outside. If someone was out there watching, they would be waiting to see Moon Ray exit. Hopefully, they wouldn't know that Carla had come in the back.

"Moon Ray, please. You've got to give me something to go on. Even one name would help," Carla whispered urgently.

"I told you, their identities are secret." The older woman pulled on a long black coat. She looked up once more at Carla, studying her face in the dim light for a long moment.

"How much you look like your mother," she said finally, sadly. "We could use her help more than ever at this moment, I fear." She put her hand on the doorknob but then looked over her shoulder at Carla, who stood in shadow. "There is one name that might be of importance."

"Yes?"

"The magical name Abaddon."

Carla fought to keep her face neutral. "How do you spell that? "

"A-B-A-D-D-O-N."

"What does it mean?"

"It is a name of great evil and great power. Be careful, Carla. Circe and I are now on our guard, but I fear that your being Gwen's sister has put you in danger as well."

"Don't worry about me. Keep yourself and the others safe. I can take care of myself."

Carla locked the door behind Moon Ray and wearily climbed the stairs to her room, using her flashlight to illuminate the way. It was now 4:30 a.m. and nothing sounded better than a little shut-eye.

She checked the safety on her Colt and tucked it between the mattress and the headboard. She placed her knife under the pillow.

As she adjusted the curtain over the window beside the bed, she glanced out onto the street in front of the Magic Shop. A movement caught her eye. Across the street and half a block down, someone was standing in the shadows. The man had shifted his position, taking the weight off his right foot.

Her green eyes narrowed. Peering through the darkness, she tried to make out the man's features. He was tall , but his face was hidden in darkness. Despite the distance and the dim light, she noted how arrogantly, how regally he carried himself.

Mark.

Had he followed her from Montecito? She'd been careful that no one had tailed her to the Magic Shop. He must have figured she'd come back here. But why would he follow her, and how long had he been standing out there? Had he seen the coven members leave the building? He must have seen Moon Ray.

She let the curtain drop and climbed into bed. The myriad questions about Mark and the Illuminati threatened to bring on a bout of insomnia. She rolled onto her stomach and punched the pillow under her head, quieting her mind. She fell asleep with her hand under the pillow, where it clenched the hilt of her twelve-inch Bowie.

CHAPTER 8

A phone ringing woke Carla. She blinked an eye at the clock on the bedside table. It was almost 11 a.m. The answering machine clicked on and Gwen's recorded message played. She stumbled down the hall to the kitchenette.

"Carla, are you there? Pick up? I need to talk to you. It's important."

Mark. What the hell was he doing, following her at night and then calling her first thing in the morning? OK, it wasn't exactly first thing in the morning, but still. He was acting like he was really worried about her, or maybe more like a guy who'd been assigned to keep tabs on her.

His voice sounded deep, husky, sexy. Her sleep-fogged brain wasn't thinking clearly. Should she pick up? What if he had information about Gwen? Her hand moved toward the receiver.

Forget it, she told herself and jerked her hand away, reminding herself of one of her mottos: keep your enemies guessing. And he could still be the enemy, especially after his refusal last night to level with her.

Besides, she going to Eye Spy later, so he could wait until then to tell her whatever it was that was so earthshakingly important.

"OK, I guess you're not there. When you get this, call me. Right away. Thanks." He hung up.

She hit the replay button and listened to his message again. His voice washed over her again, sending a delectable frisson of pleasure coursing up her spine. She realized what she was doing and cursed. Wrenching her long black hair back into a ponytail, she hurried back to her room.

She threw on her clothes, trotted downstairs and left the Magic Shop through the back door. The first order of business was to get the new Agency cell phone and touch base with Tate.

A short time later, she pulled up in front of Kristi's house. She squinted as she got out of the car. The bright Santa Barbara sun at noon was diamond sharp. A crisp breeze blew off the ocean. She inhaled deeply, relishing the fresh, marine scent that laced the air.

"There you are, Carla. We were wondering what happened to you." Kristi greeted her at the door. "Come on in. Are you OK? Where's Mark?" Her sky blue eyes sparkled with curiosity.

Carla frowned as she followed her friend into the living room. Ever since they were kids, Kristi had been trying to play matchmaker with the other members of the Cota Club.

"I'm fine, Kristi. Stop looking at me like that! There's nothing between me and Mark!"

"OK, OK," Kristi laughed. "I'll take your word for it." The gleam was still there in her eyes but she let the subject drop. "Did the lead on Gwen pan out?"

"Too soon to tell." Kristi didn't need to know the details.

"You're not telling me everything, are you?" Kristi looked at her with concern.

Carla paused, then lowered her voice. She could hear Kristi's family in the other room. "I can't. If I do, I could be putting you and your family in jeopardy."

"Don't you think you're being a little overdramatic?"

"You're eight months pregnant, Kristi, and you've got the rest of your family to worry about. Don't worry about my sister and me. I'll figure it out." She spoke with confidence, but inside she wasn't so sure. She needed a solid lead, something that would crack the mystery of Gwen's disappearance wide open. "In the meantime, I think it's better if I stay somewhere else."

"You always were so responsible. What would Gwen do without you? Remember the time she got caught trying to put a spell on that nasty old Miss Finch? If you hadn't figured out a good reason to explain why she was trespassing, Gwen would have been in real trouble. Miss Finch could've called the cops and you both might have ended up in foster care."

Carla didn't want to reminisce about the past and all the ways her sister used to get into scrapes. She needed to talk to Tate.

"Have any packages come for me?"

"Oh, I completely forgot. A courier service dropped something off for you early this morning." Kristi heaved herself up from the sofa and went to the dining room table. "It doesn't say who it's from, but the postmark shows it was shipped from Nebraska."

Carla smiled. Kristi may be mother of two little boys and eight months pregnant with twin girls, but she was still a detective.

"From the insurance company?" she asked.

Carla nodded but disliked the feeling of lying to her friend.

"But I thought you were on vacation?"

"Some vacation, huh?"

"Maybe after you find Gwen, you can stick around for a few days? It sure would be fun to get the Cota Club together again. Izzy's due back from China and maybe we could get Tate out here, too. It would be just like the old times."

"Uh, yeah. Maybe." Carla was perfectly happy not remembering the old days. "Thanks for your help with everything, but I've got to get going."

"Let me know as soon as you've found Gwen, OK?" Kristi walked her to the front door.

"Of course. Hopefully, it won't be much longer." She hugged Kristi and hurried to the car. She needed to find a private place to talk to Tate.

She drove out to the park along the bluffs of the Mesa. Except for an elderly couple walking their two Basenjis and a forty-something mother pushing a stroller, she had the place to herself. She took the cell phone and walked to a bench under one of the eucalyptus trees near the viewpoint. Pulling her leather jacket closed against the brisk ocean breeze, she hunkered down on the bench and called Tate.

"Talk to me, Tate. Gwen is still missing and I need leads. What you got?"

"Hi yourself," Tate laughed. "I'm glad to hear you got the phone."

"Thanks. You were very crafty routing it through Nebraska. I told your nosy sister it was from Morton & West."

"I wonder if she has doubts that you work for an insurance company."

"Has she said anything to make you think that?"

"No, but I find it hard to imagine you working for something so straight-laced and stodgy as an insurance company."

"You'd be surprised what goes on behind the doors of even the most innocuous insurance company. Speaking of seemingly innocuous companies, have you found out anything useful about LSA Enterprises?"

"Maybe."

"What?"

"Our assumption that LSA Enterprises is a financial

holding company was correct. The books show it's owned by a Mr. Snyder, but what I found out this morning is that Mr. Snyder is fictitious. The company is actually owned by none other than Richard Lyons."

"Mark's dad?"

"Interesting, isn't it?"

"Well, that might explain why Paul and Mark were there the other night, I suppose."

Although she'd suspected Mark from the beginning and despite her detective's brain wanting to know the facts, she hesitated. What if Tate had evidence that proved beyond a shadow of a doubt that Mark was the enemy?

"But the Lyons family owns a whole slew of companies," she reasoned. "What's the connection to the Illuminati? Were you able to analyze the photos I took of those documents from the Illumine Corporation?"

"I'm still working on the analysis, but it does look like LSA Enterprises is funneling money to the Illuminati. I'm having one of our chemists examine the scientific data you photographed in the Illumine Corporation file. Maybe that will yield some clues, too."

"Have you been able to dig up anything more on Mark?" Carla finally asked the question that had been burning in the back of her brain since the moment she'd called Tate. She hadn't wanted to appear too eager.

"I sure have. Are you sitting down?"

"Yes. What about him?" She sounded too eager, but she couldn't help it.

"He was FBI."

"What do you mean?"

"Before he dropped out of sight two years ago, he worked for the FBI. And get this, his wife was also an agent."

"No way." Carla couldn't believe her ears.

"Yes way," Tate continued. "In fact, his ex-wife is still FBI. Her name's Julie Conway. At the moment, she's on assignment at an undisclosed location."

"Could Mark still be working for the FBI?" Carla's brain spun with the possibilities. "Maybe he's investigating the Illuminati, too?"

"He's definitely no longer with the FBI. Three years ago, he severed all ties with the government. My records are clear on that point."

An unhappy thought sliced through Carla. Maybe he was still married and the divorce was a cover. "Is he really divorced?"

"You still care about him, don't you?"

"Just answer my question." She had to know.

"Yes, the divorce is valid. It was finalized about the time he quit the FBI."

"Is it possible he's working for someone else to expose the Illuminati?"

"Maybe, or maybe he's been recruited to join the Illuminati."

"Like a spy gone bad? Really?"

"It's been known to happen. You've got to admit he'd be a valuable asset to any organization with aspirations to undermine the government."

"Maybe." She didn't want to believe it.

"Watch yourself, Carla." Tate had heard the emotion in her voice. "Don't let what you want to believe color what you know to be true. At this point, the only thing we know for sure is that he is involved with the Illuminati and that he has denied the connection."

"I haven't explicitly asked him. I can't, not without dropping my cover."

"It sounds to me like you're defending him. You can't trust him."

"OK, OK, I get your point," Carla said, irritated but aware that Tate was right.

Tate cleared her throat and dropped her voice. "I've got some more information, but I don't think you're going to like it."

"What?" Carla frowned. It wasn't as if she'd liked any

of the information Tate had given her so far.

"Sam has been digging deeper into the satanic and alchemical aspects of this case. The blood symbols left for both you and Gwen were definitely warnings, and he uncovered something about Abaddon. That name has connections to a nineteenth century German philosopher named Rudolph Steiner. Steiner believed that Satanic evil consisted of a triumvirate of three powerful figures: Abaddon, Lucifer, and Sonneillon."

"So?" Carla tried not to sound impatient. Satanism, alchemy and esoteric philosophy weren't going to help her find Gwen.

"So it confirms one thing. It establishes that the Illuminati is operating within a black magic framework."

"I could have told you that already." Carla quickly filled her in on her conversation with Moon Ray. "But what I really want to know is, why would a group of powerful, influential men band together to target a coven of witches?"

"You're not satisfied with Moon Ray's explanation that it is part of the perennial battle between good and evil?" Tate asked.

"No," she snorted. "Besides, that doesn't explain why the Illuminati is after me, too."

"Do you think they still are?"

"I can't assume they aren't."

"If you're looking for a reasonable explanation, you may not find one," Tate said. "It seems plausible to me that they might be after you because of your relationship with your sister and her role in Circe. Maybe they have an occult reason for targeting you that has nothing to do with a logical motive."

"Ugh," Carla frowned. "I hate magic."

Tate laughed.

In the momentary pause that followed, Carla revolved the case over in her mind. She watched a sailboat race toward the harbor, its white sails billowing.

"Frank said something a while back about the Illuminati possibly having links to international terrorism," she said. "Have you had a chance to investigate how that might factor in?

"I'm working on it," Tate replied, "but right now, the evidence suggests the Illuminati is primarily some kind of domestic occult organization."

"What about the fact that several of those documents from LSA Enterprises were written in German and Latin? Oh, and have you found out how Charles Harrington might be involved?"

"Carla, it's only been a day since you sent me those files. Give me some time, OK?" Tate sighed in exasperation.

"I'm sorry to be so pushy. It's just that I'm getting a bit frustrated about how to proceed."

"I can relate, believe me," Tate said. "Just remember the first rule of detection."

"Work with what you've got. Right. Hey, can you get me access to a DNA analysis machine here in town?"

"Sure. Why?"

"I found some hair that might be Gwen's."

"Really? Where did you find it?"

"In one of the stables at the Lyons estate, along with some duct tape and a gag."

"You don't say." Tate sounded dismayed. "I find it hard to believe the Lyons would lower themselves to the level of brute abduction."

"It does seem a little crass, doesn't it? It's probably someone else's hair, or maybe a horse's." She spoke the words wanting them to be true, but she couldn't help wondering if Mark actually was a spy gone bad.

"I certainly hope so," Tate said. "Give me a few minutes to check and see if there's a DNA analysis facility in town. What're you going to do in the meantime?"

"Head over to Eye Spy. I may as well keep an eye on Mark. Who knows, maybe he'll let something slip."

Carla hung up and walked back to the rental sedan. The wind had shifted and clouds were pouring down the Santa Ynez Mountains. She'd forgotten how dynamic the weather could be in Santa Barbara in the spring. In her memories, the town always seemed desert dry. At the moment, a hint of rain laced the air. She got into the car just as the first clouds obscured the sun. When she reached State Street, her cell rang.

"You're in luck," Tate said. "Drighton Technologies is owned by a guy Frank knows, so discretion is assured."

"Excellent," Carla said, swinging the car off State Street and heading for the freeway. Drighton Technologies was in Goleta, the sprawling town west of Santa Barbara.

Forty-five minutes later, she was headed back to State Street and Eye Spy Private Eye. Low-slung clouds obscured Santa Barbara's spectacular scenery, and it had begun to rain. She parked several blocks over from Eye Spy.

Now that she was finally free to turn her attention to Mark, her heart kicked up in a nervous flutter. Was he possibly an ally? Angrily, she squelched the hopeful thought. He hadn't once leveled with her, and he had told her nothing to help her find Gwen.

"Hi, Mandy." She breezed by the receptionist, who was on the phone, and headed to Mark's office.

His door was closed. She knocked softly.

"Come in," he called.

She pushed the door open. He was on the computer. He looked up when she entered and immediately jumped to his feet.

"Where have you been? Didn't you get my message this morning?" He came around the desk and her pulse went into overdrive.

She was still staring at his spectacular body, dressed in a white crew neck sweater and designer jeans, when he caught her in a hug.

"I'm so glad you're OK." He squeezed her close.

Damn, he felt good. She hated being caught off guard, but she gave herself a moment to savor the feel of his body touching hers from thigh to chest, before shoving him away.

"You have a lousy memory, don't you? I told you, no manhandling." She stepped back.

"Can I help it if I'm happy to see you're OK after last night's escapade?" He held his hands up in mock surrender, grinning.

"I'm touched you care so much." The finest trace of sarcasm colored her smile, but then she realized the implication in her words. She frowned and plopped into the chair beside the desk. Dropping the bantering tone, she changed the subject.

"I got your message. Do you have a lead on Gwen?"

He returned to his seat on the other side of the desk. The grin had disappeared as though it had never been. Leaning back in his chair, he steepled his fingers together and placed them against his lips. He gazed at her pensively.

"Come on, Mark. Don't keep me in suspense. What aren't you telling me?" Her pulse quickened. Had something happened to Gwen, something bad?

He studied her a moment longer, his gaze traveling from her long black hair down to her face and then briefly down to the red turtleneck she was wearing. Under other circumstances, she might have felt flattered at his intense regard, but at the instant, fear rather than lust made her heart race and her palms damp.

"Gwen was being initiated into a coven, wasn't she?" He finally spoke. "

"Why are you speaking in the past tense? What's happened to her?"

"Sorry, it was a figure of speech," he said hastily. "I don't know what's happened to her. I certainly hope she's OK."

She stared at him hard. Did he know where Gwen was

but wasn't letting on? His silver eyes, the whole of his expression, looked sincere, like he was telling the truth. Either that or he was a consummate liar.

"Yes, she *is* being initiated into a coven." She emphasized the verb. "But what does that have to do with what you're not telling me?" She wanted to scream at him to get to the point.

"You know the name of the coven, right?"

"Do you?" She threw back at him. Two could play the interrogator game.

He looked at her wryly, obviously aware of her tactic. "Yes, I do."

"Then why are you asking me?" she interrupted impatiently.

"Look, Carla, I don't know what information you're working with, so I don't know if what I'm going to tell you will make sense."

"OK, OK," she conceded. "The coven is called Circe."

"Do you know who its members are?"

She looked at him, unable to mask the suspicion coloring her expression. There was no way she was going to compromise Moon Ray, Sally and the other witches to a man she knew was involved with the Illuminati.

"Yes, I do." She wanted to add, what of it? Instead, she sat silent, waiting for him to respond.

"They have all disappeared. I'm sorry to say it, but it looks like they've been abducted."

"What? How do you know that?"

"Eight separate phone calls were made to the SBPD by concerned family members and friends about their disappearances."

"When were the calls made?"

"Between six and ten this morning. I'm sure you know the police won't open an official investigation until they've been missing for twenty-four hours. I called the families to see if there were any witnesses, but no. That's the strange thing. It's as if they disappeared into thin air."

"Maybe it isn't foul play. Maybe they decided to go off together somewhere." She didn't believe that for a moment, especially not after her conversation with Moon Ray. The witch had been very clear about returning to the Magic Shop to perform the protection spell.

"I suppose it's possible," Mark said. "But why would they do that without telling their families where they were going?"

"You're asking me to explain the motives of a coven of witches? Believe me, I don't understand their logic even when they try to explain it to me themselves."

The intercom buzzed. Mark answered it. A dark expression slammed down across his face. As soon as he realized she was watching him, he wiped all emotion from his face.

"Show him in," he said into the receiver. Hanging up, he abruptly rose to his feet. She followed suit.

"Can we talk later?" He escorted her to the door.

"Sure," she said, standing beside the closed door. Why was he trying to get rid of her so fast?

He stood close, staring down into her green eyes with what looked like sincere concern. She thought he might try to touch her again. A rueful expression crossed his face. He dug his hands into the front pockets of his jeans.

"I've got a bad feeling about this latest development. Something tells me you will be the next target."

"Why?"

"Let's just say that I don't think the guy who attacked you in that alley was a mugger."

"You think he's involved with what's happened to my sister and the missing coven." She knew she was stating the obvious, but she wanted to nail him down. If only he would broach the subject of the Illuminati, but until then, she couldn't mention that name—not without risking her cover.

"No question about it." He opened the door and

practically pushed her into the hallway.

"Carla deVille?"

She turned around and found Mark's brother Paul standing directly behind her.

"Hi Paul, long time no see," she said.

He was dressed formally in a navy business suit, his wing-tipped shoes immaculately polished, his straight blond hair cut short. He stood only inches taller than she and his features lacked Mark's hard masculine edges. He held a black leather briefcase in well-manicured hands.

"What are you doing here?" He studied her as much as she studied him, his eyes cold and pale blue. "What are you doing with my brother?"

She felt rather than saw Mark tense behind her. Back in high school, she would have assumed Paul was mad that his brother was "slumming" with her, not that they were actually doing anything of the sort. Now, however, she had no idea why he might take offense at Mark's speaking with her. It didn't make sense. If they were both members of the Illuminati, wouldn't they know what each was up to? She didn't owe Paul any explanations, that was sure. Better to keep him guessing.

"Wouldn't you like to know?" she said saucily and sauntered down the hall to Kristi's office. She'd have loved to eavesdrop on the two brothers, but there was no way to do so unnoticed.

She left Tate voicemail about the missing coven and then spent several hours of fruitless computer research before leaving the agency. She mulled over Paul's appearance. Why was he there? And why had Mark been in such a rush to get her out of there? She thought about Mark's reaction when Mandy had buzzed him. He'd looked angry, as if he hadn't expected Paul.

She stood on the sidewalk and looked up at the agency windows. The light was on in Mark's office, but she couldn't see him. He and Paul hadn't left his office all afternoon, she'd made sure of that. She'd tail whichever brother came out first to see if that might yield any clues.

There were two exits from Eye Spy—either down the front formal staircase that emptied directly onto State Street or down the back service elevator to the alley in back. Which way would they leave?

She jogged around the office building to the alley. The main parking structure was across the alleyway. Knowing the Lyons boys, they wouldn't mind paying to park. Hell, they probably had VIP parking, or maybe their family owned the building. The parking structure emptied onto the same cross street where she'd parked her car. How convenient. A small smile touched her lips as she walked to the rental car and got in. She glanced about the street to see if anyone was watching her case the joint. What with the steady stream of weekend tourists coming into town from L.A. and the Santa Barbara rush hour, it was impossible to tell. She turned on the radio.

During the next thirty minutes, she carefully watched each car that exited the parking structure, since she didn't know what kind of car Paul drove. Living in D.C. and working on the seamier side of life, she'd forgotten how affluent most Santa Barbarans were, at least the ones that paid to park when they shopped downtown. A sparkling stream of Mercedes, Beamers, an assortment of SUVs including several Hummers, and even a Rolls Royce Silver Shadow exited the place. No sign of Mark's Porsche. Her stomach growled. Just as she was about to abandon her mission, a black H2 Hummer driven by a man with a blond crew cut shoved its way out of the parking structure and into the crowded Friday evening traffic. Bingo.

Paul was on his cell. Perhaps it was the massive size of the vehicle that made him drive so rudely. He pulled into traffic with no concern for the oncoming cars. Tires screeched, horns honked. He didn't notice. Carla smiled. He'd be trivial to tail and he was obviously oblivious to anything but whoever he was speaking to. She swung a U-turn and raced to catch up with him.

He headed east toward Montecito. Maybe he was headed home. She wondered if he had Gwen stashed somewhere out there. Maybe he'd lead her straight to her sister. For a moment, she felt hopeful, but then he turned onto San Ysidro Road and entered Montecito's posh uptown center. He pulled the H2 into the valet parking of Evvia, one of Montecito's most exclusive restaurants.

She ditched the rental in the parking lot of the pizza joint across the street and hurried around the side of the restaurant. Dressed in jeans and a red turtleneck, there was no way they'd let her in, even to get a drink at the bar, and even if they had, she'd have stood out like a sore thumb. Instead, she'd have to play Peeping Tom and look in through the windows.

The restaurant entrance faced the parking lot and teemed with a black and white mass of well-heeled diners, valet parkers and possibly a bodyguard or two. Along the opposite side of the building, a row of low bushes grew under the restaurant windows. Carla smiled. The bushes would make good cover.

Unfortunately, they were also still wet from the afternoon's rain. She darted between the bushes, grimacing as cold water dripped down her back. She poked her head up above the bushes and peered through the window. A glamorous blond was seated at a table directly adjacent to the window and saw her. The woman's finely penciled eyebrows shot up in surprise.

Whoops, Carla exclaimed under her breath and crouched hurriedly back down.

More cold water splashed her as the leaves smacked across her face. Her plan wasn't going to work if the diners saw her staring in. She crept on hands and knees further around the side of the building. Risking another peek, she looked up again. She was now at the back of the restaurant. The place was crowded and it took her several minutes to locate Paul.

He sat relatively close to her location but his back was

to her. He was seated at a table with two other men. Whoever they were, they might be important. Carla whipped out camera and took a moment to ensure the flash was off. She doubted the pictures would turn out, but she snapped a few shots of the men anyway.

Dropping the camera back in her purse, she peered through the window and studied the men as carefully as she could in the dim light of the restaurant. If the photos didn't turn out, she wanted to make sure she could positively ID them.

They were both much older than Paul, in their early to mid sixties. The older one looked vaguely familiar. She noticed the firm cut of his chin, his ramrod straight posture, and the distinguished sweep of his gray hair. She tried to make out his eyes behind the glasses he wore. It was difficult because they reflected the candles on the table. His eyes looked like twin flames. With such a proud bearing, could he be Richard Lyons?

She turned her attention to the other man. He also sat with a regal posture, his back straight, his broad shoulders squared. His hair still retained much of its original black color, though it had traces of silver running through it. He wore no glasses. Something about him compelled her gaze. She couldn't tell the color of his eyes but they seemed piercing, almost hypnotic.

Oh crap, he was staring right at her! A slight smile twisted the harsh line of his mouth upward. She dropped down beneath the window, her heart racing. She'd been so intently studying him that she hadn't even realized he was watching her.

The bushes swished nearby. A big man was forcing his way toward her. Despite the darkness, there was no doubting the massive man's identity. The Hulk. She swiveled on one knee and crawled as fast as she could back toward the street, but it wasn't fast enough. A giant hand clamped onto her sneaker.

Damn. If she'd been wearing any other shoe, she

might have wriggled free. Unfortunately, the sneaker was laced up tight. He had her.

"Come here, you little bitch. You've caused quite enough trouble," he drawled in a distinctly Texan accent. Grabbing her arm, he hoisted her to her feet.

"What, no Latin tonight?" she said, hoping to egg on his fury.

If his personality was as bull-like as his appearance, maybe he'd do something stupid if enraged. His hands, the size of baseball mitts, had her trapped.

"You think you're so smart. Just you wait," he said smugly, dragging her through the bushes toward the back of the restaurant.

In the tight space between the bushes and the building, the only way he could drag her was to walk backward as he pulled her forward. She smirked. Good thing he hadn't pulled a gun on her, she thought as she rammed her knee into his groin. It wasn't the most creative escape tactic, but it worked.

"Umph." He dropped her and doubled over in agony.

"Hope I did permanent damage," she jeered, before turning and rushing through the bushes toward the street. She didn't care if the people in the restaurant saw her now. When the Hulk recovered, he'd undoubtedly be mad, real mad. She didn't want to be anywhere near him at that point.

During the drive back to Santa Barbara, she sent the digital photos to Tate and left her a voicemail to tell her the files were on the way.

There had to be a connection between Mark and the Hulk, but tonight she'd left Mark in downtown and had followed Paul to Montecito where the Hulk had suddenly appeared. Was the Hulk Paul Lyons' bodyguard? Her stomach growled. Nothing like a little adrenaline rush to get the appetite flowing. There'd be time enough to answer all the questions she had, but first she had to eat.

CHAPTER 9

Instead of heading downtown, Carla drove to Milpas Street. At 8 p.m. on a Friday night, she didn't want to deal with the teeming throngs of people cruising State Street or the overpriced and poorly cooked tourist faire. Pedro's was one of her favorite restaurants, a little Mexican joint on the poorer East side of town. If things hadn't changed since her visit home, she wouldn't have to wait long for food.

She pulled onto a side street and parked. Walking by the restaurant to its front door around the side, she glanced in the window. What the hell, Mark was in there, and with a woman!

Carla's green eyes narrowed. The setup looked romantic. Who was that woman? There was only one way to find out. Without questioning her motives, she dug the costume rock he'd given her out of her purse and jammed it on her finger. She released her long hair from its pony tail, flipped her hair a few times to make it wild, and marched self-righteously into the restaurant and up to their table.

"Oh, there you are, honey chil'." She laid on a thick Southern accent. "I was wundrin' where you'd got yerself to."

She placed her left hand on his shoulder, making sure the rock sparkled ostentatiously toward the other woman. When Mark simply stared at her, a look of disbelief on his face, she continued.

"Well, ain't you gonna introduce me to yer lady friend? Hi, sugar." She reached her left hand over to the other woman, keeping her other hand proprietarily on Mark's shoulder. "I'm Christine Fairchild, Mark's fiancée."

The woman's hair was actually a deep shade of red, almost auburn, and she had striking, hazel eyes. Carla felt a stab of jealousy. The woman was beautiful. When she heard what Carla said, the woman's gorgeous hazel eyes widened in surprise.

"Really? Mark, why didn't you tell me you were engaged?" The woman glanced at him.

He still said nothing. Carla wondered if he was mad or amused. It was hard to tell by the slight twist of his lips and the steady glint in his eye as he stared up at her.

"Nice to meet you, Christine. I'm Julie," the other woman interjected. She paused a fraction of a second before continuing. "A friend of Mark's." She took the hand Carla offered in a firm, sure grip. "Nice ring," she said, studying the rock a moment before letting Carla's hand go.

Who was she? Julie Conway, Mark's ex-wife and an FBI agent? Unlikely he'd be hanging out with his ex-wife, but Carla saw the intelligence in her eyes. The woman knew the ring was a fake. She shot a glance down at Mark. He was now looking at Julie so she couldn't see his expression.

"Well, Mark, aren't you going to move over and make room for Christine?" Julie arched an eyebrow at him, a grin tugging at her lips. "I want to hear all the details. How did you meet? How long have you been engaged?"

Carla wondered how he was going to get out of this one. To her surprise, he slid over in the booth.

"Here, Sweetcakes, have a seat." He patted the seat beside him and laid his arm along the back of the booth.

Sweetcakes? What kind of an endearment was that? She fought to keep the vapid smile on her face as she took in the seating arrangement. If she sat down, he'd have his arm around her. He looked up at her expectantly, his silver eyes now glinting with definite humor and perhaps a challenge. She slid into the booth.

Sure enough, his arm came around her neck. His hand gently squeezed her shoulder. Before she realized what he was doing, he pulled her to him. Her eyes swept up to his. His eyes burned brighter. She dropped her gaze to his mouth, realizing he was inches from her. She licked suddenly dry lips.

"Hi there," he said, his voice low and husky.

And then he was kissing her. She couldn't believe he'd stoop to such a trick, but then all thought fled. Gone was the unsure, tentative boy who'd once kissed her long ago. In his place was a thoroughly experienced man. Mark's lips were firm and moist and tantalizingly delicious. His hand on her shoulder tightened and crept into her hair as his tongue brushed her lips, seductively seeking entrance.

Flames licked through her. She tried to tamp them down. She didn't want to give him the satisfaction of knowing he affected her, but then she remembered Julie was watching. If she pulled away or resisted in any way, she'd blow her cover as the loving fiancée. Damn. She'd gotten herself into a bind. She opened her mouth.

Maybe that was a mistake. He instantly claimed the advantage, his tongue sliding between her lips and stroking her tongue. He tasted of Mexican food, of corn and beer, and of something else, something delicious that she suspected was the taste of him. She sighed and gave up the fight. She returned the kiss with enthusiasm.

The sound of someone clearing their throat brought her back to consciousness. What the hell were they doing? She was practically sitting on his lap and her hands were tangled in his hair. She wrenched her mouth from his and stared at him. His eyes met hers, dark with desire, and those dangerously delicious lips were parted with what she could swear was surprise.

"Well, well, well," Julie said. "You two really are in love, aren't you?"

Carla wriggled off his lap and put some space between their overheated bodies. She was trembling and her mind refused to cooperate. The only thing that registered was that whatever had transpired between them wasn't love. Lust definitely, but not love. She wanted to kick Mark for taking advantage of the situation, but damn it, she was the one who had created the situation. Fighting the urge to grit her teeth in frustration, she pasted a syrupy smile on her face and looked across the table at Julie.

"Oh, yer right, chil'. We wouldn't be gitten married if we weren't, now, would we?" She laid on the thick accent, wondering again if this were Mark's ex.

Had he been in love with her when they married? He didn't seem to be in love with her now, nor her with him for that matter. But then with her body trembling and the heady taste of him still on her tongue, she was having trouble objectively assessing anything.

Julie was looking at Mark. Something abruptly registered in her eyes. The next moment, she rose to her feet and made a point of looking at her watch.

"Congratulations to you both," she said. "I've got somewhere I'm supposed to be right now. I'll catch you later."

She rushed off. The moment she left the restaurant, Mark turned on Carla.

"What are you doing here?"

"Can't this wait for just a moment? I'm starving."

Carla dropped the accent and moved quickly away from him to the other side of the booth. She signaled the waiter and resolutely ignored Mark while the waiter took her order and cleared away Julie's dishes. Once the waiter was gone, she glared at him.

"How dare you kiss me like that!"

The memory of the kiss started her knees trembling again and she found her eyes dropping to his lips. Impatiently, she jerked them back up to look him in the eye. He stared back at her with a mixture of incredulity and residual desire.

"You asked for it, posing as my fiancée. What on earth possessed you to do such a thing?"

"You were the one who started the whole fiancée business last night."

"Yes, but that was to give you a cover. I was trying to keep you safe."

"I know, and I appreciate your concern for my well-being." She tried to sound suitably appreciative, although she still doubted his motives.

"But we're not under cover right now," he continued. "Hell, except for that phony ring and your silly accent, you're not even in disguise, so why tell Julie a bogus story about our relationship?"

"Our relationship, is that what we have?"

"You saw me with Julie and you were jealous, weren't you?" His studied her, a new light dawning in his eyes.

Of course she wasn't jealous of that woman, she told herself. She just wanted to know what he was up to and if Julie had something to do with his involvement in the Illuminati. She realized she could use his thinking she was jealous to her advantage. She wanted him to answer some questions of her own.

"Who is Julie? Does she have a last name?" she asked as she dug into the chicken enchilada the waiter had placed in front of her.

Mark watched her shove more food into her mouth and laughed. "You weren't kidding. You're starved."

"Pedro's is the best," she said between bites.

"Well, that's one thing we have in common, at least. I love the food here." He sipped a cup of coffee.

"You still haven't answered my question."

"What, about Julie's last name?"

"Yes."

"Her name's Conway, Julie Conway."

Carla choked. Whatever she'd expected him to say, she hadn't thought he'd actually tell the truth.

"Hey, slow down. Inhaling your food isn't good for the digestion."

She wiped her mouth with the paper napkin and took a sip of soda. If he was in such a truth-telling mood, she wondered what else he'd tell her.

"So, how do you know Julie Conway?" She lifted her gaze from her almost empty plate to look at Mark.

He sipped the coffee, his silver eyes studying her over the rim of his cup.

"She and I have been friends for years."

"Is that all?" Maybe ex-wives could be friends, but she'd never heard of such a thing.

"Like I said, we're friends. Now I could use your help tomorrow on the Dupree case." He placed the cup back on the table and leaned forward, dropping his voice. "I've got a lead on Sebastian Dupree's missing artwork."

"Really?" she said. He had adroitly changed the subject, but why? Why hide the fact he and Julie had been married?

"Since you have such a flair for undercover work," he continued, grinning, "we'll go in disguise. You up for it?"

If she went with him, she could keep tabs on him. Besides, she was still waiting on the intel analysis from Tate. "OK. Are we posing as the Fairchilds, or do you have something else in mind?"

"We're going to attend the Jackson fundraiser tomorrow afternoon. It's being held at Charles Harrington's estate."

"How interesting," she murmured. "What does Harrington have to do with the Dupree case?" Her brain was already spinning with ways she might be able to combine working on the Dupree case with her own interest in Charles Harrington. He'd been at LSA Enterprises just minutes before Paul and Mark had shown up.

"He's hosting the fundraiser." He drained his cup of coffee and looked at her. "You want dessert?"

Was she imaging the suggestive tone in his voice?

"No, thanks," she said. "But what's Harrington got to do with the artwork?"

"Let's talk about that somewhere else." He stood up and offered her his hand.

He glanced around the restaurant. Santa Barbara was a small place, and who knew who might be listening to their conversation. After all, hadn't she just run into him here at Pedro's?

She took his hand and they headed outside. The night had grown colder. The cloudless sky twinkled with distant stars, barely visible through the glow of the orange streetlights. His hand was warm and firm. She pulled free.

"Where are you going to spend the night?" he asked as they approached her car.

"Don't worry about me. I'll be OK."

She unlocked the door and made to slide into the driver seat. He put a hand on her arm, stilling her movement.

"Be careful."

"I'm always careful." She saw the concern in his eyes. "Why are you so worried? What's going on?"

"They came for your sister." He pulled her closer, his deep voice a whisper. "They came for Circe." His voice dropped lower, barely a rumble in his chest. "They are going to come for you."

His silver eyes pinned hers with the intensity of his gaze. A shiver ran down her spine. He was warning her, but would he finally level with her?

"Who is coming for me? Who are 'they'?" she demanded. "What aren't you telling me?"

He abruptly dropped her arms and backed away. He passed a hand over his face before looking at her again. His expression had shifted. He looked sad, but resolved.

"I can't tell you, Carla. Believe me, I wish I could. But I can't. Just be careful, OK? Don't let your guard down."

He spun away and headed down the street, presumably to his car. She watched him turn the corner before getting into her own rental car. She had a feeling he'd come as close to an admission of his involvement with the Illuminati as he could risk at the moment.

Taking his warning to heart, she decided not to go back to the Magic Shop. Instead, she headed for the Riviera and Henry Lee's Green Dragon School of Martial Arts. By the time she reached the school, it was 10 p.m. No lights were on in the main building.

She took the path through the garden to the back where Henry and his family lived. Not much had changed since the days when she and Gwen used to come over for an occasional home-cooked meal. The cactus lining the space between the path and the school building had grown a bit higher, but the grassy knoll with its spectacular view still remained. This time of night, the Channel Islands weren't visible, but the long line of off-shore oil wells twinkled brightly along the Santa Barbara Channel. She knocked on the door. Isabelle McCormick opened it.

"Izzy, what are you doing here? I thought you were in China," she laughed in surprise.

"I could ask you the same thing!" Izzy grinned and enveloped her in a big hug. Unlike her two older sisters, Izzy was tall, almost as tall as Carla, but like her sisters she also had curly blond hair.

"Come on in." She led the way into the Lee's living room.

"Where are Henry and Patricia?" Carla asked.

She sat down cross-legged on one of the zafus scattered about the living room floor. She smiled, remembering all the times Henry had tried to teach her the correct posture for sitting on the little round cushions during meditation.

"They took off to visit some of their folks back East." Izzy rejected the zafus in favor of lying sprawled out full-length on the carpet. She tucked one of the zafus under her head. "I just got back from China yesterday. They wanted me to housesit. You know how Pat is about her orchids."

"I remember." Patricia Lee's international reputation as an orchid expert was fully merited. Her orchids were spectacular.

"Kristi tells me Gwen's missing and that you're working with Mark Lyons to try and find her. How's it going?"

Carla was glad Izzy didn't rib her about Mark. Maybe she didn't remember the feud that used to rage between them back when they were students at the Green Dragon School. She looked at her friend, thinking. Like Kristi, Izzy didn't know she was CIA and only knew her cover story.

"I haven't found her yet, so I wouldn't say it's going very well." She kept her answer vague.

"Do you think someone could have abducted her? Has anyone asked for ransom?"

"I wish it were as simple as that." Carla shook her head. "Let's just say that like my mom, Gwen has gotten herself mixed up in the occult."

"I'll buy that." Izzy's straightforward response reminded Carla of why she liked Izzy. She and Tate shared the same kind of level-headedness.

"Do you mind if I crash here for the night?"

"Sure, it would be fun to have the company. But I'm curious, why did you come here tonight?"

"I was hoping Henry and Pat might let me stay here for a few nights."

"Really? What's wrong with the Magic Shop?"

"Mark says it isn't safe. He's worried someone might

be after me."

"Has someone threatened you?"

"Don't worry. I can handle myself."

"It sounds like you're giving me a snow job." Izzy held up her hand in protest when Carla made to interrupt. "Don't worry. I'm the queen of discretion and I know when not to ask certain questions. But if Mark's concerned, you make sure to watch your back."

"I never knew you thought so highly of his opinion," Carla couldn't resist throwing out.

"You and he had some problems when we were kids, but that was a long time ago. He's a good guy, Carla."

"How do you know?"

"Well, for one thing, he sits on the board of the School and he's been a generous donor."

"Aren't all the Lyons?"

Izzy ignored the snide remark. "Since he came back to town, he's also volunteered to lead some of our classes," she said. "You remember he was a black belt in Green Dragon technique?"

"How could I forget," Carla quipped, remembering their recent sparring match at the farmhouse in Virginia.

Izzy rolled her eyes. "All I'm saying is, don't be too quick to jump to conclusions about the guy, OK? But enough about that. Come on and let's get your bed set up."

As they unfolded one of the futons from the living room into a bed, Izzy regaled Carla with stories about her trip to China. Her travels had taken her to several of the leading Chinese martial art schools, where she had the opportunity to invite several top martial artists to visit the Green Dragon.

"It would be so cool if we could make the Green Dragon one of the best martial art schools in California, if not the whole country," she said, tucking in the sheet. "It's great to see you again, Carly. Sleep well tonight. And hey, maybe tomorrow you'll get lucky and find Gwen."

"I wish it was as simple as good luck," Carla sighed.

After Izzy left, she had trouble falling asleep. She had to get Mark and that mind-bending kiss out of her head. She rolled onto her back and stared blindly at the dark ceiling, carefully reviewing the facts of the case. Something had to break soon in the case. She could feel it. She just hoped it was in time to keep Gwen safe. She punched the pillows under her head and closed her eyes.

#

Carla slept until noon, awoke thoroughly refreshed, and shared a delicious brunch with Izzy before going into the lush gardens of the Green Dragon School to call Tate. She had the place to herself, since Izzy had left to run errands and the school was closed. She took a seat on the stone bench by the small koi pond. Hummingbirds and butterflies flitted among the vibrantly colored flowers.

"Hey Tate, I need leads. Anything new?"

"Yes, it looks like we're finally getting a few leads." Tate's usually cheerful voice sounded somber.

"What's wrong?" Carla's pulse jumped.

"Frank called. Apparently, his buddy James Drighton of Drighton Technologies called him this morning and gave him the DNA results on that hair sample you dropped off yesterday."

"Wow, that was fast. What did he find?"

"Carla, the hair you gave him to analyze was Gwen's."

"Oh." Her heart stopped.

"You know what that means, right? It means that someone held your sister captive in the Lyons' stables. This is proof positive that she really was abducted, and most likely by a Lyons or one of their employees."

"Crap."

"Did the other coven members turn up?"

"No. Nothing has been heard from them since they disappeared."

"I've got a bad feeling about this."

"What're you thinking?"

"Harassing you and abducting your sister is one thing, but to abduct eight women, all within two hours and in broad daylight with no witnesses, is quite a feat. It'd require careful planning and coordination, and why would they do it? My guess is that they've got something planned for the coven, something bad. And judging by the timeline of these abductions, they're planning to do something sooner rather than later."

"Damn. I bet you're right." Carla pushed her hair away from her face, frowning.

"I have some more information," Tate continued.

"What?"

"I was able to positively ID one of the two men Paul Lyons had dinner with last night. There's no question that the older man was his father, Richard Lyons."

"I suspected as much. He looked familiar, though I don't remember ever having met him before. What about the other guy?"

"I'm not having much luck IDing him. When I cross-checked the photos we have on file with the photos you sent, I thought the man you photographed might've been Jonathan Carter, but Frank tells me that's impossible."

"Why? Who's Jonathan Carter?"

"I've never heard of the man myself, but Frank says he's one of the masterminds of Wall Street. He says there's no way Jonathan Carter would've been having dinner in Montecito last night."

"Why not?"

"Because he never leaves New York."

"How does Frank know that?"

"I asked him the same question. I even showed him the photos you took. He said there was no way to verify Carter was the man. Apparently, the most recent photo on file of Jonathan Carter was taken over ten years ago. The man is extremely elusive."

"All the more possible he could have snuck out to California for a clandestine dinner with Richard and Paul."

"Come on, Carla, think about it. How clandestine is it to have dinner in a public restaurant in a relatively small town? If they were going to have a clandestine meeting, don't you think they could've just video-conferenced from their private offices or something? I think Frank's right. The guy was probably just some personal acquaintance of the Lyons. They were probably just having dinner."

"Maybe, but it doesn't explain why the CIA doesn't have a record of the guy."

"Hey, this is a free country! We don't keep records on everybody."

"OK, OK." Carla changed the subject. "What else have you got for me, any other leads?"

"Yeah. Sam's been researching the Illuminati and traced it back to the Middle Ages. Apparently, as early as the fifteenth century, a mysterious organization calling itself 'the Illuminati' surfaced in Europe. Its members practiced alchemy and an assortment of black arts. But get this," Tate paused, her voice dropping. "They believed that by utilizing the power of polar opposites they could obtain vast amounts of psychic power."

"'Polar opposites'? 'Psychic power'? What the hell does that mean?"

"Sam couldn't find specific details about that. But I have a theory."

"Go on."

"Those guys at that farmhouse chanted about 'the light inside reflecting the light outside' and they chanted in Latin. They were talking about opposites—the inside and the outside—and Latin was the preferred language of priests in the Middle Ages. I'll bet you the men we're dealing with are part of some kind of modern day reincarnation of the very same Illuminati Sam found in his research."

"I suppose it's possible." Carla thought over her friend's theory. "If what you say is true, what do you think it all means?

"I don't know, at least not yet. I just don't understand their motive for targeting you, Gwen and Circe. One more thing." Tate paused and cleared her throat. "What about Mark?"

"I knew you were going to get around to asking about him." Carla stood up and walked back along the gravel path through the garden.

"The evidence is stacking up that the Lyons family is directly involved with the Illuminati and with Gwen's abduction," Tate said. "You know as well as I do that Mark is involved and that he probably knows where your sister and the other Circe members are."

"It's possible," Carla granted reluctantly. "But if he really is a member of the Illuminati and if they really are after me, too, then why hasn't he tried to abduct me? He's had plenty of opportunity."

She didn't want to sound like she was defending him, but she couldn't help it. He hadn't harmed her. If anything, he'd consistently been concerned for her welfare—and her pleasure.

"Have you tried straight out asking him about his involvement?" Tate asked.

"Come on, Tate. You know I can't do that," she said impatiently. "What possible reason could I give for suspecting him without blowing my cover? I can't risk letting him find out I'm CIA. It would jeopardize our entire investigation, especially if he really is the enemy."

"I suppose you're right." Tate didn't sound very happy about it. "Whatever you do, Carla, be careful, OK? The Illuminati came after you once before, and I'm more convinced than ever that things are coming to a head. You could very well still be a target."

"Don't worry so much, Tate. Haven't you heard, too much stress leads to premature aging?" She headed inside to the bathroom for a shower. It was time to get ready for the fundraiser. "I'll catch you later. And as I said, don't worry. I can take care of myself."

CHAPTER 10

An hour later, Carla sat with Mark in his Porsche as they drove to the Harrington estate for the Jackson fundraiser. She shot a glance at him, wishing she could ask him straight out the question that kept running through her mind. The DNA evidence proved her sister had been held in one of the stables of his family's estate. Did he know where she was? Keeping him close was one way to find out.

She straightened in the car seat. Maybe this afternoon she could play double-agent. Sleuthing in Harrington's house might not just uncover the Dupree's stolen goods. It might also reveal information about the congressman's connection to LSA Enterprises and possibly the Illuminati.

"So, you never did explain why you think Harrington has Dupree's stolen artwork. Care to elaborate?" She fiddled with the curly auburn wig of her disguise.

"A lead came in yesterday. I've got a hunch Harrington's got the painting."

"Just a hunch?" She didn't put much faith in hunches.

"A source confirmed the painting was sold yesterday and Harrington was party at the sale."

"OK, then what's the plan for tonight?"

"We need to check Harrington's safe. That's the most likely place for him to stash it."

"How big is the painting?"

"Small enough to fit in a standard issue safe."

"Where's the safe?"

"In his study on the second floor."

"So when do we go upstairs?" She checked her makeup in the car's vanity mirror before turning back to him. It was difficult to resist the urge to rub her eyes. The false eyelashes made her eyes itch.

"Let's mingle with the other guests for a while and get the lay of the land. After the meet and greet and the champagne's been flowing a while, Harrington will probably give a speech. That'll be the perfect distraction for us to do some safecracking."

"Sounds like you're familiar with these kinds of fundraisers." She ruthlessly quashed the memory of the only fundraiser she'd ever attended, the night at his family's estate when her girlhood dreams had come crashing down.

"Of course," he grinned, obviously not sharing the memory. "It comes with the territory of being a Lyons, don't you know." He waggled a gray eyebrow at her.

She studied him a moment. He'd donned a gray wig and moustache. A pair of slightly tinted, designer glasses disguised his distinctive eyes. He wore an impeccable, soft gray silk suit. If she hadn't been so familiar with the proud, almost arrogant way he held his body, she might have been fooled into thinking he was a distinguished older gentleman.

"Not a Lyons, a Townsend," she said. It felt good to correct him. It showed he wasn't perfect.

"How could I forget? Must be my advanced age," he laughed good-naturedly.

"So, let's say we locate the painting." She changed the subject. "How do you propose we smuggle it out of the house?"

"We'll use that laptop case." He gestured to the storage well behind the front seat. "The painting is only about a square foot, so it should fit quite snugly."

He piloted the Porsche up the long winding drive of the Harrington estate. The party was in full swing and they parked at the end of a vast line of luxury automobiles.

"Welcome, friends." A flamboyantly dressed older woman greeted them near the front door, a clipboard in hand. "May I have your names, please?"

"Samuel and Joyce Townsend," Mark said.

The woman ran a long magenta nail down the sheet. "Ah, there you are." She checked off their names. "I'm glad you could make it. Here are some nametags."

They quickly wrote their pseudonyms on the tags, put them on, and then sauntered into the mansion. A crowd of Santa Barbara's elite thronged about in the foyer. Mark guided Carla through the crowd to where a large sweeping staircase ascended to the second floor. Several large pots filled with broad-leafed tropical plants stood at the base of the staircase.

"This should do it," Mark said under his breath.

He abandoned her elbow for a moment to deposit the laptop case between the fronds of one potted plant. Carla darted a glance around the foyer. No one seemed to notice. Moments later, he had her by the elbow again and steered her into an enormous ballroom.

Banquet tables of food and wine lined one side of the room, attended by a host of formally dressed caterers in chef's whites. On the other side, people accepting contributions to Jackson's campaign stood behind tables covered in political materials. Enormous banners hung on the walls behind the canvassers. A band played dance music on the stage at the far end of the ballroom, where a number of the guests were dancing.

In her spiky heels, Carla towered over most of the women and many of the men. She had to laugh at the incongruity of being among so many of Santa Barbara's well-heeled elite. Mark might move through the place with cool aplomb, used to such ostentatious displays of wealth, but she couldn't. She felt like a fox in the henhouse, or perhaps a wolf in sheep's clothing.

"What're you smiling at?" Mark whispered in her ear, causing tingles of awareness to dance through her.

"I'm thinking how a deVille from the wrong side of town is infiltrating Santa Barbara's upper crust." Her teeth gleamed white behind the deep burgundy lipstick of her disguise.

"You're not a deVille, my dear. Tonight, you're Joyce Townsend, a beautiful billionairess." He lifted a canapé from one of the many trays being carried through the crowd and held it to her lips.

"How could I forget?" She opened her mouth and accepted the delicious morsel.

The three-inch heels put her almost at his height. She looked him directly in the eye as she chewed, thinking again what a remarkable color his eyes were, like the color of clouds passing over a midnight sky. His eyes darkened perceptibly as she swallowed the canapé. She licked her lips.

"Let's dance." He took her arm and guided her through the crowds to the dance floor.

She'd never danced with him before, but it was as if their bodies had been made for each other. Whirling, her body raced with excitement whenever it came into contact with his. She tried to ignore how big and warm his hand was in hers, the other against her hip, but it was impossible. Distracting herself, she discreetly studied the faces in the crowd, looking for the key players in the Dupree case as well as for those in her own. She noticed Mark was also observing the crowd through his phony glasses.

Martin Jackson stood near the political tables, greeting people and working the crowd. Richard and Barbara Lyons stood prominently in the small circle of dignitaries around him. Senator Charles Harrington and the Santa Barbara Mayor were there. When Mark twirled her to the other side of the room, she saw Paul helping himself to a plate of food.

She scanned the crowd, looking for the man she'd seen last night, the man Tate said could not be Jonathan Carter, but he wasn't there. She did another scan. As her eyes moved past Paul again, she suddenly recognized the Hulk. He was standing not far from Paul, and he was staring right at her!

Tightening her hold on Mark, she twisted her head away from the Hulk. The music had changed to a slow number. Ignoring convention, she led the dance and pushed Mark toward the other side of the room and away from the huge man.

"You're leading," he said. Their bodies were pressed so close she could feel his voice rumble through her.

"Do you mind?" She kept moving them across the room.

"Not at all. I like it when you take charge." He nuzzled the side of her neck just beneath the wig. "You feel so good," he whispered against her ear.

His lips moved tantalizingly along her sensitive flesh and his arm circled her waist, pulling her closer to his hard heat. If she didn't do something and do it quick, she'd go up in smoke.

"Aren't you forgetting our mission?" She cleared her throat and pulled back far enough so she could look up at him.

"Our mission?" His eyes were unfocused.

It was obvious he was suffering the same onslaught of lust that was making it hard for her to think. They were getting way off track. The Hulk was somewhere in the crowd, watching them, and for an instant there, she'd forgotten everything but being in Mark's arms.

Not good. She had to keep a clear head. She had to do something fast to distract them both.

"I'm thirsty.   Let's get something to drink."   She steered him toward the bar, which was to the right of the stage and on the opposite side of the room from where she'd last seen the Hulk.

"What'll you have?" Mark asked, his voice still husky.

"A glass of Chardonnay sounds good."   When he ordered a tonic and lime for himself, she said, "You don't drink on the job?"

"Not if I can help it," he said. "Besides, it might lower my inhibitions." A wicked grin curved his lips and he shot her a sultry glance.

"Would that be such a bad thing?" She batted the fake eyelashes at him, the urge to flirt overwhelming.

"Don't tempt me." He curled his arm around her waist and guided her toward the large ballroom doors.

Their path brought them directly alongside Richard and Barbara Lyons and Charles Harrington, who was now speaking with Jackson and another woman.

"See that woman standing next to Jackson?" Mark whispered in her ear. When she nodded, he continued, "That's Marie Dupree, Sebastian's wife. As you can see, they're definitely an item."

Marie was watching Jackson like she was starving and he was a delicious meal. Jackson seemed oblivious to her devotion. He was in deep conversation with Harrington, a serious expression on his face.

"I'm not convinced," Carla said after they passed the group. "I think she'd like to be an item, but he's got other things on his mind."

"Really? What gives you that idea?"

"Call it intuition," she lied. Intuition had nothing to do with it. She recognized the desire on Marie's face. It was all she herself could do to keep from drooling all over Mark, despite the fact she knew his motives toward her were suspect.

They came to the edge of the crowd near the ballroom doors. Mark casually draped his arm about her waist.

"Funny, I didn't think you believed in intuition." He turned his head and brushed his lips against her neck as he spoke. His hand stroked her waist and she felt compelled to look up at him. His face was inches from hers, his eyes riveted on her mouth.

Do something, fast, she told herself, but her overheated brain refused to function. His head dipped closer. In seconds, their lips would touch.

"Ladies and Gentlemen," a loud voice squeaked over the PA system.

The music stopped abruptly and her eyes flew to his. He was still looking hungrily at her lips.

"Mark, it's time." She let out a shaky breath.

"So it is." He gave her a rueful smile and gently squeezed her waist one last time before he turned his attention to the stage. An emcee, dressed to the teeth in a black tux, addressed the crowd.

"I would like to welcome you all this evening to honor Martin Jackson and his run for Congress."

Cheers and applause erupted from the crowd. Carla glanced around the room and observed that everyone's attention on the stage.

"Let's go." Mark placed his hand once more under her elbow and guided her out the door.

"The caterers must use the servants' entrance," she noted when she saw the empty foyer. "Don't you want to pick up the laptop case for the painting?"

"That might be a little too obvious, especially if anyone catches us leaving Harrington's study. Don't worry, it's a small painting. I'll be able to get it downstairs without anyone seeing."

He led her up the sweeping staircase to the second floor, decorated in a heavy Victorian style. The wood trim was dark mahogany, including the ornately carved banister. Crimson velvet drapes adorned the windows on the second floor landing. Dark hardwood lined the second floor hallway. She wondered if Mark was at all conscious of the mansion's opulence or if it was merely business as usual for him.

He walked quickly to the second door along the hall. He paused outside to listen and removed two pairs of latex gloves from his pocket.

"Thanks," she whispered when he handed her a pair.

He twisted the crystal doorknob and hurried into the room. She followed, closing the door quietly behind her.

"Should I lock it?" She noticed the old-fashioned brass key protruding from the lock.

"Too risky. We'll just have to take our chances. When music starts playing again downstairs, we'll need to get out of here," he said, already moving across the luxuriant Persian carpet to the other side of the room.

He lifted a seventeenth century Dutch landscape painting away from the wall. Even without being an art expert, Carla could tell the thing was a masterpiece.

"Where did you learn how to safe crack?" she asked, knowing he'd probably learned the skill as part of his FBI training but patting herself on the back for phrasing the question so casually.

"It's a long story," he said. He pulled a small device from his pocket and attached it to the front of the safe. "I'll tell you later if you're interested, but right now I need to focus." He began fiddling with the electronic controls.

Well, if he doesn't need my help, I may as well help myself, she thought, and moved to the desk.

Fortunately, the drawers weren't locked. The top drawers contained the usual: bills, statements, receipts. Toward the back of the middle drawer, however, she came across several interesting files. She glanced up. Mark was still on the other side of the room, completely absorbed with his safecracking.

She extracted three folders and placed them on the desk. One had HARRINGTON written across the top. Opening it, she realized she was looking at documents from LSA Enterprises. From the very first page in the file, it was obvious this was an accounting of the financial contributions Harrington had made to LSA Enterprises.

Well, well, well, what do we have here, she thought to herself as she checked the dates and amounts.

Harrington had contributed almost ten million dollars to LSA Enterprises over the last ten years. How had Harrington come into possession of LSA Enterprise documents? Had he stolen them, maybe that night she saw him at LSA Enterprises? Regardless, the document confirmed he had long-standing ties to LSA Enterprises.

The next folder was unlabeled. Inside were five sheets of paper, printouts of a Web site. Each sheet contained a list of instructions, but unfortunately, none included the Web addresses they'd been printed from. Carla scanned the instructions on the first page.

What the hell? These were directions for how to get to the farmhouse in Virginia! Bingo. Here was solid evidence linking Harrington with the Illuminati.

She quickly scanned the other sheets. They included directions to three different locations, two in California, one in New York, and one in Switzerland. All five pages had dates. The date listed on the first page was the same date she'd been taken captive at the farmhouse.

Oh hell, she thought as she looked at the second sheet again. Today's date was listed at the top. The instructions described how to get to a location off Ladera Road in Montecito.

She hastily flipped open the last folder. Like the previous one, it too was unlabeled. Inside was a single sheet of letterhead with the words 'JC & Associates' embossed across the top and a peculiar image stamped just beneath the heading. The image looked like a hexagram made by interlocking a black and a white triangle together, with a strange image of an eye at the center.

"I got it!" Mark said jubilantly, causing her to jump in surprise.

Damn, there wasn't time to look further at that final

piece of paper. She quickly slid the files back into the drawer and hurried across the room to Mark's side. Peering over his shoulder, she looked into the safe. Boxes and papers were stacked neatly inside. Sure enough, against one wall leaned a small, gilt-framed painting.

"Is that it?"

He pulled the painting out. "Yes. Dupree's going to be a happy man."

"So how are we going to get it out of here?"

"Don't worry. I've got a plan," he said, just as they heard footsteps approaching in the hall.

"Quick, behind the curtain!" She sprinted for the thick, floor-to-ceiling velvet drapes that shielded deep set casement windows.

Mark swiftly closed the safe, slid the Dutch landscape painting back into place on the wall, and followed her behind the curtain. Too late she realized the open drape barely left room for one person to hide. The doorknob turned. Mark laid Dupree's painting on the window sill and pulled her into a tight embrace. She stiffened, wanting to keep some space between them, but it'd be impossible if they were both going to fit behind the one open drape.

His breath came hot and fast against the side of her neck. Her heart pounded wildly. She tried not to think about the steady, growing pressure rising against her belly, but it was mighty difficult. His breathing suddenly stopped. Belatedly, she realized he was listening.

Damn. She'd been so flustered by his proximity that once again she'd forgotten where she was. Who was in the room?

The soft whisper of footsteps moved across the carpet and someone picked up the phone.

"Hi, it's me, Charles," a man's voice spoke. It was Harrington.

Carla resisted the urge to squirm in Mark's arms. The hard press of him against her was causing liquid heat to pool between her legs.

"Yes, everything is a go," Harrington said, responding to the person on the other end of the line.

There was a pause.

"Just one more and the circle will be complete," Harrington said.

Another pause.

"Yes, that should do it," Harrington finished and hung up.

What was that about? Carla wondered, but it was hard to stay focused. Mark was hot and hard against her.

It was only when the study door closed and Mark let out a long breath that she realized he'd been holding it almost the entire time. Thank goodness he had, because now as his breath moved along her skin in an elevated, uneven cadence, she felt the last vestiges of her self-control spin away. She squirmed against him but that only served to increase the friction of his erection against her.

"Let me go of me." She tried to pull back. "He's left the room."

"Not yet," he said, his voice a husky growl.

"What?" She looked up, surprised and outraged he'd disobey her command, but then she saw his expression.

"I have to kiss you."

"You what?" She studied his face, incredulity, astonishment, and finally wonder racing through her as she realized this was no ploy to distract her or fool someone else. He really did want to kiss her. Desire burned in his eyes and she felt it pulsing through the rigid length of him.

Oh what the hell, she thought. They had enough time to steal a quick kiss before getting out of there.

She wrapped her arms around his neck and pulled him in, trying to take control, but the kiss was nothing like the one they'd shared as inexperienced high school students or the one at Pedro's.

His tongue thrust boldly into her mouth. She barely registered his hands stroking across her back, one coming to stop low on her hip and press her closer to him, the other moving up to caress the side of her breast. She purred with delight. The fake moustache tickled her cheek.

"Let's make this even better." A seductive smile curved his lips as he leaned back slightly and removed his latex gloves.

"Good idea." She chuckled at having forgotten she was even wearing them. She yanked hers off. With eager hands, she reached up underneath his wig, dislodging it, and dug her fingers through the thick hair at the base of his neck.

The kiss spiraled out of control, their tongues dueling in a sensual battle. This was liquid fire, lighter fluid to an already raging inferno. The blaze shot higher.

He slid her blouse from her skirt and stroked up the bare flesh of her back. Just as impatient, she tugged at his shirt, desperate to feel his skin under her hands.

"Do you know how much I want you?" he groaned and grasped her around the waist, hoisting her up.

Before she could answer, he was kissing her again, deeply, passionately, pressing himself more firmly against her. Her full skirt parted and she gasped in startled pleasure. His blunt heat pushed into her damp flesh. She wriggled against the window sill to better position him.

Just then, the sharp window locking mechanism jabbed her between the shoulder blades. The stabbing pain brought reality crashing down like a bucket of cold water.

"Stop, Mark. Stop!" She wrenched her mouth away from his.

What the hell are we doing, she wanted to scream. They were supposed be recovering the stolen artwork and she was supposed to be looking for her sister, but instead they were practically having sex. It didn't help that one of his hands was cupping the full weight of her breast, his thumb rushing lightly over her desperately sensitized nipple.

She pulled her hands off the rippling, tensile strength of his back and clenched them at her sides, fighting to tamp down her body's wild response to him.

He stared back at her for a moment, his eyes still glazed. She saw the instant they cleared. Gingerly, he removed his hand from her breast and slid it out of her blouse.

"Um, I got a little carried away," he said, his voice thick with self-mockery.

"You think?" She bit her lip to keep it from trembling.

He stepped back, breaking physical contact, but his eyes continued to hold hers. "You OK?"

"Just peachy," she lied, breaking eye contact and moving hastily away on shaky legs. She straightened her clothes with businesslike efficiency.

But her body felt cold and bereft without his heat. Regret chased through her, and to her mortification, tears stung her eyes. *Ridiculous*, she told herself, *deVilles don't cry, especially when a Lyons is involved.*

She took a deep, shuddering breath and willed herself to relax. Damn, unfulfilled desire was a drag.

"I can't apologize," he said, adjusting his wig, his eyes still looking at her searchingly.

"Let's just get out of here," she said, picking up the latex gloves she'd dropped during their X-rated kiss and hurrying to the door. It was time to take control of the situation. She immediately felt better.

She listened at the door for a moment to verify the second floor hallway was silent, cracked the door and peeked out.

"All clear," she whispered over her shoulder, but then jumped in surprise. Mark stood directly behind her. How could he move so quietly? She'd have to ask him, but not now. Right now they had to get the hell out of there.

"Where's the painting?" she whispered as they walked swiftly down the hall to the staircase.

"Under my shirt."

That's not all you've got stashed under there. A fine tremor passed through her fingertips at the memory of his firm, silken flesh under her hands. She clenched her fists.

They arrived at the head of the staircase. Music wafted up from the open ballroom door. A few people had begun leaving the party and were walking through the foyer toward the mansion's front door.

"Now, Mrs. Townsend, let's behave properly like the aged billionaire and billionairess we're supposed to be," Mark said.

"As if anyone would believe two people our age would sneak upstairs during a party for a quickie."

She stopped him to rub her thumbs across his lips and remove the smeared lipstick. His eyes sparked.

"Stranger things have been known to happen," he said as they descended the staircase.

"What, like two people who used to hate each other getting dressed up as old people and then making out?"

"I never hated you."

Before she could ask him to clarify, they'd reached the bottom of the staircase. He walked away to the potted plant where the laptop case was hidden. A huge man suddenly appeared in one of the doorways.

Oh hell, only one person could be that huge.

The Hulk moved toward her. She couldn't risk calling to Mark. He was somewhere behind her, hopefully hidden behind the large potted plants. Maybe the Hulk didn't recognize her in the disguise. He continued to approach. Then again, maybe he did.

She pivoted and headed for the nearest door on the opposite side of the foyer, hoping she walked in a suitably calm and stately fashion. Swinging open the door, she found herself in a large powder room. Another door led into a bathroom. She tried the handle. Damn. It was occupied. She hurried back to the powder room door. If she was lucky, it would also have a lock.

Before she got half way across the room, the door burst open. The Hulk's vast bulk filled the doorway. He was so tall he had to stoop to enter the room. A malevolent smile creased his beefy face and his beady black eyes stared aggressively down at her.

Oh crap. Trapped in such tight spaces would make fighting difficult. Her costume didn't help, either. The skirt was a hindrance, as well as the three-inch heels. She kicked off the shoes and assumed fighting stance.

"You've had your fun." He smiled maliciously as he pulled a syringe from his coat pocket. "Now it's my turn."

"Just try it, you big fat oaf," she tried to goad him, swinging a brutal kick at his left knee.

It was like kicking a rock. He didn't budge, and before she could recover her balance, he plunged the needle into her neck. The drug acted almost instantly. Her legs collapsed out from under her. The last thing she heard before her head hit the floor and her consciousness departed was the Hulk saying, "The circle is complete."

CHAPTER 11

The next thing she knew, Carla was bumping along in the windowless rear compartment of a van. Her head ached and her mouth tasted like cotton. She lay there for a moment to get her bearings and unstick her tongue from the roof of her mouth. Her memory came back in a flash: the fundraiser, Mark, their kiss, her going to the powder room, a syringe, the Hulk. Damn. For once, the Hulk had bested her.

The van bounced over another rock. Her hands were tied behind her back, but she managed to brace herself against the side of the van and sit up. Anything was better than having her head smack against the bare metal floor as the vehicle moved over uneven terrain.

She peered through the darkness and tried to assess her surroundings. There was nothing to see. The inside of the compartment was pitch black. Her hair brushed across her face and she realized the wig was gone. The engine whined as the van climbed up a steep, rocky slope. She heard muffled voices up front, but it was impossible to understand what they were saying.

How long had she been out? There was no way to access her wristwatch with her hands tied so tightly behind her back. Based on the steep and rocky terrain, she could only guess that they were headed up into the mountains behind Santa Barbara. Unless, of course, she'd been out longer than an hour or so. In that case, they might be as far as the Sierras. She doubted it. She'd bet good money they were headed toward the location off Ladera Road that she'd seen on the printout in Harrington's office. The Illuminati had made their move, and at least for now, she was at their mercy.

The van came to an abrupt stop. She slumped over, feigning unconsciousness. The rear doors opened. A guttural voice spoke in German, another of the five languages she knew fluently.

"You get the girl," the guttural voice said. "I will check in with the others."

"Wait," a higher-pitched man's voice said. "She's still out like a light and she's big. I can't carry her by myself. Can't you help me?"

"You're such a weakling, Hans. If you worked out more, you could do it yourself."

Carla felt hands grip her by the shoulders and another set of hands take hold of her ankles.

"She is heavy, isn't she," the guttural voice said.

I'm not that heavy, she frowned, and risked a peek at the men carrying her. The full moon had risen high overhead and the landscape was brightly lit. Both men looked as German as they spoke. They had blond crew cuts and cold blue eyes, but they were both quite short and stocky.

"Welcome, Hans and Karl. Bring her in here," a third voice spoke in German.

She kept her eyes shut as she heard a door creak open and the two men lugged her inside.

"Oh my Goddess, Carly!" Her sister's voice was a welcome sound, but she kept her eyes closed, unwilling to let her captors know she'd regained consciousness. Better to let them think she wasn't a threat.

"What have you done to her?" Gwen sounded

terrified.

The Germans either didn't understand English or chose not to respond. The two men dumped her unceremoniously on the ground. Straw tickled the side of her face. She resisted the urge to sneeze.

"You brutes! You can't leave her like that. Make sure she's all right!" Gwen demanded.

"Do not worry, *ma belle*. She is unharmed." Moon Ray's voice came from some distance off.

Carla listened carefully. The straw rustled all around her and she heard the crunch of retreating footsteps as the men left. The creaky door sounded again. She opened her eyes.

As she suspected, all eight members of Circe were seated on the floor of what appeared to be a barn. Gwen sat not more than six feet away from her. They were peering through the dim light at her.

"Gwen," she whispered. "It's good to see you again." She struggled to right herself.

"Thank the good Goddess you're all right. What are you doing here?" Gwen wriggled closer. Like Carla, she and the other witches had their hands tied behind their backs.

"I'd like to ask you the same question," she said. "Who are those Germans? Why did they kidnap you?"

"You remember when I told you someone was practicing bad magic against us? They are a group of dark sorcerers seeking power. They call themselves—"

"The Illuminati," Carla said.

"How did you know?" Gwen asked, surprised.

"No thanks to her." Carla shot Moon Ray a dark glance. She hadn't forgotten Moon Ray's refusal to level with her. All the troubles with the Illuminati started when Moon Ray resurrected Circe. What wasn't the witch telling her or the other coven members?

"I've been doing everything I can to find you, Gwen," she continued. "Why has the Illuminati abducted you?

What are they hoping to accomplish?"

"Night Rose, be careful what you say." Moon Ray cut into their conversation. "Your sister is an unbeliever. She will not understand what you tell her. The information could be dangerous if it falls into the wrong hands."

"Oh, for crying out loud." Carla fought to control her temper. "How can I save all your sorry butts if I don't know what I'm up against?"

"Carly, she's right," Gwen said. "There are forces at work that would only make sense to someone in the Craft."

Carla couldn't believe her sister was siding against her. She bit her tongue, resisting the urge to tell them how ridiculous they sounded, but she knew that questioning their belief system wouldn't help her get them to safety.

"The Illuminati is utilizing powers against us, powers we haven't been able to fathom," Gwen continued. "We think they plan to harness our coven's magic for some yet as unrevealed dark purpose."

"You really don't know what they want from you?" Carla looked pointedly at Moon Ray. "Are you telling the coven everything you know?"

Moon Ray calmly returned her stare but did not respond.

"Of course she is!" Gwen's outrage colored her whisper. "Why wouldn't she? She's our coven leader. You sound paranoid."

"Believe me, Gwen, a healthy dose of paranoia is a good thing. It keeps you alive." She looked meaningfully at her sister but didn't elaborate. She may not know much about magic, but she did know about survival. Now was definitely not the time to share the contents of her previous conversations with Moon Ray. Not only were the other seven coven members an avid audience, but they were also running out of time.

"We've got to come up with an escape plan." She changed the topic. "Do you know where we are and how many men we're up against?"

"I'm not sure exactly," Gwen said. "I have no memory of getting here. The last thing I remember clearly was trying to get away from a huge man who broke into the Magic Shop and stuck me with a syringe. Everything's blank after that, until I woke up here in this barn with Circe. I haven't seen that big man again. I've only seen those three guys who were just here, plus another man when they took me outside to use the bushes. That guy had a big gun hanging from his shoulder."

Carla mulled over this information. She had distinctly heard the third man tell the other two that he was going to check 'with the others,' which meant there were more men lurking about. She tried another tack. "Did you get a look around when you were outside?"

"A little," Gwen said. "We're definitely somewhere on the front range, but I couldn't see either the ocean or any identifiable peaks. We could be anywhere from Hollister Ranch to Carpinteria."

Carla nodded. They had to be in Montecito above Ladera Road, as per the intel she'd found in Harrington's office. Unfortunately, knowing where they were wasn't going to help get them out of there. The land above Montecito was rugged and isolated country.

"Did any of you see other men besides the ones Gwen did?" She addressed the question to the other coven members, but they all shook their heads in the negative.

She'd bet good money the Hulk was one of the men, and at least a few of them were armed. If she alone had been captive, things would have been easier, but with eight other bound women to assist, the odds weren't so good. Her mind ran through possible escape scenarios. The first thing to do was get free of the ropes.

"Don't worry, I'll think of something." She tried to sound reassuring, knowing that fear would only put them all at a disadvantage when the time came to move.

"Thinking will not save us." Moon Ray spoke softly,

calmly. "We will need to use other methods."

Carla ignored her and focused on freeing herself. She wriggled her wrists around so she could reach her watch. Flicking a button on its side, she released a tiny razor blade from the other side of the watch. It was one of the more ingenious devices thought up by her cohorts at the CIA. She smiled grimly as she set about sawing through the rope.

The door creaked open and the two stocky men reappeared. They approached the two women closest to the door.

"Please don't," one woman cried out before the man bound a gag over her mouth.

"Stop it!"

"Leave them be!"

Several coven members shouted at the men, who ignored them. When they were done gagging the two women, they jerked them to their feet and pushed them out the door.

Crap. Time was running out. The ropes were thick and Carla couldn't tell how much more she had to go. She got to her knees and shuffled across the floor to the back of the barn. With luck, she'd just bought herself some more time.

"Until I know what Magicks they intend, we can't use a counter spell." Moon Ray spoke softly to the remaining witches. "The most we can do right now is to keep the circle strong."

At these words, Carla suddenly remembered something. She stopped sawing on the rope for a second.

"Wait," she said to the others. "This might not mean anything, but a huge man, probably the same guy that went after Gwen, said something to me right after he stabbed me with a syringe. He said something about a circle."

"*Oui, ma belle?*" Moon Ray said. "What did he say about circles?"

"I passed out right afterwards, but I'm pretty sure he

said, 'the circle is complete'."

"But she's not part of Circe," Gwen broke in.

"You are right, Night Rose, to think that he was speaking of Circe," Moon Ray said. She looked back and forth between the two sisters, her expression shrouded by the dim interior of the barn. "You are both Madeline's daughters. Because of this, it is possible that these men think you are both members of Circe. Whatever magic they have planned, it is now most evident that they plan to use the power of our coven as a whole."

"But what can we do?" another of the women said, her voice no longer a whisper.

"Keep quiet," the guttural-voiced, slightly taller German spoke.

The men had returned. They gagged and left with another two of the coven members. The fact that only the same two men had come back was encouraging. Most likely there wasn't a whole army outside to contend with. Carla kept sawing on the rope. It had to give way soon.

Once the men left with their captives, Moon Ray whispered to the remaining witches, her voice quietly urgent.

"Tonight is Ostara," she said. "It is the turning point of the Light over the Dark, of the Spring Equinox. We can appeal to the power of Ostara and the full moon to aid us in keeping Circe strong."

Carla tuned out their conversation about protection spells and focused on getting free of the rope. In minutes, the two men were back. This time, they took Moon Ray and another woman. Gwen got to her knees and moved back to where Carla sat.

"Carly," she whispered. "Do you have a plan?"

"What, you don't trust your magic to save you?" She tried not to sound bitter, but she was still mad at Gwen for siding with Moon Ray against her.

"I'm not worried about myself. I want to know if you'll be OK."

"Thanks for the concern, sis, but I'll be fine. I always am." She sawed more vigorously. "My main concern is making sure that none of you get hurt. As you said, at least one man out there has a gun. Not all the magic in the world will stop a bullet."

The two men returned. They gagged and removed two more women. Gwen and she were the only ones left.

"Look Gwen, I've got a plan, at least the beginnings of one, but I'll need your help."

"What do you want me to do?"

"Move closer to the barn door. When the men come back, we need them to take you out first. Once you're outside, move as fast as you can away from here. Can you do that?"

"Sure. But what's your plan?"

"I'm going to get out of these ropes. Then I'll figure out the specifics."

Gwen wriggled toward the front of the barn. In minutes, the two men were back. The shorter one grabbed Gwen. The taller headed her way.

"Get up," the guttural-voiced German said as he grabbed Carla by the upper arm and hoisted her to her feet.

She still hadn't cut through the rope. She had just enough time to flick the metal lever on her watch to conceal the razor as the man secured a gag over her mouth. It smelled musty and tasted faintly salty, like sweat. Ugh. She hoped the gag didn't come from something one of the men had worn.

The man pushed her ahead of him out of the barn. Neither he nor the other man was armed. They obviously weren't expecting any trouble from a bunch of women. She tossed her head back to move her long black hair away from her face. Her green eyes glinted in the darkness.

Outside, the night was quite bright. The full moon had almost reached its zenith. The Channel Islands were dark humps rising above the shimmering ocean, and the surrounding hillside practically glowed under the radiant moon. She continued to wriggle her hands. The frayed rope had loosened her bindings and her hands were almost free.

Gwen and the other man disappeared down a narrow path in the chaparral. The surrounding vegetation was thorny and densely packed. Not good for running through, if it came to that. Adjacent to the barn was a large paddock containing several horses and a dirt road heading west. Carla got one last glimpse at the vicinity around the barn before the German pushed her down the narrow path. Neither the van nor any other vehicles were in sight.

She frowned. It would be difficult to transport so many people down to town without some kind of vehicle, but she'd think of something.

"Keep moving." The man gave her a shove.

The gag made any verbal response impossible. Gwen and the other man disappeared around a corner in the path. Now was the time to act.

She pretended to stumble, slowing her pace even more. The three-inch heels had disappeared sometime during her abduction. Her bare feet were nimble and sure-footed over the sandstone terrain but the German didn't need to know that. She limped and pretended to stumble again.

"Hurry up," he said.

If you say so, she thought. She instantly changed pace, charging forward at a jog and twisting frantically at the ropes binding her hands. Abruptly, they gave way.

Excellent! She was isolated on the trail with a single adversary and both her hands and feet were free. A dangerous grin curved her mouth. The German lumbered unsteadily over the uneven ground, trying to keep up with her.

"Not so fast," he commanded, breathing heavily.

Carla spun around, using the momentum to throw a vicious kick at the man's thighs. He let out an "umpf" and fell forward onto his knees. Immediately, she delivered a second kick to the side of his head. There was the dull thud of contact and he dropped like a rock.

Checking his carotid, she verified he was unconscious. She yanked the disgusting gag out of her mouth and with an appreciative sense of justice jammed it into his. She bound his hands with the remaining rope and dragged him into the chaparral beside the trail. She cursed silently as the sharp thorns gouged her skin, but there was no avoiding it. She had to hide him before proceeding.

Quickly and quietly, she moved on bare feet down the narrow trail. The smell of smoke laced the air. Ahead, the chaparral gave way to a large open space. Voices carried toward her on the slight breeze. She crouched behind the bushes and peered through the thorny branches.

A peculiar collection of boulders stood in the clearing. They were large, flat on top, and placed in a ring around a giant bonfire. The coven members sat on eight of them, all still gagged and with their hands tied behind their backs. The biggest boulder, which was closest to the fire, had no one on it. Her sister sat on a boulder about ten feet from where Carla crouched.

Inside the ring of rocks, a group of men stood around the fire. They wore long crimson robes that looked identical to the ones worn by the Illuminati at the Virginia farmhouse, and they wore the same black masks. Carla's eyes narrowed as she counted the men. There were only five. Assuming this was the Illuminati, what had happened to the other six members? She spotted four other men lurking in the shadows. They weren't wearing robes. Probably henchmen.

One of the masked, robed men moved toward her. Was he going to come up the trail? Gritting her teeth, she pressed her body more firmly into the thorny chaparral to ensure she remained in shadow. Instead, the robed man approached Hans, the shorter German, who was standing beside the rock where Gwen was perched.

"Where is Karl? Where is the other woman?" The man spoke flawless German, but even so, Carla could tell he was not a native speaker. The way he inflected the words indicated he was American.

"I do not know, *mein Führer*," Hans said.

"Damn it!" the masked, robed man exclaimed. "Go find her, now!"

"Yes, *mein Fuhrer*." Hans moved toward Carla.

She quickly hurried up the trail around the first bend and waited, breath held and body poised. The moment Hans rounded the corner, she leapt forward and delivered a double karate chop to both sides of his neck. She caught him as he fell and quietly laid him unconscious on the ground. She then darted back down the trail to her hiding spot.

"We must begin without her," the man was saying to the other masked, robed men standing around the bonfire.

One of the men was significantly larger than the others. She'd bet good money he was the Hulk. Could any of them possibly be Mark? She searched each of the masked faces, but it was impossible in the firelight and at such distance to see the color of their eyes.

The man who'd spoken to Hans pulled a black snake dagger from the folds of his cloak. He raised it high above his head and pointed its sharp blade toward the flames.

"Lord of Light, of infinite power and might, the Illuminati has gathered together on this most auspicious of nights, the night of coming Light. We pay you tribute."

The man didn't speak in Latin, but plain English. He reached into a small pouch tied to the rope about his waist and withdrew something Carla couldn't see.

"We honor you, oh bringer of purity, of truth, of infinite justice. We are ready to accept the mortal responsibility you demand of your most ardent followers. In the name of Abaddon, Sonneillon, and Lucifer, we make to you, our Lord, this Offering."

He threw whatever he was holding into the fire. The

other four men began bowing repeatedly toward the flames, their hands clasped together in the folds of their robes.

"Hail, hail, oh Mighty One," they chanted in unison.

Stifled shrieks came from the witches. They writhed precariously atop the boulders. Carla's eyes shot to the fire. A weird, thick black smoke rose from the bonfire and curled into eerie, snakelike shapes.

A shiver ran down her spine.

Stop it, she told herself, *it's just smoke*. But whatever the man had done, she couldn't deny the instinctive dread her body had of the creepy blackness. Like the black thing she'd seen rising from the pit at the farmhouse, this was something bad, something evil. The same desperate urge to flee surged through her as her survival instinct kicked into high gear.

She clenched her fists against her sides and fought the wildly disparate urges to either rush in and stop the ritual or run away as fast as possible.

Fleeing wasn't possible. She had to help her sister and the other women. Stopping the ritual wasn't an option yet, either. She had to find out what the men were going to do, and she had to wait for the opportune moment to intervene.

The men began to circle the bonfire. The black smoke obscured their movements. As the leader passed in front of Gwen's rock and not far from her hiding place, Carla saw him gesture with the long black knife toward her sister.

"In the name of Abaddon, Sonneillon, and Lucifer," he said, his voice rising almost to a shout. "We make to you, our Lord, this Offering. Bring forth the power of nine, the power of the moon. Strengthen our pentangle, steel our power of five."

"Hail, hail, oh Mighty One." The men chanted, continuing to circle the fire.

Dimly through the thick smoke, Carla saw the man

reach into the pouch at his waist and toss something else into the fire.

"Forge together the force of our power. Bind it. Bring together the forces of Light," the man shouted above the loud popping sounds erupting from the fire.

Suddenly, a brilliant flash, brighter than lightening, burst from the fire and rent the night.

Carla screamed, unable to control her reaction. The light stabbed her eyes, blinding her completely. She stumbled backwards and fell against the sharp manzanita.

"No, no! Stop! Please!" Screams echoed off the boulders and around the clearing. Something terrible was happening to the coven, to her sister, but she couldn't see a damned thing.

She groped about blindly, trying to right herself. More popping sounds echoed off the surrounding hills. These were different. Gunshots. Instinctively, she fell to the earth, feeling the dry Santa Barbara sandstone rough against her cheek.

What the hell was going on? She blinked desperately and rubbed her eyes, trying to restore her vision, but all she could see was that blinding white light.

CHAPTER 12

The gunshots stopped, and then she heard fighting. Someone grabbed her and hauled her to her feet. Her vision had cleared enough to see the stocky shape of a man in front of her silhouetted by the bonfire. Without thought, she delivered a one-two karate punch with her fists to his face. The man doubled over. Her knee finished the job. The man crumpled to the ground.

Her sight had returned. Around the clearing, a large number of people were violently battling the Illuminati and the henchmen. She ignored them and looked for Gwen. Her sister was slumped over on the boulder above her.

"Gwen, are you OK?" She climbed up onto the rock.

The gag prevented her sister from answering. Her dark blue eyes were wet with tears. Cursing, Carla carefully removed the gag from her mouth.

"Are you OK?" she asked again, setting to work on the ropes binding Gwen's hands.

"No, I'm not." Gwen's voice was a hoarse whisper. Her voice broke and she hid her face in her hands. Her shoulders shook and Carla realized she was crying.

"Don't cry, Gwenny. It'll be OK." She didn't know what else to say, so she put an arm around Gwen and hoped it would give her some comfort.

A helicopter appeared overhead, drowning out the battle cries and her sister's sobs. It hovered, shining a bright spotlight down on the clearing and illuminating the hand-to-hand combat that was quickly subsiding. One group had emerged victorious.

"I bet that helicopter means the police are here. Look Gwenny, it's all over. See?" Carla squeezed her shoulder and encouraged her sister to look up.

Gwen sat up. She wiped away the tears and met Carla's eyes, her own were intense.

"It isn't over." She shrugged Carla's arm from her shoulders, her expression grim. "It won't ever be over, don't you see?"

"Of course it's over. Look, we've been rescued," Carla gestured at the clearing. "Let's get off this rock. Here, let me help you."

She grasped Gwen around the waist and helped her down.

"Thanks." Gwen swayed unsteadily. "I am weak, very weak. They took a lot of our power. Are the others OK?"

"See for yourself." Carla looked at the helicopter and the swarm of people busily handcuffing men and freeing the other women.

"Did you plan all this?" Gwen asked.

"Not exactly."

A blond-haired woman dressed in a black Wu Shu martial arts outfit approached, a big grin on her face.

"Hey you guys, it's great to see you!"

"Izzy!" Carla and her sister exclaimed simultaneously. They each hugged her.

"What are you doing here?" Carla asked.

"Coming to the rescue, of course," Izzy smiled cheekily. "I brought along a few of my friends from the Green Dragon school to help out."

"Yeah, but how did you know where we were?" Carla shot her a speculative glance. "Did Tate tell you what was going on?" She couldn't keep the accusation from her voice. If Tate had gone behind her back again, she was going to be royally pissed.

"I've got my sources," Izzy laughed, but didn't answer her question.

"What about the helicopter? That's not Green Dragon property," Carla asked, once Gwen had left to talk to the other coven members.

"Nope," Izzy said. "We had help from some special reinforcements."

"You're not exactly a fount of information. What's with all the mystery?"

A tall man appeared out of the darkness.

Mark.

"What's he doing here," she scowled at Izzy, feeling betrayed.

"You told me you were in trouble the other night. I wasn't going to leave you in the lurch." Izzy touched her arm lightly. Her blue-eyed gaze was earnest and caring. "I really don't see why you're upset, Carly. Mark's on our side."

"That's right, I'm on your side. You can trust me." Mark broke in and pulled her into a tight hug. "I'm glad you're OK." His voice was warm against her ear and his body burned against hers.

She shivered, aware for the first time that night that she was cold. The adrenaline had worn off and the silk blouse and skirt she'd been wearing since the fundraiser offered little warmth against the chill mountain air.

"Trust you? I don't think so." She pushed out of his embrace and stepped back a few paces. She crossed her arms over her chest and rubbed her arms through the flimsy material of her blouse. She avoided his gaze, feeling just the tiniest bit self-conscious. The fact that Izzy was beaming at them didn't help.

She ignored them and looked about the clearing. Gwen stood nearby, talking with the other members of

Circe. A group of men were being led away in custody. Carla frowned. They weren't the five masked, robed men, but the other henchmen. She looked again at the other men in the clearing and realized she recognized one of them. What the hell was Dan Moreno doing there? He was from the LA office.

"Izzy, who are all these people?" She turned on her friend.

She figured Izzy must have called Tate for help but wasn't about to mention the Agency by name in front of Mark. It wouldn't take a rocket scientist to know that the helicopter and the men in the clearing weren't from the Green Dragon.

"I told you, we had help from some special reinforcements," Izzy said.

"Tate?" She hoped that was cryptic enough.

Izzy nodded. "She had a crew from the local bureau to come help."

Carla shot a glance at Mark. He was looking at her in amusement.

Damn it! Izzy may not know she was CIA like Tate, but Mark was no idiot. He had to suspect she had ties to the government at this stage of the game.

She grabbed Mark by the arm. "If you'll excuse us, I need to speak to him."

She pulled Mark away from Izzy and the other people in the clearing. "It's time we had a talk."

"Hold on," he laughed. He pried her hand from its viselike grip on his arm and took it in his. He stopped walking and looked down at her. "We do need to talk." He squeezed her hand gently, his expression earnest. "And we will, but not now. I need to be somewhere, fast. I've got to go."

"No, Mark. Not yet." She kept hold of his hand. She couldn't let him leave, not until she had some answers.

"I promise, we'll talk. It just can't be right this moment. Oh, before I forget—" With his free hand, he swung a bag off his shoulder and thrust it at her. She dropped his hand in order to catch the bag.

"I thought you might want that."

"What's in it?".

"Your street clothes. I thought you'd also like your sneakers rather than those man-killer shoes you were wearing earlier." His eyes dropped to her bare feet and then slowly traveled up her legs, revealed beneath the hemline of her skirt. "But I see you lost those."

"They weren't exactly good for kicking ass in." She hitched the bag onto her shoulder.

"Honey, you can kick my ass anytime you like, if you wear shoes like that."

"What?" Her jaw dropped in surprise as he shot her a cocky grin and waggled an eyebrow suggestively at her.

Before she could think of a good rejoinder, he spun away and disappeared up the trail through the chaparral.

Damn it, he'd done it again! He'd distracted her with a silly, suggestive comment. But the outrageous image his words evoked made her grin.

Chuckling, she dug into the bag and found her shoes and fleece. As she shrugged into the jacket, she patted the pocket to confirm her cell phone was still there. Come to think of it, maybe it would be better to touch bases with Tate before confronting Mark, especially after what had gone down tonight.

She checked her watch. It was still a little too early to call Tate, so instead she headed over to her sister and the other members of Circe, who were being directed toward the dirt road out of the clearing.

"Hey Sis," she said. "Mind if I tag along?"

"Not at all, Carly." Gwen sounded weak and tired. "They're giving us a ride home."

"Where did Izzy and the other Green Dragon fighters go?"

"I don't know." Gwen looked around, surprised. "They were just here."

Carla smiled as she followed the other women to the waiting vehicles. One of the first rules she'd learned from Henry Lee at the Green Dragon School was that the best fighters come and go like the wind. She'd have to thank Izzy later for the save, though it rankled that she'd needed the help.

The ride down the mountain was quiet. The driver was not inclined to chat. The four Circe members in the back were exhausted. Gwen's head lolled against the seat as she slept. A slight frown creased her forehead and her lips moved every so often, as though Gwen were speaking in a dream. Whatever had happened in that clearing had exacted a huge toll from the witches.

Carla frowned as she remembered the ritual. She could explain the black smoke and blinding flash as some kind of chemical reaction, probably some kind of pyrotechnics used by the group's leader for effect.

What she couldn't explain was why the witches were so exhausted. It was late at night and none of them had gotten any sleep, but that wasn't enough to explain their weakness and abnormally extreme fatigue.

When the driver dropped them off at the Magic Shop, Carla had to help her sister down from the SUV.

"Careful." She caught Gwen before she stumbled.

"Thanks, Carly. Would you mind helping me up the stairs?"

"No problem."

They entered the Magic Shop. Carla glanced around quickly. Thankfully, nothing seemed out of place. She helped Gwen to her room, where she sank down onto the bed.

"I'm glad you're OK," Carla said. "Make sure to pull the blinds and get some sleep." She moved toward the door.

"Carly, wait." Gwen struggled into a sitting position and spoke with renewed urgency. "I saw you with Mark."

"He came to help out." She spoke dismissively, not

wanting to discuss him with her sister. Too much had been left unsaid between them.

"He's not all he appears to be." Gwen ignored her tone.

"If you're telling me he's involved with the Illuminati, I already know that," she said impatiently.

"Then you must know he's dangerous." Gwen's blue eyes met hers, surprised.

"Can you give me one good reason why I should be afraid of him?"

"Oh Carly," Gwen sighed. "You've always had a thing for him. That's what makes him dangerous."

"What do you mean?"

"Do you really want to know?"

"Of course."

"I'm exhausted and need to get some sleep." Gwen lay back against her pillows. "But I'll tell you what I know, if you promise to listen and not give me any grief."

Carla nodded, despite knowing she was about to hear a lot of magical mumbo jumbo. She had to know how Mark factored in, and maybe her sister had the answer.

"After what happened up there on the mountain, we all talked about it," Gwen said. "Moon Ray told us that the ritual confirmed her suspicion. The Illuminati has modeled itself after the hierarchical structure of hell, of Satan and his minions."

"What?" Carla couldn't keep the incredulity from her voice.

Gwen continued, unperturbed. "Satan has many guises. Lucifer, Sonneillon, and Abaddon are just a few of the names he goes by."

Carla stared at her, surprised to hear the names so often invoked by the Illuminati.

"His minions, his evil-doers, are too numerous for me to recall right now. What matters is that you must not trust Mark. He holds an extremely powerful position within the Illuminati."

When Gwen didn't continue, Carla prodded her. "What's his position?"

"Can't you just trust me on this?" Gwen studied her eager expression and looked unhappy at having to say anything more.

"No, I need something solid," Carla insisted. "You need to give me a reason, something tangible, even if it's one of your magical explanations. Otherwise, I just won't buy it. I can't."

Something about the tone of her voice made Gwen look up sharply.

"Carly, don't let your past history color your relationship with him now. He's not an innocent teenager anymore."

"What do you mean?"

Gwen let out a sigh and ran a hand over her face. She looked exhausted. After a moment, she brought her midnight blue eyes back up to meet Carla's gaze.

"He is Lucifer in the Illuminati triumvirate of power," she said softly.

"What?" Carla wasn't sure she'd heard her correctly.

"Lucifer, Abaddon and Sonneillon form the three points of power the Illuminati is using to call Satan. Mark is Lucifer."

"You're joking, right?" It sounded too ridiculous, too far-fetched to be true.

"I wish I was." Gwen let out a deep breath, her expression grim. "He's made a pass at you, hasn't he?"

"What does that have to do with anything?" Carla wasn't about to discuss the intimate details of her interactions with Mark. Intimate details, good grief. Memories of how intimate that last kiss had been caused a flush to creep up her neck.

"Lucifer is the Bringer of Light." Gwen looked at her seriously. "He is the Great Seducer. He inspires human hot-bloodedness and the fanatical pursuit of hallucinatory pleasures. Mark is working to seduce you."

"Oh come on, Gwen. This is too much. Even if Mark were trying to seduce me, why would the Illuminati care? What on earth would they hope to accomplish or gain by his trying to get me into bed?"

"It has nothing to do with this earth and everything to do with matters of heaven and hell." Gwen paused. "I am so tired," she leaned back against the pillows. "I know if I tell you to avoid him you'll ignore me. So Carly, please, just promise me you'll be careful where Mark is concerned, OK? Don't trust him."

"I always watch my back." Carla walked to the door. "Sleep well. I'll see you in the morning."

She closed the bedroom door and went to her own room. She threw off her clothes and fell into bed, her mind turning over what Gwen had said. She couldn't deny that Mark had been on the make with her, and that more often than not his sexual advances seemed as much attempts to distract her from her mission as actual seduction. One thought remained clear as she drifted off to sleep. Whatever role Mark might be playing in the Illuminati, he wasn't Lucifer, not really.

\#

It seemed like seconds later that her cell phone rang. Bright light streamed through the window and the bedside clock told her she'd slept longer than she'd meant to. It was almost 10 a.m. The phone rang insistently. She pushed aside the pile of clothes she'd unceremoniously dumped on the floor last night and found the phone in her fleece pocket.

"Hello?"

"Sorry, I thought for sure you'd be up by now." It was Tate.

"I had a late night."

"I know."

"Yeah, about last night. Damn it, Tate. How could you have gone behind my back again?" The words came out in a furious flow. "Do you even know what the hell you did? I just can't believe you'd jeopardize my mission like that. I thought we were friends!"

"Wait, Carla, you're blowing everything out of proportion." Tate's voice was smooth, reasonable.

Reason and logic be damned. Carla wasn't having any. "I am not," she shouted into the phone. "By calling in Dan Moreno and his men, I'm pretty sure you blew my cover with Mark. I may as well kiss my whole investigation goodbye, thanks to your so-called concern for my welfare."

"Stop it!" Tate interrupted loudly. "You're making a whole lot of assumptions based on a lack of information."

That stopped Carla up short. "What aren't you telling me?"

"You've been too busy hurling accusations to let me get a word in edgewise," Tate said with a sigh.

"Oh hell, Tate, I'm sorry." She exhaled and tried to get a grip on her emotions, being half awake didn't help. "You're right, I'm out of line. I need a cup of coffee."

"Actually, I'd probably be as upset as you if our situations were reversed, so don't sweat it, OK? Izzy called me last night and told me you'd been abducted."

"How did she know?"

"Mark called her. "

"Why would he call her?"

"Apparently, he witnessed your abduction. When Izzy told me Mark knew you were in trouble, I figured he must have inside information, which would mean you were in really serious trouble. That's why I called Dan. I wasn't going to take any chances."

"I'm touched by your concern, Tate, but—"

"Hold on," Tate interrupted, growing impatient. "It was a very good thing I called Dan, because he recognized Mark. It turns out that Mark is on our side. He's working undercover to expose the Illuminati."

"What? I don't believe it!"

"Believe it. Apparently, Dan and Mark worked on a

few coordinated agency assignments several years back. When Mark left the FBI, Dan knew where he went."

"How?"

"Because Dan was solicited to join the very same organization Mark joined when he left the FBI."

"What organization?"

"I'll tell you, but it's highly classified, OK?"

"Sure."

"The group calls itself the Phoenix. Everything I'm telling you I learned this morning when Frank debriefed me."

"The Phoenix?"

"That's their code name. According to Frank, it's an extremely covert association made up of agents who take on sensitive assignments our government doesn't want to touch."

"You're kidding."

"Nope."

"But if that's really true, then why did Frank assign us to investigate the Illuminati? Why have two independent agencies conducting two separate investigations? Wouldn't it be better to pool resources?"

"Of course it would, it's just that apparently we didn't know the Phoenix was involved. Now that we do, Frank wants you to work with Mark on the investigation."

"You're joking, right?"

"You said it yourself, it would be better to join forces and pool our resources."

"There's no way I'm going to work with Mark Lyons."

Suspecting him had kept him at a safe distance. Now, she was being told she'd have to work with him, which meant trusting him, too. No way.

"I'm afraid you don't have a choice," Tate said. "I already spoke with him this morning. He's going to call you today to set up a meeting so you can coordinate your efforts."

"Oh hell," Carla cursed. "You didn't give him any of

the clues we've uncovered so far, did you?"

"What's gotten into you, Carla? I thought you were the mistress of cool-headed reason and logic. That's what's always made you such a kick-ass operative. It only makes sense to work with him, so why are you so bent out of shape? You're taking the situation with him too personally."

If she only knew!

"Enough about him," Carla snarled. "Let's get down to business. What more have you uncovered about the Illuminati? Did you ever get the analysis back on those documents I photographed from LSA Enterprises?"

"Yes, I just got the results from the Chem department today." Tate sounded relieved to at last be talking shop. "As we suspected, the financial reports verify that LSA Enterprises has been funneling money to the Illuminati, but what's intriguing about the scientific documents is that they include data for building different kinds of nuclear weapons."

"You don't say." Carla's green eyes narrowed. The occult was one thing, nukes were something else entirely.

"I'm afraid so. This confirms Frank's theory that the Illuminati has links to international terrorism. The documents are in German, indicating the Illuminati has ties with Germany or possibly Switzerland."

"That would explain the thugs who held me and Circe captive. I'm pretty sure they were German nationals. They were arrested last night, so we can verify their identities and interrogate them for leads about the Illuminati. Did you hear, the five Illuminati members disappeared?"

"Yes, strange considering the mountain was swarming with agency personnel."

Strange, indeed, Carla thought, wondering yet again about Mark's involvement. He, too, had disappeared that night.

"Listen," Tate continued. "Sam has dredged up more

information about the medieval sect that called itself the Illuminati. It was based out of what is now present-day Switzerland. Its members believed the world needed purification. The only way to do this, they believed, was to cleanse it by fire."

"What does that mean?"

"According to Sam's sources, the Illuminati was an apocalyptic cult. Its members believed that the world had been blackened by the sins of men. They believed that the only way to save the world was to eradicate its darkness. They wanted to purify it and return it to the light. In order to do this, they planned to harness the power of alchemical fire to burn away the evil."

"'May the light within reflect the light outside.'" Carla remembered the words the members of the present day Illuminati had chanted.

"I think it's safe to conclude that the modern day Illuminati is a reincarnation of that same organization."

"Did you know that Lucifer is supposedly the Bringer of Light?" Carla remembered her sister's words.

"What?"

"Gwen is convinced Mark is evil. Last night, she warned me in no uncertain terms that he is Lucifer in the Illuminati. She told me that he is the Bringer of Light. What do you think that means?" She left out the part about him being the Great Seducer.

"I think you'd better ask him."

"Could he be a double-double agent?"

"Hell if I know, Carla. Anything's possible. But you've said it yourself a million times, trust the facts. Trust what you know, not what you believe, right?"

"Of course. I'll make sure I keep an eye on him," she said. "Hey, before I get off the phone, I just remembered a few more things you should hear about."

She quickly described what she'd found in Harrington's study, including the strange letterhead and the five sheets of locations, dates, and instructions.

"Excellent work," Tate said. "This confirms Harrington's ties to the Illuminati. Why don't you check with Mark to see who else he may have identified as members? In the meantime, I'll run a check on 'JC & Associates' to see if I can find out who they are."

"Let me know what you find," Carla said. "According to those docs, the next meeting of the Illuminati is in New York. I plan to be there."

"Sounds good. You will coordinate your effort with Mark, right?"

"Sure," Carla lied.

There was no way she was going to divulge all she knew to him, not yet. She had scoffed at her sister's occult explanation of the threat Mark posed, but that didn't mean she wasn't going to take Gwen's warning to heart. Until Mark proved himself to be a true ally, she had no intention of trusting him.

CHAPTER 13

When Carla finished her conversation with Tate, she hurried out of her bedroom and into the hall.

"Gwen, where are you?" She called for her sister, but the place was quiet.

The door to Gwen's room stood open. She glanced in, but there was no sign of her sister. "Gwen?" She checked the kitchenette. Her sister was nowhere to be found. As she turned to leave the room, a piece of paper on the small kitchen table caught her eye.

She quickly scanned the note.

"Carly, don't worry about me," the note said. "I'm safe with Circe. We're in hiding while we regain our strength. Stay safe and remember what I said about Mark."

Damn. Now she wouldn't be able to ask Gwen why she'd visited their mom at the clinic, or if Gwen knew something more about their father than what Moon Ray had reluctantly revealed.

She opened the refrigerator to see what she could eat, when a hand clamped over her mouth.

"Not this time." Mark slipped his arms around her waist and lifted her bodily off the ground. "I don't think my feet can handle any more stomping."

Carla wriggled furiously in his grip. Who the hell did he think he was, manhandling her again?

"I'll let you down, but keep very quiet. We've got trouble." Mark's lips brushed the delicate shell of her ear. She squirmed. Fury warred with desire as her body caught fire where he held her firmly against him.

"Promise to keep quiet?" His voice was a sibilant hiss. Anything to get away from him! She nodded, her long black hair swinging across his face.

The instant her feet touched the ground, she spun around.

"What the hell?" Her jaw dropped in surprise.

The man standing in front of her had black eyes and long, straight black hair tied back in a ponytail. He was dressed in clothes appropriate for someone half his age, an oversized football jacket, baggy jeans and basketball shoes. Except for his height and the fact that she'd recognized his voice and the feel of his body against hers, she wouldn't have recognized him.

"We're out of time," Mark whispered. "We've got to get out of here, now." He pulled her toward the kitchen door.

"What's going on?" She yanked her arm from him.

Before he could reply, they heard the Magic Shop's doors crash open downstairs, followed by the sound of breaking glass and the heavy tread of shoes rapidly approaching.

"They're coming for you," he said and forcefully grabbed her by the arm again, this time not allowing her to shake him off.

It didn't take a genius to know that trouble was on its way up the stairs. She followed swiftly behind him. As they passed her room, she veered to the side.

"One second."

"We don't have it."

"I don't care." She ran and grabbed her duffel bag. She also grabbed her Colt Defender. There wasn't time to shove it in her bag, so she slung the bag over her shoulder and into the hall, gun in hand.

"Follow me," she said, hurrying down the hallway, Mark on her heels. "We can get out on the roof."

They raced to the end of the hall. She jammed the gun into the rear waistband of her jeans and shoved open the window to the fire escape. It screeched loudly.

"Damn it!" she cursed. She climbed out onto the fire escape, Mark on her tail.

Below them on the street, a large black SUV and several men waited outside the Magic Shop. One of the men was looking up.

"Stop them!" he yelled, pointing.

They rushed up the metal ladder to the roof. Footsteps thundered up the metal ladder after them.

"This way." Carla tore across the black emulsion roof in the dazzling midday sunlight.

"I've got a car parked at the other end of the block," Mark said as they ran.

"We can jump to the next building," Carla shouted. As a kid, she'd played on the roof of the Magic Shop and the other buildings along the short commercial strip. "Make sure to get up enough speed."

She charged ahead of Mark, her long legs eating up the distance, and then she launched herself across the eight-foot space between the storefronts. Mark landed with a heavy thud beside her on the next roof.

"Excellent," he grinned, and they set off at a sprint across the next string of rooftops.

Carla looked over her shoulder. No sign of their pursuers on the roof, but she knew they weren't out of the woods. The men on the street were looking for them.

"This is our best bet down." She looked over the edge of the commercial strip's last building. A dumpster sat directly below. She jumped agilely down the six-foot drop onto the dumpster lid and bounced off. Mark followed.

"The car's over there," he pointed. A silver Maserati

Coupe was parked in the alley.

"Not so fast," a voice commanded. Spinning around, they faced the Hulk and five other men, who stood at the alley entrance. The Hulk cracked his massive knuckles.

"Run." Mark tossed her a set of keys. "Don't wait for me."

"Like hell." She pulled the Colt from her waistband and leveled it at the Hulk.

"Back off. Now," snarled. "I'll use this if I have to." Her eyes shot molten emerald fire at the men. "Go, Charlie." She made up the alias on the fly, assuming he was undercover, and tossed the keys back to him. "Get the car started."

She didn't take her eyes from the men. The engine roared to life. Slowly backing up, she moved toward the waiting car.

"Get in." Mark swung open the passenger side door.

Spinning about, she jumped in. Mark gunned the engine. The Hulk and his henchmen jumped aside as the car shot off like a bullet, tires screeching as it skidded out of the alley and around the corner onto Cota Street.

"Nice car," she quipped, strapping herself into the leather interior and placing the Colt across her lap. "Another rental?"

"Not exactly," he grinned. "It actually belongs to a friend of mine."

"Not a member of the Illuminati, I assume, or your disguise has already gone to waste."

"Don't worry. I sincerely doubt any of those guys back there recognized this car."

"At least one of them was Illuminati." She glanced in the rearview mirror. At the moment, none of the cars behind them looked suspicious.

"Yes." He downshifted the Maserati as they pulled up to a crowded stoplight on State Street. "Thanks for coming to my rescue back there." He looked pointedly at the gun in her lap. "You can put that away now."

"I don't think so," she said. "Tate told me she had a little chat with you this morning." She took comfort in the gun's solid weight and enjoyed the fact she was making him uncomfortable. Serves him right, she thought. Maybe he'd finally answer some of her questions. "She tells me I'm now supposed to work with you on this case."

"You don't like the idea?"

"Come on, Mark. How can I work with someone I don't trust?"

"Why don't you trust me?" He maneuvered the car around a double-parked van and hung a quick right onto Anacapa Street. "Can't you see that I trust you? I'm letting you hold a gun on me and I'm not complaining."

"Damn," Carla ignored him, looking out the rearview mirror. "We've got a tail."

A red pickup truck had run the light into oncoming traffic in order to keep up with them.

"I know," Mark said.

"Where are we going?"

"We've got to get to New York as soon as possible."

"What?" she blurted. "Wait just one minute. Why the hell do we need to go to New York?" She knew the Illuminati planned a meeting there, so he must know, too, but then why wasn't he telling her so? Was he simply a double agent, or was he a double-double agent? She leveled the gun at him.

"Has anyone ever told you that you curse a lot?" His black eyes met hers for a split second and then dropped to the gun. "Can you please put that away? I really am on your side."

"You're avoiding my question." She kept the gun where it was.

"Hold on." He floored the Maserati, ran a red light and slammed a hard left down the State Street underpass. "Did we lose him?"

Carla looked over her shoulder. The traffic had started to move on State Street, which had effectively blocked the truck from following them.

"It looks that way, but if you're trying to get to 101, why are you going this way?"

"A diversionary tactic."

"You're good at that, aren't you?"

"What?"

"Diversionary tactics."

"What do you mean?"

"Every time I try to get a solid answer out of you, you change the subject," she paused. "Or other things." A slow heat crept up her body, memories of their last kiss burning through her.

"Other things? What other things?"

"You know damned well what I mean." Her eyes traveled involuntarily down his body. His big hand firmly gripped the stick shift and the muscles of his legs flexed under the jeans as he expertly downshifted at the next light.

"There you go again," he said.

"You're doing it again, too," she said, wanting to shout, or at least grab her gun and point it at him again. Instead, she clenched the gun in her lap.

"What, diverting you?" he grinned cockily, his eyebrow quirking up suggestively.

"Yes," she ground out. "Enough banter, Mark. You need to give me some real answers. No more stalling."

"OK, OK, lady. What do you want to know?" he laughed as he hung a right onto the Milpas Street onramp.

Carla's body sagged back into the leather seat as the Maserati shot forward from 10 to 75 mph in less than five seconds. There was so much she wanted to ask him that for a moment she was speechless. She studied him as he focused on the road. She had to give him credit. His disguise really was clever. The black hair and clothing was one thing, but the black eyes were truly ingenious.

"I didn't know they made black eye contacts," she said, thinking aloud.

"Special issue."

"From the Phoenix?"

"I'm perfectly happy talking to you about the Illuminati and answering any questions you might have about the case." His eyes met hers, a slight smile on his lips. "But the Phoenix is off limits. I can't speak to you about that." He pulled on a pair of black shades and returned his gaze to the road.

They were pushing 90 mph and the Rincon sped by. Carla ignored the spectacular scenery, her attention focused entirely on Mark. She wanted to ask him more about the Phoenix but that was not top priority. First and foremost was the issue of Gwen's whereabouts.

"OK, I'll save those for later," she said. "How about you tell me where my sister is?"

"What?"

"You heard me, where the hell is Gwen? She left me a note this morning saying she and the rest of Circe have gone into hiding. Do you know where?"

"No." He gave a slight shake of his head.

"No what? No you didn't know they'd gone underground, or no you don't know where they are?"

"I knew they went underground. That's why I knew the Illuminati would be after you."

"But do you know where they are?"

"No, I don't."

"Good."

"What do you mean 'good'?"

"I mean I don't want you letting any of your buddies know where they are. I want my sister safe."

"My buddies? What the hell are you saying, that I'm buddies with the other members of the Illuminati?"

"Hey, watch your cussing." She couldn't resist the jab.

"Not funny," he scowled. "Look Carla, we've got to trust each other. It's the only way we're going to work together and take the Illuminati down."

"OK, then tell me this, why is the Illuminati so bent on

capturing me?"

"Because you are the Offering."

"What the hell does that mean?"

"How much do you know about the Illuminati?"

"Enough to know they're a bunch of loonies obsessed with the occult and the alchemical properties of light."

"Don't you think you're being a little simplistic?"

"No, actually I don't. But I know what you're doing, Mark."

"What?"

"You changed the subject again."

"What do you mean?"

"I asked you a question, but you didn't answer it. Instead, you turned around and asked me a question. Is this part of your strategy to keep me in the dark?"

"Now you're just being paranoid," he snapped. "Look, I don't want to waste time telling you stuff you already know."

"Yeah right," she said.

The ringing of a cell phone interrupted them. Mark dug inside the football jacket and pulled out a tiny phone.

"Yes?" he spoke into it. "Yes, she's with me. Don't worry, everything is going according to plan."

"What plan? Who are you talking to?" Carla demanded. Mark shook his hand to silence her as he listened intently to whoever it was on the phone.

Carla fumed. Was it his superiors at the Phoenix, or was it the Illuminati on the line?

Two could play that game. She grabbed her phone from her duffel bag. Tate answered on the second ring.

"Hey there, it's me," Carla said.

"Hi girlfriend, what's up?"

"Why don't you tell me?"

"What do you mean?"

"Mark's telling me that we've got to go to New York. He's not telling me why." She didn't elaborate, because Mark had just hung up. He was focused on driving, but he could also now hear every word she said.

"He hasn't talked to you about his involvement with the Illuminati? You know Frank wants you two to work together," Tate said reasonably.

"Enough about him," Carla frowned. "My sister and the other Circe members have gone into hiding until this whole Illuminati thing is cleared up."

"That's probably not a bad idea, considering."

"I agree, but the thing is, she never got my new cell phone number, so she has no way of reaching me now that I'm leaving town."

"I'll have your old phone number forwarded in case she tries to contact you, and don't worry, I'll let you know if I hear anything, OK?"

"Thanks."

"Hey, while I've got you on the phone, I've got some interesting info," Tate said.

"What?"

"You'll never believe it, but that JC & Associates letterhead you saw in Harrington's office belongs to none other than Jonathan Carter."

"The guy Frank told us about?" Carla glanced over at Mark. She'd have to keep her side of the conversation vague.

"None other," Tate said. "And get this, it looks like Jonathan Carter has an interest in the occult."

"Why do you say that?"

"Sam researched those symbols you described and he's pretty sure they're satanic."

"Really," Carla said skeptically. "It sounds like his imagination is working overtime. Maybe he's become susceptible to the power of suggestion, what with all the research you're making him do."

"You're impossible!" Tate said angrily. "Why don't you get it, that even if you don't believe in some things, other people may?"

"It's serious with him, isn't it?" She refused to take

Tate's bait.

"What do you mean?"

"You and Sam," Carla said. "You really like him, don't you?" She felt Mark glance her way.

"Yes, but that has nothing to do with what we're talking about."

"I guess not, but I'm more interested in talking about you and Sam," she said, especially with Mark seated right next to her. She had no intention of him overhearing anything really important, not yet. "I'm really happy for you, Tate." She meant it. It was about time one of them succeeded in the man department.

"Thanks, I guess." Tate's phone clicked. "I've got another call coming in. While you're in New York, I'll arrange for you to visit Jonathan Carter. Hopefully, the recluse will agree to see you."

"Sure thing." She hung up. Glancing out the window, she noticed they were about to merge with the 405 and begin the climb up over the Hollywood Hills. At this rate, they'd be at LAX within the half hour.

"So, are you going to tell me who you were talking to?" She cast a quizzical glance at Mark.

"Why do you want to know?" He kept his eyes on the busy freeway ahead of them.

"Why don't you just answer my question?" she said impatiently. "Were you talking to the Phoenix or the Illuminati?"

"Neither."

"Then who the hell were you talking to?"

"Your boss, Frank Carson."

"Frank? Why were you talking to him?"

"You know as well as I do that our two organizations are coordinating the next leg of this investigation. I was briefing him on this morning's events and what our plans are for going forward."

"Great. You plan to clue me in?"

"Well, first of all, do you see that bag in the back seat?"

"Yes."

"It's got your disguise for our trip to New York."

"Who am I supposed to be this time, and who are you?"

"I'm Geoff Martin and you're my aunt, Trina."

"Kinky." She put the gun on the seat beside her and reached for the bag. "Am I your *older* aunt?" She shot him a devilish glance.

"I don't have a problem with older women." He returned her glance with an equally devilish grin.

"How much older?" Her question was answered when she pulled the gray wig from the bag. "I don't know about this pantsuit," she muttered. The pantsuit was light brown polyester. It was accompanied by a pair of bulky brown shoes. "No three-inch heels?"

"I'll miss the man-killers you were wearing the other night," he said regretfully, glancing down the length of her jeans to her feet, currently encased in white sneakers.

"Hush puppies are perfectly fine for kicking ass."

"You may as well change now," he said. "We're going to drop the car off in a lot outside LAX and approach the terminal on foot. I don't want to take chances that someone might recognize you."

There was no back seat in the Maserati, so it looked like she'd have to do it in the front.

"Sounds like a plan, but only if you promise to keep your eyes on the road, buddy."

"Hey, I told you, you can trust me."

"Yeah, right," she said under her breath as she began wriggling out of her jeans. To distract him, she changed the subject. "You never did explain exactly why the Illuminati is so set on capturing me."

"I told you, it's because you're the Offering."

"You never explained to me what the hell that is."

"I can't give you an exact definition. What I can tell you is that you're very special. You may not realize it, but an enormous amount of magical power resides in you.

The Illuminati wants to harness your power in order to raise its Deity."

"Magical power. How absurd." Carla rolled her eyes.

"It's not absurd to them. That's what matters, isn't it?"

She finished zipping up the polyester pants and grimaced. His explanation didn't explain a damned thing.

"If I'm so important, then why the hell did they go after Circe and my sister?"

"Ideally they wanted all of you. They wanted the circle complete. With Circe's disappearance and their failed attempt last time, you're now their last hope. They'll try to raise the Deity tomorrow night at the next ritual. We're going to be there. I'll present you as the Offering, and then we'll take them down."

"You mean they're going to try something like what they tried at that place in Virginia?" Memory of the blackness rising from the fire on the mountain and from the pit in Virginia shuddered through her.

"Yes."

"So you were there?"

"Of course, I thought you knew."

"I suspected as much. But come on, Mark. How was I to know it was you? We hadn't seen each other in what, ten years? And we certainly hadn't parted on the best terms."

"I'm sorry about that." He glanced her way.

"Hey, no looking!"

He ignored her, a serious expression on his face as he watched her shrug into the white polyester blouse. When her fingers finished buttoning it closed, he reached over and took her hand. He brought it to his lips.

"I really am sorry about that." He kissed her hand.

She watched his mouth move over the back of her hand, flashbacking to Harrington's study. Heat flooded through her and the delicious feel of his lips on her skin almost succeeded in distracting her.

"How did you get involved with the Illuminati?"

She wanted to pull her hand from his, but when he placed it on his thigh, she couldn't pull it off the warm, hard flesh. He lightly stroked her hand along his thigh.

"It's a long story, and I'll tell you, but we're almost at LAX." He put his hand back on the stick and downshifted as they exited onto Century City Boulevard.

In minutes, they arrived at the parking structure. As Carla transferred the relevant items from the black duffel to her new purse, an oversized red leatherette affair, she realized he'd once again manipulated her attraction to him to avoid answering her questions. At least he was telling the truth about the Illuminati's next meeting. What he'd said matched the intel she'd uncovered in Harrington's office.

"So how do you propose we take them down?" she asked, getting out of the car.

"Let's talk about that later, OK? We're running late." He set off at a brisk pace toward the airport shuttle stop.

She hurried after him in the brown Hush Puppies, frowning. She still had so many questions, but she knew that speaking in public about confidential affairs was risky. Damn. It was going to be a long flight to New York, and she still didn't know where the hell they were going to stay once they got there.

\#

They made the flight with seconds to spare. As they strapped into their seats in business class, Carla leaned close to Mark.

"I'm impressed."

"About what?" He turned, his face now intimately close.

She shifted in her seat, moving back and adjusting the gold-rimmed eyeglasses of her disguise. She was supposed to be his older aunt, after all.

"You must have powerful connections if you can get the TSA to wave their anti-terrorism security precautions." She spoke under her breath.

"Oh Aunty, don't be silly," he grinned, his mouth devilishly sexy. He didn't whisper. "I'm sure your connections are just as powerful as mine."

She nodded, realizing he was attempting to maintain cover. As the flight attendant told them to prepare for takeoff, her stomach grumbled loudly.

Oh hell. It was going on 2 pm and she'd completely forgotten about food.

"Aunty, are you hungry?" Mark's eyes drifted down to her belly and then slowly back up to her face.

"I never had breakfast, or lunch for that matter."

"Now that you mention it, I'm pretty hungry, too." His finger lightly grazed the back of her hand where it lay on the armrest.

"For what, a hot tuna melt?" She fought to stifle a giggle. Starvation was turning her silly.

"That would be delicious," he chuckled. "But I checked the menu. It looks like we're stuck with roast beef."

"I like red meat." Her green eyes twinkled.

"I'll just bet you do," he muttered under his breath, his hand sweeping across her body to her safety belt resting in her lap. "Let me make sure this is secured correctly." He leaned over, his lips dangerously close to hers, his black eyes focused on her mouth.

"What are you doing?" she whispered urgently, shocked he'd risk blowing their cover by taking their sexual banter so far.

"Now you're strapped in good and tight, Aunty." His hand caressed her hip and he ran his fingers along the belt where it lay low across her lap.

"Thanks, Geoff." She tried not to squirm. "What would I do without you?"

"I don't know," he breathed, his eyes catching hers with a burning intensity.

The plane took off and she heaved a sigh of relief. Maybe teasing him wasn't such a good idea. She remembered what Gwen had said about Lucifer's seductive power. If anyone could be described as a Great Seducer, it would be Mark.

She let out a deep breath and turned away from him, pointedly looking out the window. The plane left the coast and curved in a great arc eastward, back over land. LA disappeared in a haze of murky smog.

Carla stared blankly out the window, revolving all the questions she had over in her mind. Fundamentally, she wanted to know if she could trust him, if she could believe what he told her, but she couldn't very well ask him straight out. Any answer he gave would be suspect.

She thought about the evidence she'd found in the Lyons' stables as a good test. Did he know Gwen had been a captive there? How good a liar was he? She glanced at him, trying to figure out how to ask without blowing their cover.

"I was wondering," she said, carefully watching his expression. "I went to the stables." She quickly scanned the cabin, but none of the other passengers seemed interested in their conversation. The businessman sitting directly across the aisle had his headphones on. The couple in front of them was involved in their own conversation. They were at the back of business class.

"Your stables," she continued. "I found things there. My sister had been there."

Was that surprise flitting briefly across his face? But surprise about what, that Gwen had been held captive there, or that she'd discovered the fact?

"Was that the night I saw you at my folks' place?" he asked, keeping things vague.

She nodded.

"No, I didn't know."

"Really, you have no idea who held her there?" She whispered.

"No," he said blandly. "I have no idea."

"Oh come on, Geoff," she glared through the phony

glasses at him. "It had to be someone in your family. What about your brother, or your father?" His expression was still a blank mask. She scowled. How could she make him lose his cool and draw him out?

"I know it couldn't be your mother, not with her drinking problem," she hissed, raising the old ghosts. "As I recall, she could barely stand on her own two feet when she hit the gin."

"Let's get a few things straight, shall we, *Aunty*?" He emphasized the last word harshly under his breath. "I won't talk about your mother if you don't talk about mine."

"You always made it clear what a whack job my mother was." She forced herself to stare at the blank TV screen in the back of the airplane seat in front of her.

"Damn it," Mark ground out in a barely controlled whisper. "How many times do I have to apologize for what an idiot I used to be?"

"You're certainly no idiot now, are you?" She muttered. "I know when you're working me, so don't even think of trying it."

"I'm not working you. I never have."

"Don't make me laugh. You made my life a living hell from the first moment I met you."

"I was a stupid, hormonal teenager." He leaned back against the passenger seat, running his hands down the length of his thighs, a grim expression on his face. Then he turned to face her, his voice dropping to a barely audible rasp. "You got under my skin. You always have. You still do. You probably always will. Can't you see that I teased you because I couldn't think of any other way to talk to you?"

"What?" She fought to keep from looking at him. "Are you trying to tell me that all those times you kicked my ass at the Green Dragon School you were just trying to 'talk to me'?"

"For such a smart cookie, I'm surprised how obtuse

you can be sometimes."

"What the hell does that mean?"

"I wanted any excuse to touch you. God, I still do."
He clenched the armrest between them.

"You've got to be kidding." She struggled to keep her
voice quiet and turned to stare at him, incredulous. "You
had one hell of a bizarre way of showing it."

"What do you mean?"

"You ran off and left me. That night." He had to
know she was talking about that fateful night in August, so
many years ago. It still stabbed like a red hot poker to her
heart.

"I did no such thing."

"Yes, you did." Her voice rose and her cover slipped.
"Your mother told you to go to your room and you did.
You left me there with her and she made it quite clear how
little I meant to you."

"What did she make clear?"

"That I was just your summer fling and that you'd
move on to, what did she say, 'bigger and better things
than some lowlife piece of trash from the wrong side of
town.' She said I was nothing more than some summer
fun before you left our provincial backwater to go East
and join the Ivy League."

"Would you like to order some food?" The flight
attendant's voice cut into their conversation.

Carla stared up at the woman for a moment, unable to
process what she'd been asked, her mind still deep in the
past.

"She'll have the roast beef sandwich. I'll take the
chicken." Mark covered.

The attendant handed the boxes to them and moved
on to the next row of passengers.

"Funny, I never figured you for a chicken," Carla said
bitterly. She'd been hungry, but now she was ravenous.
She tore hungrily into the sandwich.

"What?" she said, when she realized Mark was staring

at her.

"Nothing."   His voice was velvety deep, his eyes focused on her mouth.

She swallowed with difficulty, acutely aware of him watching her. She took a hasty swig of cola and started coughing.

"Easy there, Aunty," he laughed and patted her on the back.

"I'm fine." She shrugged him off. "Eat yours."

"I will." He grinned and picked up his sandwich.

She ignored him and quickly polished off the sandwich and the butter cookies, and then dug out the headphones from the seat pocket in front of her. She put them on, selected a movie, and forced herself to tune him out. She mulled over what he'd said as the movie washed over her.

Was it true? Was all the attention he'd paid her when they were young due to real attraction, or was her sister right? Was he making it up now to establish an intimacy he could later use against her for the Illuminati?

CHAPTER 14

The movie finished as the plane began its descent into Kennedy Airport and Carla removed the headphones.

"You didn't give me a chance to explain." Mark spoke softly, his deep voice causing tingles of awareness to shimmer down her spine. Damn. She couldn't wait to get off the plane and away from him, his tempting lips and his seductive voice.

"Damn it, do we have to keep beating dead horses to death?" She twisted her head away from him and shoved the headphones into the seat pocket.

Would she be able to believe any excuse he might offer for his behavior, either as a kid or now, or would it all just sound like one more of his damned diversionary tactics?

"Yes, we do," he said, keeping his voice low. "I'll keep on beating them until you understand."

"Understand what?" She knew perfectly well what he was referring to.

"I had to leave you that night. I didn't have a choice. You said it yourself. My mother is impossible when she's been drinking." His voice dropped and he leaned close, his breath warm against her wig. "I thought you knew how much you meant to me. I thought we could talk in the morning and clear things up."

He paused and she felt her heart in her throat. Did he really mean what he was saying?

"But you didn't return my calls." He sat back in his seat.

"Why on earth would I, Geoff?" She held their cover firmly in place. "As I said, your mom spelled it all out."

"Why did you believe her?"

"You never gave me any reason to believe otherwise." She remembered with bitterness how naive she'd been.

She glanced out the window. The plane was taxiing into the terminal at JFK. She was surprised to see how dark it was and then realized it was late, just past 10 p.m. The trip had been the shortest continental flight she'd ever taken.

"I'm sorry," he exhaled quietly. "I had no idea how much you'd misread my feelings." His fists clenched on his thighs, as if he was doing everything he could to keep from touching her.

"Did you even know what you felt?" She forced herself to speak quietly, though her voice vibrated with anger. "As you said yourself, you were a hormonal teenager. Maybe your mother wasn't so far off the mark."

"You've got to be kidding." He twisted in his seat to face her again, his cover slipping, his voice rising in frustration. "Tell me something, will you? What did you feel for me?"

She risked looking at him, ignoring the black contacts and trying to read what really lay behind his eyes. Could she trust the vulnerability she saw there? A Lyons vulnerable? No way. It had to be some kind of act. There was no way she was going to tell him the truth. Not now, not ever. She had to get away! The plane arrived at the gate and she launched herself to her feet.

"Let's focus on the task at hand, shall we?" She

grabbed her duffel bag from the overhead bin and stalked up the aisle toward the exit.

#

An hour later, the taxi dropped them off in front of one of Manhattan's many high rise buildings. It was just past 11 p.m., but despite the late hour the city teemed with life. People milled about the sidewalk, horns blared, and drunks stumbled out of alleys.

"What is this place?" Carla asked as she followed Mark through the massive bronze and glass entry doors and into a silent space.

"A place we can spend the night."

They crossed the vast marble foyer, lit by crystal chandeliers suspended some twenty feet above them, their footsteps echoing in the silence.

He pulled a keycard from his back pocket and slid it into the elevator card reader. The door opened instantly.

"This is a safe house." He spoke quietly once they were inside the elevator, his voice not more than a whisper.

"Provided by your company?" She kept it vague. Even elevators could be bugged.

"Yes."

Great, she thought, time alone with Mark and nothing to interrupt them. Could she trust him to behave? Could she trust herself?

"This place must cost a fortune." She entered the apartment, surprised at its size for an apartment in downtown Manhattan. She quickly checked each room. Besides a living room, dining room and fully appointed kitchen, there was a luxurious bathroom that included a sunken tub. The bedroom was massive. She stared at the king-sized bed.

Uh oh. Were they supposed to share?

She dropped the duffel bag on the bed and headed back into the living room, looking for Mark. He was in the kitchen, brewing a pot of coffee.

"Don't you think it's a little late for that?" She perched a hip against the counter and watched him pour water into the machine.

"You know as well as I do that we've got some unfinished business we need to clear up before we work together any further." He passed by her into the living room. "I don't know about you, but I want to get out of this blasted wig and take out these contacts." Not waiting for her response, he headed into the bathroom.

She had to agree. Her own wig itched unbearably. She went back into the bedroom, whipped off the phony glasses, and quickly changed out of the polyester pantsuit and into black yoga pants and a tank top. Removing the wig and releasing her hair from its constricting pins, she sighed in pleasure as she ran her hands through her hair and massaged her scalp. The door opened and she whirled about.

"Do you mind?"

"Much better." He stood, one shoulder braced against the doorway, his arms crossed over his chest. His silver eyes traced her face, her long black hair, and her body encased in the form fitting outfit. His lips kicked up in an unholy grin. She felt naked, exposed. Her heart started to race.

"How about some coffee?" Instead of coming into the room, he turned away.

"Sure." She exhaled, telling herself it wasn't disappointment she was feeling, and followed his tall form toward the kitchen. He was still wearing the black jeans and T-shirt, but the black wig was gone and his hair shone golden in the light.

Moments later, they sat facing each other at opposite ends of the couch in the living room. Carla nursed the steaming mug in her hands and studied him, thinking of all the questions that lay unanswered between them.

"Why did you join the CIA?" He took a sip of coffee.

"Ugh." She coughed over a mouthful of too hot

coffee. Whatever she'd expected he might ask, this question hadn't been one of them.

"All the usual reasons, I guess," she said when she'd recovered. "I wanted to get as far away as I could from home. I wanted adventure. I wanted to align myself with people who value the powers of reason, deduction, and the truth of empirical evidence. Yes—" she said when she saw him nodding. "I know what you're thinking. I was looking for something different than the world my mother and sister believed in. What about you?" She changed the subject, not wanting to dwell on what had been a sore point between them. "Why did you join the FBI?"

"I wanted to get as far away as I could from home. I wanted adventure." A slight grin twitched his lips as he parroted her answer. "But I also liked the satisfaction of solving cases, of finding clues, of putting the pieces together and solving puzzles. Speaking of that," he put the coffee mug on the table and stood up. He pulled his wallet from his back pocket and extracted money.

"For services rendered." He handed her the bills.

She counted out five hundred dollars in hundreds.

"What's this for?" She arched a black brow inquisitively at him, aware he'd diverted the conversation away from the topic of him joining the FBI.

"We solved the Dupree case, remember? With everything that's been going on, I forgot to tell you. I returned the stolen painting to Dupree."

"What about Harrington?"

"What about him?"

"Did he suspect anything? He must realize the painting is missing from his safe."

"I'm sure he does, but that's not our problem, right?'

Right, she thought. But Harrington was their problem. He was a member of the Illuminati.

"Enough chitchat, Mark." She drained her mug and placed it on the glass coffee table. "It's time we get down to business. On the plane, you claimed you didn't know my sister was held captive in one of the stables at your family's estate." She looked at him, her green eyes serious.

"That's true." He nodded.

"I had a DNA test run on the hair I found there. It confirmed the hair was Gwen's. Someone definitely held her there. You want to tell me who else in your family is involved with the Illuminati?"

His silver eyes met hers for an instant, sharp and assessing, and then he finished his cup of coffee. "You want another cup?"

"No," she said, "I want you to answer my question."

"OK." He heaved a sigh and leaned back against the couch, running both his hands through his thick golden hair. It was obvious he was reluctant to speak.

"If you want me to trust you, you're going to have to tell me what you know." She spoke softly, encouragingly. Whatever happened now, she wasn't going to let him back out or distract her.

"I honestly don't know who was keeping Gwen in the stables." His eyes met hers and she wanted to believe him, but there was too much missing information.

"It had to be someone in your family. Tell me something," she said, sifting through the facts of the case. "How did you become involved with the Illuminati in the first place? I know the Phoenix must have assigned you to the case, but why you? Was there some reason, a family connection perhaps, to justify your involvement?"

"You're smart," he said, a spark of admiration offsetting the obvious tension tightening his face.

"I'm CIA, what can I say?" She smiled, accepting his compliment, but then resumed her questioning. "What was the reason you were assigned?"

"It's complicated."

"Clue me in."

"The Phoenix got a lead several years back about a clandestine organization that was utilizing aspects of the occult in an effort to gain power."

"What kind of power? Why would the Phoenix be interested in a bunch of fringe occult types?"

"Careful, Carla. You've got to watch your assumptions."

"Why?"

"Because not everyone involved in occult activities is deluded."

"What do you mean?"

"I mean that at first we thought the Illuminati was simply a group using aspects of the occult to influence financial markets and the like."

"The occult can influence financial markets, really? That's absurd."

"Not in the case of the Illuminati. Things started to happen."

"What kind of things?"

"Mysterious disappearances of prominent members of Wall Street, rumors of bizarre rituals, things of that nature. When some of the men resurfaced, we had reports that their personalities had greatly altered, that they were behaving strangely and that vast sums of money were disappearing. There was no proof that any actual crimes had been committed, and everyone wanted to avoid publicity. That's why the Phoenix was called in."

"So why were you assigned to the case? Was your dad or your brother involved?" She wanted to know who had taken her sister, and it was becoming obvious that he was trying to protect someone.

"My dad's not involved," he said quickly, adamantly.

"What about Paul?"

Mark expelled a deep breath and his expression turned grim. "I was assigned to the case because we had evidence linking Paul with the organization. I went undercover to Santa Barbara to investigate exactly how he's connected."

"So, is he a member? If you joined the Illuminati, wouldn't you know for sure if he was a member?"

"It doesn't work that way." He shook his head. "The

Illuminati is an anonymous organization."

"How does that work?"

"It's a highly selective, highly secretive group that strives to protect the anonymity of its members. You've seen how it works. The members always meet in cloaks and masks. They use the Internet both to screen potential members and to arrange locations and meeting times."

"Someone has to be in charge of all that. Someone must know the identities of all the members." Carla stretched, feeling the caffeine coursing through her body.

"I would assume so, but I've been unable to find out who that person is. All other members are anonymous to each other."

"I take it they accepted your application?"

"Yes, but they are highly selective, as I said, and it costs a small fortune to join."

"So you and Paul could both be members but not know it?"

"It's possible."

She shot him a perplexed glance. "So what's the scam?"

"What do you mean?"

"Why would anyone pony up a huge amount of dough to join such a group? What's the payoff?"

"Enormous financial gain, world domination, stuff like that." He shrugged.

"So what did you uncover about your brother's involvement?"

"I'm still working on that," he said. "I'm sure you can understand that this has been a difficult assignment. I love my brother." He broke eye contact and ran his hands distractedly through his hair.

As she watched him, she abruptly saw the situation from his perspective. Damn. Of course he loved his brother. She'd been so focused on her own line of questioning she'd been unaware of how increasingly uncomfortable and tense he'd become. He was sitting now with his hands clenched tightly into fists on the tops of his thighs. His jawline stood out in sharp relief and his gray eyes were dark, bleakly austere.

"I'm sorry." She reached out and gently touched his clenched fist. "It must be really tough investigating your own brother." She remembered all the times she'd had to help her sister out of scrapes.

He unclenched his fist and rotated his hand so that he could grasp hers, interlacing their fingers.

"I want this whole thing over." He exhaled. "The sooner we blow the lid off the Illuminati's anonymity, the sooner we can stop them, and the sooner I can get my brother out of this mess."

She heard the honest pain expressed in what he said, and though questions still lay unanswered between them, she realized he was finally telling her the complete truth about something.

His love for his brother would also explain why he'd been so unwilling to discuss the case with her. It must be really galling for a Lyons to have a criminal in the family.

In the small paranoid part of her brain, she knew it was possible that his love for his brother overrode his duties to the Phoenix and that he could still actually be a double agent, but she doubted it.

"You never answered my question." His voice interrupted her thoughts.

"Which?"

"On the plane, when we were talking about the past. I asked you what you used to feel for me."

"Oh geez, Mark. Let's not bring up the past, OK? It's dead and gone and completely irrelevant now."

"That's not true and you know it."

"Why?"

"Because you feel this as much as I do." He took her hand and pressed it between both of his. She felt the electric current pulsing between them.

"I don't want to talk about it." She yanked her hand

away as if burned.

"You were just as eager to battle me at the Green Dragon as I was." His voice dropped low, growing intense. "I'll never forget how you responded to me that night when we kissed."

"I said I don't want to talk about that!" Their more recent kisses had singed the specific details of that first kiss from her memory.

"Why, because maybe you cared as much as I did about what we shared?"

"Damn it, Mark. All that happened almost ten years ago. Why the hell are you bringing it up? What the hell does it have to do with what's going on now, huh?"

"Don't you see, honey, it's key." He reached out and took her hand in his again.

"What's key? And don't call me 'honey,'" she scowled. "Let go of my hand." She pulled her hand free and jumped to her feet. She had to get away from the heated intensity emanating from him.

"You don't trust me now because you never have, have you?" He looked up at her, meeting and holding her gaze.

"Why should I?" She stared defiantly at him, her arms crossed against her chest. "You were always the one holding all the power, Mark. You had everything: the money, the prestige, the family connections. Compared to you, I was nothing."

"But you were, don't you see?" He rose to his feet and moved toward her. His eyes traveled over her face, a thoughtful smile on his face.

"You were independent and strong and completely able to take care of yourself. I'd never met anyone like you. You're right to think I was born with a silver spoon in my mouth, but that's part of why you so fascinated me. You had none of my advantages and yet you were proud and capable, and you were hot, Carla. You still are." He reached out and wrapped his arms around her waist, pulling her close.

"Stop it, just stop it." She jerked away again and paced over to the large, floor-to-ceiling windows that looked out on the bright lights of the big city.

She stared out into the night, unseeing. How could he say such things to her? Did he have any idea how much what he was telling her was what she'd always wanted to hear?

She heard him pick up the coffee mugs and go into the kitchen. Her brain was spinning. Was it possible that he actually was telling the truth? Had her own sense of inferiority kept her from trusting him, all those years ago, and led her to completely misread his intentions? What about now?

Damn. Maybe she was still misreading him. She revolved the evidence, the facts, over in her mind. Ever since he'd surfaced at the farmhouse in Virginia, he'd done nothing to jeopardize her safety. If anything, he'd acted consistently on her behalf, if a little arrogantly at times. She couldn't avoid comparing her own behavior to his. She'd been so eager to accuse him of duplicity and of being unwilling to level with her, but she herself had only leveled with him under direct orders from her supervisor.

She turned away from the window, having made up her mind to answer his question. She'd at least give him that. He wasn't in the kitchen or the bathroom, so she walked down the hall to the bedroom. She stopped dead in her tracks.

He stood by the bed with his back to her. He pulled off the black T shirt. His back was a broad expanse of masculine muscle and sinew, of broad shoulders tapering to a lean waist, the black jeans riding low over narrow hips. Her mouth went dry.

"Carla?" He turned.

She struggled to raise her eyes from the delicious contours of his chest, his lean belly, his jeans. She had never seen him shirtless before. The sight stole her breath. She swallowed with difficulty and finally managed to pull her eyes off his body.

"It's nothing," she said, chickening out in the face of such tempting male flesh. "We can talk about it in the morning."

"No way." He approached. "What's on your mind?"

"Oh hell," she swore under her breath. All judicious intention fled and she succumbed to temptation. "Let me show you."

She pulled him to her and dug her fingers into the thick golden hair at the base of his neck. She reached up on tiptoe to kiss him.

"Carla!" He pulled back. His hands came up to her shoulders and he held her slightly away from him. "What are you doing?" His voice was unsteady, his eyes burning into her.

"Isn't it obvious?" She yanked him close again.

They had talked enough. It was time for action.

"Kiss me." She whispered against his lips.

"Yes." He took possession of the kiss, pulling her against him. When his tongue slipped into her mouth, the kiss spiraled out of control.

All her reservations, all the questions and concerns she'd harbored about him, everything took flight and disappeared in a rush of desire. Nothing remained but the wild electricity sparking between them, igniting their bodies into a single burning flame of sensual need.

The next thing she knew, she was topless, lying draped across the bed, and he was leaning over her, stroking and cupping the fullness of her breasts as she writhed sinuously against him, her body on fire.

He broke off the kiss and looked down at her, reluctantly removing his hands from her as he did so.

"You know where this is headed, don't you?" His breath was husky and uneven, a heated flush rode his cheekbones.

"Of course," she said impatiently, her body desperate to feel him again. "We're going to finish something we started ten years ago." She reached out to the top button of his jeans.

"Wait just a moment, honey." He stilled her movement, taking her hands and bringing them to his mouth. "Believe me, there's nothing more I'd like to do right now." He pressed a kiss to each palm. "But you know as well as I do that it wouldn't finish anything between us. If anything, we'd just be getting started." He released her and ran his hands through his hair in a distracted motion.

"So what are you proposing then, more talk? More analysis of our history?" She could feel the heat radiating from him and her body craved the burn. "Damn it, Mark." She grabbed his shoulders and pushed him back against the bedcovers. Her hair curtained his face as she leaned over him. Her bare breasts brushed his naked chest.

"I'm sick to death of talking." She struggled for words as desire pumped through her. "I'm sick to death of analyzing and dissecting everything you say for ulterior motives. I don't care about the past, or the future. For once, let's just be here, together, just the two of us, right now, OK?"

She climbed on top of him, straddled him, and then gasped in excitement as she felt him hot and hard between her legs. Consequences be damned! She was sick and tired of trying to maintain control around him. With a sense of heady delight and freedom she leaned over to kiss him again.

"Oh yes," he growled in masculine pleasure as her breasts swung low across his face. "Do you have any idea what you're doing to me?" He clasped her hips and seized a nipple in his mouth, lathing it with his tongue.

"Yes," she cried out in pleasure. Molten fire erupted through her body. They had to get naked, now. "Take off your pants," she commanded.

"If you take off yours," he grinned wolfishly, his hands

stroking ceaselessly over her hips, his groin lifting in a suggestive rhythm against hers.

"You drive a hard bargain, mister," she laughed and sprang from the bed.

"All the better to please you," he chuckled.

While he dug into his bag to find the necessary protection, she shucked her sweatpants and threw back the bedcovers. She lay back against the sheets and pillows, naked and unabashed as she watched him. He watched her watch him. He unbuttoned his jeans and pushed them down.

"Do you have any idea how beautiful you are?" he said quietly as he slid onto the bed to join her.

"No more than you." Her mouth went dry as she drank in the glorious lines of his body. He was big and muscular, everywhere. Her eyes dropped below his waist and desire loosened her knees. It was a good thing she was already lying down.

He pressed an intimate kiss to her left breast. "Am I dreaming?" he whispered against the silken swell. "Would you believe me if I told you I've dreamed of this moment since the first day I met you?" He rolled between her thighs.

"You're kidding, right?" she gasped as she felt him push intimately against her.

Romantic declarations aside, why on earth did he want to keep talking? Her body was mindless with desire. It was time to get down to business. She moved her hips against his and tried to pull him into another kiss.

"No, I'm not." He rolled off her, resisting her desperate efforts to kiss him again. "I've never been more serious in my life."

He propped himself up on an elbow. He looked down into her flushed face, smoothing her hair aside. "Tell me, honey, did you ever want me like this?" He moved himself suggestively against her hip, his flesh hard and hot where it rubbed. "Did you want me so much you burned, so much you ached for me? Did you, ever?" His silver eyes met hers, dark and serious, and vulnerable.

Vulnerable? Was that really what she was seeing? A Lyons vulnerable to a deVille?

She stared back at him, her passion cooling for a moment as she realized with surprise that he was telling the truth. She heard the uncertainty in his voice and saw the naked honesty in his eyes. Finally, there was no more pretense, no more obscured truth, no more diversion between them. He was admitting how much he wanted her to want him.

With the realization, something abruptly shifted deep inside her. The balance of power tipped. All her inhibitions, all her prohibitions and fears, all of it disappeared in the face of his honesty. The walls melted and her heart opened to him.

She met his gaze with her own, honest and open and with no walls between them.

"Oh Mark, you have no idea how much I want you." She touched him intimately, her body instantly reignited with desire at the thick hard heat of him pulsing in her hand.

"I've hated you like no one else I've ever met." She pushed him back into the pillows and slid her lips along the heated column of his throat. "I've wanted you like no one else I've ever met." She straddled him and slowly sank down his rigid length.

"Carla!" he gasped, thrusting up and meeting her in a passionate kiss, their bodies one.

CHAPTER 15

Carla wasn't sure what woke her the next morning. One moment she was wrapped in the deepest, most blissful sleep she'd had in months, and the next she was sitting bolt upright in bed. She tossed her long black hair out of her eyes and realized she wasn't alone.

Oh hell. She'd completely forgotten about last night.

She looked at the man sleeping peacefully beside her. Mark lay sprawled on his back. The blankets rode low on his flat belly and his lips curled in a slight smile. Her heart skipped a beat. She fought the urge to lean down, kiss him, and start all over again. There wasn't time. The clock on the bedside table read 8:30 a.m., and she had to get going.

They may have broken down many of the barriers between them during the long hours of loving last night, but it didn't change the facts. Mark's love for his brother was a liability that could jeopardize his objectivity in the investigation. Besides, Jonathan Carter might refuse to see her. Or he could be a red herring. She didn't relish that possibility, or how Mark might laugh if that were the case. Better to keep him in the dark until she had something solid on the guy.

She slid naked from the bed, careful not to jostle it, and picked up her bag on the way to bathroom. From the duffel, she pulled out her trusty janitor disguise and within minutes had transformed herself once more into the elderly man who'd infiltrated LSA Enterprises.

She checked her cell when she reached the crowded street. Tate's message said she had an appointment scheduled with Jonathan Carter at 10 a.m. Good, the recluse had agreed to meet her.

As she slid the phone back into her pocket, she noticed a huge man towering over the crowd and moving toward her on the busy sidewalk. No way! But it was. The Hulk was there in New York. She'd recognize him anywhere. But did he recognize her in disguise?

She pushed out into the hordes of morning rush hour pedestrians and moved down Barclay toward Wall Street. Surreptitiously, she glanced over her shoulder. Damn. He was still there, moving along at the speed of the other foot traffic. She couldn't be sure if he was following her, or if it was simply a bizarre coincidence.

No way, there were no such things as coincidences.

Right before the corner, she hurried with a few other foolhardy jaywalkers across the street and onto Broadway. Not wasting a moment to see if he was following, she jogged a block and slipped into an alley. She pulled out her cell and called Tate as she walked toward the street at the far end of the alley.

"Hey, Tate, I got your message. Who am I supposed to be when I meet Carter?"

"Good morning to you, too," Tate laughed.

"Good morning," she managed a quick smile. "Look, I'm sorry I don't have time for chitchat, but I've got someone on my tail. I'm gonna have to split in a moment. What's my alias?"

"Carl Costa."

"Excellent. I've already dressed the part."

"I know how much you like to go in drag. I'll send you

a text file with your cover story. Keep out of trouble." Tate hung up.

Carla had just reached the other end of the alley. Glancing back, she saw the Hulk's enormous shadow enter behind her. She hung a right on Trinity Place and broke into a run.

An hour later, she'd given the guy the slip and had helped herself to an excellent breakfast at a little diner in a crowded section of the financial district. She paid the tab and headed across Wall Street to the high rise where JC & Associates was located.

As she rode the elevator to the top floor, she adjusted the baseball cap and made sure her long hair was still hidden under the gray-haired wig. As per Tate's instructions, she was an irate stockholder from one of Carter's numerous investment accounts, though the janitor disguise didn't easily jibe with her cover story. She'd have to rely on her acting skills to carry it off.

When she reached the executive floor, she detoured to the men's bathroom to check her facial hair. Good, the place was empty. Her moustache had come slightly unglued, probably at breakfast. She quickly reattached it and then headed for the door. Just as she was about to open it, the door swung open. She found herself face-to-face with none other than Paul Lyons.

What the hell was he doing here?

She broke his steely blue gaze and hurried passed. Adrenaline pumped hard and fast through her as she rounded the corner to the executive offices. A spark of recognition had fleetingly crossed his face when he'd seen her. Had he placed her? Would he follow her into JC & Associates?

Damn. She should have worn a different disguise, but how the hell was she to know he'd be here?

Her green eyes narrowed as she walked into the office. If Paul was there, then it was pretty safe to conclude that Carter was also working with the Illuminati, but how on earth would she be able to ascertain the level of his involvement?

"May I help you?" asked the receptionist.

"I am Carl Costa." She gave her voice a slight Latin inflection. "I am here to see Mr. Carter." She tilted her head proudly and thrust her shoulders back, getting into her character.

"Yes, he's expecting you. If you'll follow me." The woman rose and led Carla down a hallway.

Like LSA Enterprises, JC & Associates radiated the understated opulence of an affluent financial company. Most of the glass doors along the hallway were closed, but looking in where she could, Carla saw the offices occupied by conservatively dressed executives all appearing diligently at work on JC & Associates business.

One strange thing she noticed was that on the walls directly above each door were peculiar symbols that looked similar to the strange image on the JC & Associates letterhead. She wanted to stop and photograph them, but the receptionist had charged indomitably on.

Turning a corner, they headed down another hallway, but this one was very long and had no doors off to the sides. Carla glanced up and noticed state of the art security cameras discreetly mounted near the ceiling along the walls, strategically placed to expose every inch of the hallway. Their footsteps echoed in the silence as they walked to an enormous black lacquered double-door. The door was at least fifteen feet high and reached to the ceiling, where several more cameras watched their every move.

"Mr. Carter?" The receptionist knocked firmly. "Mr. Costa to see you, sir."

"Enter," a deep voice called from the other side.

"Please go in," she said to Carla and hurried away.

Carla opened one of the enormous doors and found herself in the strangest executive office she'd ever seen. The walls were a deep blood red. The upper reaches of the office were shrouded in complete darkness. She had to assume the ceiling was painted black because she couldn't actually see it. The floor was painted in black enamel and long black drapes completely blocked the daylight from entering the vast office. Brilliant chandeliers hung suspended on lengthy iron chains. The room was bathed in an artificial, electric light.

"Please come in." Across the room, a man rose to his feet behind a large ebony desk.

The door clicked closed loudly behind her, but Carla hesitated before moving deeper into the room. Goosebumps ran down her spine and the hair at the back of her neck rose. On the walls nearest her hung stuffed animal heads, human masks, and a selection of other fetishes.

Beside her on a pedestal was a delicate crystal sculpture of a naked woman's body contorted into an impossible shape. It might have been beautiful in a disturbing sort of way, if it hadn't been for the face. The woman appeared to be in agony as her head twisted backwards and her eyes pointed skyward in wild desperation.

Get a grip, she told herself. She tore her eyes from the sculpture and the strange wall hangings.

There was no reason to feel so spooked. She'd seen a ton of stuff like this during her years at the Magic Shop— well, maybe not the priceless crystal sculpture—but whatever she'd been expecting, it wasn't this blatant display of occultism. What the hell did other Wall Street executives make of it?

She forced herself to walk across the room.

"How good of you to come. I've been expecting you," Carter came around the desk approached her. He was tall and dressed in a formal black business suit, white shirt and silver tie.

"Uh, yeah," she said noncommittally.

His black hair had gone silver at the temples and she met his piercing black gaze. No question about it, this was the same man she'd seen at the restaurant in Montecito. She reached forward to shake his hand.

"What the—?" she gasped. Some kind of weird electricity arced from his body into hers, using their joined hands as a conduit.

Her eyes shot to his and she felt trapped in their hypnotic black depths, unable to withdraw her hand from his strong grip.

"Yes, it is good to see you." Carter released her hand. His voice held no accent, but he phrased his speech as if English wasn't his native language.

Her legs went limp as noodles and she almost collapsed into one of the black leather armchairs. Something strange was going on, some kind of unseen power struggle was being waged. She didn't believe in the occult, but nonetheless, she knew she had to remain standing if she wanted to stay on par with this man. She braced her hands against the chair and stayed on her feet.

"Perhaps you would like a drink?" He moved, tall and regal, to a bar at the far end of the room.

"Isn't it a little early?" she croaked, her throat unaccountably hoarse.

What the hell was going on? She forced her hands off the chair and commanded her legs to behave as she drew herself up to her full height, trying to maintain her cover. This wasn't like any other business meeting she'd ever had.

"I suppose, but you will feel better if you have a little something," he said. "Come, share a drink with me."

A tall chrome lamp arched over the fully stocked bar where the cut crystal glittered. He handed her a small tumbler.

"It is good to see you again," he said, clinking her glass and then raising his own to his mouth. He held the glass against his lips and watched her.

A distant voice inside her head screamed a warning not to drink the amber liquid, but as if possessed, she raised the glass to her mouth.

She cautiously sipped the amber drink. The man smiled. Surprisingly, it didn't burn going down. Whatever it was, it wasn't alcohol. The taste was slightly sweet with a faintly metallic edge. Oh hell, was she drinking something laced with blood?

"What do you mean, 'again'?" she said, hastily putting the tumbler down on the bar.

He followed suit and then closed the distance between them. "Do you really think all this can fool me?"

Before she knew it, he had pulled off her baseball cap and yanked off her moustache.

"Ow!" she yelled and jumped back.

Her long black hair tumbled down. She whipped off the thick-rimmed glasses, aware that the gray goatee probably looked preposterous.

"What the hell do you think you're doing?" She ripped off the goatee, jammed it into her coveralls, and took another step back.

"You are indeed beautiful." Carter studied her face. He smiled, but there was something sinister in the hard lines of his thin lips. "You are the very image of your mother." He picked up their drinks and moved toward her. "Come, let us not stand on formality, my dear. Bring your drink and let us have a seat." He handed the glass to her.

Once again, she found herself following him as if some inexorable force compelled her to obey. Damn it, she didn't like being out of control. Was the drink drugged? Her brain seemed to be losing some of its clarity.

"Who the hell are you?" she managed to demand as her body sank helplessly down into the soft leather armchair.

She looked up and noticed a large image, a symbol, painted on the wall directly behind and above him. It was a giant version of the one she'd seen on the JC & Associates letterhead and over the doors in the outer offices.

Inside a huge black circle, white interlocking triangles

formed a hexagram. At the hexagram's center was an eye, but unlike the other, simple ones she'd seen, this eye seemed weirdly, disturbingly real. It felt like a malevolent consciousness was peering out and watching their every move.

This must be drugged, she thought, and put the glass on the desk.

"You know who I am, Carla." The man's deep voice brought her back to the moment. "I am Jonathan Carter."

"How do you know my name?"

"I know many things about you." His black eyes bore into hers. "You have come to ask me a few questions, have you not?"

"Yes, but how do you know who I am?" She passed a hand over her face, trying to stay on topic.

Carter broke eye contact and glanced at the expensive watch on his wrist. "I have another meeting shortly. Let us focus on your more pressing questions."

She swallowed, her mouth dry, her brain strangely foggy. No point beating around the bush since he obviously knew who she was and most likely why she was there.

"What's your involvement with the Illuminati?"

"Ah yes, the Illuminati." He took another sip of his drink and looked absolutely unperturbed by her question. "It is a remnant of a secret and ancient occult society, is it not?"

"You tell me."

"Yes, but you already know this to be true." His black eyes met hers again and she struggled to maintain the focus of her questioning. There was something damned distracting about his hypnotic stare.

"So, how are you involved?"

"Wouldn't it be wiser for you to be concerned with how the Illuminati plans to use nuclear arms?"

"What?"

"You already know that the Illuminati is working to

acquire nuclear weaponry, do you not? So, what you should really be asking me is what I know that will help you stop them from committing the heinous crime of nuclear terrorism."

"What do you know about their efforts to acquire nukes?"

"They have stockpiled an arsenal at Chateau Falkenstein in Switzerland. You have very little time to stop them. Even as we speak, they are putting into place the necessary delivery system for implementing their first planned assault."

Carter looked at his wristwatch again and stood. "It has indeed been a pleasure, however, I have another meeting."

He came around the large ebony desk and held out his hand. Despite her misgivings, she took his hand. The moment their hands touched, the peculiar electricity once again shot from his body into hers, but this time she felt power surging through her. He released her hand, but her body still felt weirdly supercharged. The power seemed to intensify her every movement.

"Thanks for meeting with me, Mr. Carter," she said.

Instantly, it seemed, she arrived at the huge double-doors of the office. She whirled to face him. The action caused her arm to swing wide and hit the crystal woman on the pedestal.

"No!" he shouted, rushing forward, trying to catch the art piece as it fell. Gone was the cool, regally sophisticated man. He flung himself toward the sculpture in a desperate attempt to stop its fall, but he was too late. It smashed, scattering crystal shards across the black enamel floor. They lay glittering like a thousand diamonds on black velvet.

"I'm so sorry," Carla exclaimed, but he didn't hear.

"No, no, no, no!" he cried wildly on hands and knees, crawling across the floor and frantically attempting to retrieve the myriad crystal fragments and put them in a crimson cloth he'd pulled from his pocket. There was something unsettling about such a dignified man crawling about so distraughtly on his hands and knees.

"Let me help." She kneeled and reached out to pick up one of the shards.

"Don't touch it!" He lunged at her, shoving her hand away before she could touch the piece. "Don't you see you've caused enough trouble?" He looked up at her in agony.

"I said I was sorry," she replied. "It was an accident."

"An accident? An accident?" he laughed bitterly. "Do you have any idea what you have done, Carla?" His eyes shot black fire at her. "No, of course you do not. Please leave, just leave."

"OK." She stood up and walked to the door. "Thanks for the information about the Illuminati."

"The Illuminati, hah!" he muttered to himself as he crawled away from her, resuming the painstaking process of recovering the destroyed sculpture.

Carla took one last look at the strange man before she swung open the double doors. The strange power still seemed to surge through her body and the doors exploded open with wild force, crashing against the outer walls.

"Oh, sorry," she whispered, hurrying from the office and not waiting to see Carter's response. She was startled once again to find her legs carrying her at an incredibly fast pace through JC & Associates and out the door to the foyer.

It wasn't until she stood waiting for the elevator that she realized she'd moved so fast that no one in the office had actually seen her. The elevator door swung open.

"Carla, what are you doing here?" Paul stood inside the elevator, an angry look on his face. Beside him stood the Hulk, who immediately lunged at her.

"I don't have time for this," she said, dodging the Hulk and giving him a kick as he flew past. He slammed headfirst into the wall on the opposite side of the foyer.

She then grabbed Paul unceremoniously by the front of his suit coat and hurled him out of the elevator. She heard more than saw him hit the far wall as she entered the elevator.

Whoa, what the hell was going on?

She tried to make sense of the last hour as she rode the elevator down, but very little made sense. So much of what had happened she had no explanation for, like that strange sculpture, like that weird all-seeing eye on the wall, like her suddenly becoming superwoman, not that she was complaining. The superwoman thing had come in handy. Maybe she'd been drugged. Maybe that was it.

She hurried out onto the busy sidewalk, her head now clear and her body feeling more normal, and headed toward the safe house. She pulled out her phone as she walked. Mark had left three messages demanding to know where she was. Someone else had just left her a message. It sounded like a crank, but given the circumstances, the caller had to be someone from the Illuminati. She stepped into a storefront and out of the traffic noise and replayed it.

"Offering, your time is nigh. Prepare yourself for the Sacrifice to the Lord of Light."

She frowned and played the message a third time. The male voice sounded familiar.

Damn, if it wasn't Paul Lyons. She'd put good money down that it was his voice. It certainly seemed like no coincidence that she'd just encountered him and that now she received this threatening message, but it also meant that he'd managed to break into the CIA's secure line. She frowned as she forwarded the message to Tate and then dialed headquarters.

"Tate."

"Hey, what's up? How'd your meeting with Carter go?"

"I'll tell you in a minute, but first, check your messages."

"Sure, why?"

"I just got a crank call from someone in the Illuminati, most likely Paul Lyons. I don't know if you've got his voice in a database somewhere, but it'd be great if you could determine if it's really him."

"I'll check."

"Thanks. You know what this means if it's true, don't you?"

"That Paul and Abaddon are probably the same guy?"

"Damn, you're good," Carla smiled. "That's my guess, considering that Abaddon was also able to break through our firewall when he sent me those threatening emails. But if it's true, it also means Paul's a lot smarter and a lot more dangerous than I've given him credit for."

"It sure sounds like it. Did you learn anything from Carter?"

"Yes." She glanced outside the doorway to make sure no one on the crowded street could overhear. "He told me the Illuminati is stockpiling nuclear weapons at a castle called Chateau Falkenstein in Switzerland. He also said they're planning some kind of military action pretty damned soon."

"Wow, this is good intel," Tate exclaimed, taking notes. "But I'm curious, did he explain how he knows all this? Why would he rat on the Illuminati if he's one of its members?"

"Damn it!"

"What?"

"He never told me."

"Did you ask?"

"I tried, but it was a weird meeting."

"What do you mean?"

"The guy's a bit of a nut. He's definitely into the occult."

"So? You don't believe in any of that, right?"

"Oh hell," Carla let out a frustrated sigh. "I don't, but things got really strange in there, Tate. I mean really strange."

"You want to talk about it?"

"Not now. The most important thing is to stop the Illuminati, assuming they really are planning on starting some kind of nuclear apocalypse. We need to find out if Carter is telling the truth."

"I'd love to know what Carter's motives were for sharing this intel with you," Tate said. "But you're right, we've got to stay on target. I'll get the ball rolling over here. If any of what he says is true, get ready for a trip to Switzerland."

"Thanks, Tate. What would I do without you?"

"Suffer terribly," Tate laughed and hung up.

Carla pocketed the phone. She took a circuitous route back to the safe house, keeping a close eye to see if anyone was tailing her.

The energy that had supercharged her was gone. She felt tired and worn out. She also wasn't looking forward to seeing Mark again. They'd broken down so many walls between them last night, but he was sure to see her behavior today as a defection.

Ten minutes later, she knocked on the apartment door.

"Where the hell have you been?" He quickly closed the door behind her and turned, facing her, his hands across his chest, his face all hard lines and angles, looking as angry as she'd expected.

"I had to go out. Boy do I need to sit down." She collapsed onto the sofa. She leaned her head back against the cushions and looked up at him. His face was an open book of betrayal and hurt.

"I'm sorry I didn't wake you." She closed her eyes to avoid seeing his pain.

Why was he acting so hurt? Where had the proud and arrogant Mark Lyons she knew so well gone?

"You were sleeping so soundly, I just didn't have the heart to wake you."

"You could have left a note." He sat down beside her,

tension emanating from him in palpable waves.

She wanted to reach out to him, to touch him and restore some of the intimacy they'd built last night. Instead, she leaned back deeper into the plump sofa cushions.

"I didn't have time," she sighed. "Besides, it didn't seem all that important. I was simply going to follow up on a lead I thought would be a red herring."

"Was it?"

"No, actually it wasn't." She heaved herself up and turned to look at him. His expression hadn't softened. "Have you ever heard of a man named Jonathan Carter?"

"Of JC & Associates?" he asked. When she nodded, he said, "He's a Wall Street legend. Quite the recluse, but a brilliant money manager. What about him?"

"He's involved with the Illuminati. Did you know that?"

"No, but don't you think that's a bit far-fetched? From what I've heard, he's not been seen in public for about ten years. What evidence do you have?"

She studied him for a moment. He still looked unhappy, but at least he looked like he was telling the truth.

"I guess I should feel honored," she said.

"What do you mean?"

"I've seen him twice in the last week. Once in Montecito having dinner with Paul and your dad, and then this morning."

"Really?" He looked genuinely surprised, but then his silver eyes sharpened and she could see his brain working, processing the information. "My dad has done business with him in the past, but like I said, he's a financial genius. That meeting you saw in Montecito could have been about my family's finances."

"Maybe." Skepticism colored her voice. She wasn't sure how to break the news about his brother.

"Why did you go see him? I'm surprised he'd even

grant you an interview. From what I've heard, he doesn't meet with just anybody."

"I guess I must be somebody," she sighed again, her body and her emotions feeling drained. "Do you have any more of that coffee?" She struggled off the couch.

"I brewed a fresh pot this morning."

He followed her into the kitchen. She poured a cup and stuck it in the microwave.

"So what happened with Carter?" He braced his shoulder against the refrigerator and watched her, the lines of his face less rigid than before.

"I really don't want to talk about it," she grimaced. "The guy's a freak, OK? He's up to his eyeballs in weird occult stuff. What's relevant is that he said the Illuminati is planning a nuclear strike. He told me they're storing the nukes at a castle in Switzerland." She took a sip of the hot coffee and headed back into the living room.

"How do you know he's telling the truth? If he really is a member of the Illuminati, why would he give you this information?"

Damn. He was asking the same question Tate had, and she, like an idiot, had let Carter get away with not answering.

"Does it matter? Tate is checking the intel. I'll go with whatever she finds." She drained the coffee.

"Aren't you assuming a lot about this guy?" He took her empty mug, placed it on the table, and then lifted her onto his lap.

"I'm not assuming anything." For a minute, she let herself snuggle into his hard warmth, but then she braced herself against his shoulders and tried to stand up. What she had to say next would best be said at a formal distance. His arms were around her waist. She couldn't budge.

"Mark, please let me up. I've got to tell you something else, something important. You may not like what I'm about to say."

He released her instantly. She moved away from him

and ran a hand through her hair as she thought about how best to tackle the subject. She reached out and took his hand in hers, squeezing it gently.

"I know you love your brother, but Paul's in deep. Really deep, I'm afraid."

"What do you mean?" He removed his hand from hers and stared at her, his expression guarded.

"It's complicated." She held his gaze. "He keeps showing up in places he shouldn't. Like that dinner with Carter, then today I saw him outside Carter's office. He was none too happy to see me. In fact, his bodyguard or henchman or whoever the hell that no-neck guy is tried to attack me again. And then, just minutes later, I received a threatening message on my secure cell. I'm pretty sure it was Paul."

"Wait, what do you mean 'again'? When were you attacked before?"

"He was the one who abducted me at the Harrington fundraiser."

"You sure?"

Carla nodded. "Do you remember that guy who attacked me in the alley outside the Magic Shop? It wasn't a mugging. It was the same guy, and I'd seen him before that, too."

"Where?"

"LSA Enterprises. He was there with your brother." Her green eyes met his. "In fact, you were there, too. So do you know who that guy is?"

"When were you there? I don't remember seeing you."

"You're doing it again, Mark."

"What?"

"Using diversionary tactics to avoid answering my questions. Do you know him?"

Mark shrugged. "His name's Garrett Oswald. He's a friend of my brother's. I think it's safe to assume he's also a member of the Illuminati."

He studied her for a moment, seeing her gray coveralls.

"You were that janitor, the one going through the files." A slight grin touched his lips and his eyes twinkled.

Damn, I must be losing my touch, she thought, considering that Carter hadn't been fooled by her disguise, either.

"So, if you've known all along that Garrett was working with your brother, why did you pretend you didn't know him that night in the alley?" she demanded.

"I was undercover, remember?" He was now grinning openly.

Was he teasing her, or toying with her? She couldn't tell.

"You're really good at that, aren't you?" Frustration colored her voice and she met his gaze, her green eyes narrowing in speculation. "How can I ever know if you're really telling me the truth?"

"You want the truth?" His eyes darkened as he focused on her mouth. "The truth is there's so much more I'd like to do with you than talk about my brother, or the Illuminati. You'll probably call this a diversionary tactic, but I'm being as honest as I know how to be." He wrapped his arms around her and pulled her into another spellbinding kiss.

CHAPTER 16

The next thing she knew, her cell phone rang and Mark had his hand inside her coveralls. He was cupping her breast and his thumb was teasing her nipple, brushing across the fine silk of her bra.

"Hey, Tate." She managed not to gasp as she tried unsuccessfully to remove his hand. He rotated her on his lap to face away from him so he could inflict the sensual torment with both hands. He nuzzled the side of her neck. She had to brace her free hand against his hard thigh to keep upright.

"Is this a bad time?" It was Tate.

"No, not at all." She let out a gush of air as Mark nibbled on her ear lobe, his breath causing hot flames to lick up her body.

"Are you sure?" Tate sounded curious. Only an idiot would miss the huskiness in her voice. Tate was no idiot.

"Yes." It came out a sibilant hiss.

Once again she tried to twist away from him, but he had her pinned firmly onto his lap. It was impossible not to feel the hard length of him pressing into the small of her back. She swallowed, her mouth going dry.

"OK, I'll take your word for it," Tate continued,

amused skepticism lacing her voice.

"Your mom disappeared a short while ago from the clinic in Atascadero. None of the staff has been able to locate her. With you and Mark out of town and Kristi out of commission, I'm going to have Izzy investigate and see if she can find her, OK?"

"Cool." Carla bit her lip. She was anything but.

She had a gut feeling that Gwen and Moon Ray had something to do with her mom's disappearance, but at the moment, it was almost impossible to speak, much less think. Mark's hand was traveling southward across her bare belly, his other hand held her breast captive, and his tongue traced the delicate shell of her ear. Would Tate ever get off the phone?

"Another thing," Tate said.

"Yes?" Carla gasped, startled to feel Mark's hands suddenly on her naked breasts. He'd released her bra and was now inflicting an even more exquisite torment.

"The intel Carter gave you about the Illuminati and the Falkenstein castle seems promising. I ran it by Frank and he wants you and Mark in Switzerland ASAP to check it out."

"OK." Carla all but groaned as Mark gently rocked against her, his mouth burning a trail of fire along her neck. Her brain had turned liquid, and she struggled to stay on topic. "What about the ritual tonight?"

"Don't worry about that. Frank wants me to head up the recon mission. I'll finally get the chance to get away from this desk and out of my office."

"Great."

"I'd like to ask how it's going with Mark, but I get the feeling I'd better wait and have you fill me in later, right?" Tate was laughing openly now.

Carla hung up, tossed her phone on the coffee table, and let out a shaky breath, willing her body to calm down.

"Enough, Mark. Let me go." She glanced over her shoulder and met his dilated gaze. "We've got to go to

Switzerland, now."

He tightened his hold on her breasts.

Damn he was good. It took everything she had to keep from pressing herself more fully into his big warm hands and melting all over his lap.

"I want you." His voice was deep, sexy.

"I know what you mean." She expelled a long, shaky breath, then struggled against him. "But we don't have time. We've got to go."

He released her reluctantly and she got unsteadily to her feet.

He followed her into the bedroom, his hands buried deep in the front pockets of his jeans. She fought to keep from staring at the tantalizing way he filled them. She shook her head, trying to clear it. She was on a mission to stop an international nuclear incident. Sex was the last thing she should be thinking about right now, damn it!

She pulled a pair of black slacks and a dark green blouse from her duffel bag. Mark put his travel bag on the bed and pulled out his own disguise.

"My brother's in trouble, isn't he?"

His words stopped her short. She looked at him. His eyes were still dark with desire, a heated flush high on his jawline, but his expression was dead serious.

"Yes, I'm pretty sure he's in deep."

"He is." Mark's shoulders slumped and he sat down on the bed. He stared at the floor and ran his hands through his hair.

"What do you mean, 'he is?'" She sat down next to him.

"I'm going to level with you about him." He looked earnestly at her. "He's always been brilliant, much smarter than Nick or I ever was."

A faraway expression crossed his face and he dropped his gaze again to the floor.

"He was always different than we were. Remember when I told you he majored in physics at Princeton?"

When Carla nodded, he continued. "Well, when he finished the Ph.D., he came home to stay with my folks for a while. It didn't take long for them to notice he was stranger than usual. My mom called me and I came home to see if I could help."

"Was this before or after the Phoenix assigned you to investigate the Illuminati?"

"About the same time."

"Your brother knows you're a member, right?"

"Yes, he was the one who encouraged me to join." He looked sad. "He's always felt the little guy in our family. My dad and he have never had the best relationship and Paul's always felt at a disadvantage. Maybe it's because he's the youngest or something. Bottom line is that he's always wanted power. He believed—he still believes—the Illuminati is the key."

"Where do the nukes fit in?"

"I don't know, I really don't. But it can't be anything good," he said, his eyes sincere as he looked at her.

She nodded. Maybe she was being stupid, but she believed him. "You've been trying to protect him, haven't you?"

"A lot of good it's done. I thought I could head him off and stop him from messing up his life, but you're right. It looks like he's gotten in too deep." He rose. "I'm supposed to call him and confirm I'm bringing you to tonight's ritual. What do you want me to tell him?"

"Tell him we'll be there, otherwise he'll suspect something. Our people will be there to apprehend him and the others."

"So we're setting him up." He looked defeated.

"I'm sorry, Mark, I really am, but what other choice do we have?"

"I had a feeling it was going to come to this." He picked up his travel bag and headed into the living room.

Carla quickly changed out of the coveralls and into her street clothes. Her hands still shook slightly as she buttoned the blouse, and her legs trembled. Damn it, here Mark was about to betray his brother and her unruly body couldn't stop thinking about sex.

She grabbed the gray-haired wig. It was unlikely anyone would recognize them en route to Europe, but it was always better to be safe than sorry. Slinging the duffel bag over her shoulder, she headed for the living room. Mark's voice stopped her short. He was still on the phone, speaking softly.

"She won't be a problem, Paul. I can manage her." He hung up.

Was Mark talking about her? A dark thought slithered through her mind. Was he still playing her? Was all the supposed intimacy, all the seduction, just more of his tricks to distract her, to 'manage her' for the Illuminati?

A tightness welled in her chest, somewhere in the region of her heart. She was shocked to feel the sting of tears. No way. She wasn't going to let him do this to her, not again.

She straightened her spine and remembered Gwen's warning about Mark being Lucifer, the Great Seducer. That had all been just her sister's occult mumbo jumbo, right? Of course. There was a perfectly logical explanation for the power he exerted over her. It could be summed up in one word: sex.

Nonetheless, she couldn't discount the fact that she'd forgotten to drill him further about his own role in the Illuminati. And he still hadn't satisfactorily explained why the Illuminati had targeted her in the first place. Enough was enough. It was time to stop thinking with her body and start using her mind.

He turned and saw her standing in the hall. "Ready?" he asked.

"You bet." She pasted a smile on her face that did not meet her eyes.

\#

Carla found herself once more seated beside Mark on a

long plane ride. She studied him as the plane took off. He'd abandoned the black contacts but had kept the rest of the disguise he'd used on the earlier flight. His brilliant golden hair was hidden under the long black wig, and for this trip, he'd also donned a black goatee. He could pass for a pirate. So, was he friend or foe?

"It's too bad we didn't have time to finish what we started this morning," he whispered, dipping his head close.

What they had started? Damn him! Like the naive fool she'd been as a kid, she'd once again been the sucker, falling for his come-ons. Sex, that's all it was. Nothing more. Hell, behind that too-smug smile, he was probably laughing at what an easy make she'd been. She'd heard enough of his lies.

She ignored the shimmer of desire that danced down her traitorous body as his breath tickled her neck. She tilted her head away and reached for the in-flight magazine.

There had to be some way to draw him out, some way to figure out when he was being honest, or not. Their location wasn't appropriate for asking him about the Illuminati, but there were several other questions she could think of that would simply sound like idle gossip to anyone who overheard. She flipped open the magazine on her lap.

"So, you never told me about your marriage."

"What?"

She didn't meet his gaze, focusing instead on the magazine's crossword puzzle. "You were only married a year. Why didn't it work out?"

"Where's all this coming from?"

"You want to talk about starting something between us?" She purposely misinterpreted what he'd whispered. "If we're going to embark on a relationship, doesn't it make sense to talk about who we've been involved with? I'd really like to know why your marriage was such a failure."

She knew she was provoking him, but she couldn't resist. Maybe if he got really mad, she'd get some real answers.

"You don't know what the hell you're talking about," he bit out, his voice dropping so low it sounded like gravel. His hand closed over hers with a firmness that threatened pain.

"My, my, have I touched a sore spot?" She filled in the first answer to the puzzle with angry strokes of her pen. Reading the next clue, she shot him a narrow glance. "What's another word for 'mendacious'?"

"Dishonest, why?"

"Fancy that," she said bitterly. "It fits." She filled in the second answer.

"What's gotten into you? I thought we were finally getting somewhere. Didn't last night mean anything to you?" His grip loosened and his hand now caressed hers.

She pulled her hand away and tucked it safely under her leg. There was no way she was going to talk about last night. Hell, remembering it was bad enough. If it had really all been just a performance, some kind of lie on his part, then it was way too humiliating to think about.

Ignoring his attempt to divert her, she said, "And if your marriage was such a failure, then why were you having dinner with Julie at Pedro's the other night? That was your ex, wasn't it?"

"That was her." He didn't look overly surprised that she'd recognized her. "But I don't see how she has anything to do with us."

"Humor me. We've got a long plane flight ahead of us and you've got to admit there's a lot we don't know about each other." She looked up from the crossword puzzle.

"I'm honored you were curious enough about me to run a background check," he said, a glimmer of his good humor returning.

"It was just part of my job. I had to know who I was dealing with."

"Of course. That's why you went to all the effort to look up my marital status." A tinge of irony colored his voice.

"OK, OK, I admit, I was curious," she scowled.

"You've never married."

"You ran a background check on me?"

"Of course. I had to know who *I* was dealing with." He cocked a grin at her. "Why didn't you ever marry anyone? Were you waiting for me?"

"You wish," she snapped. His arrogance was appalling. She wanted to punch him or get her gun, something to wipe that smug grin off his face. Instead, she soldiered on with her questioning. She didn't ask herself why she needed to know so much about his first marriage.

"You married Julie while you were with the Bureau. She worked there, too. You divorced right about the time you quit, right?"

"What's up with the third degree?" He looked defensively at her, but then his expression shifted and his voice dropped. "Why talk about her when we can talk about us?"

"Yeah, right." Her words dripped sarcasm. Just like a man to avoid talking about the other woman. "I must be getting close to the truth if you're trying so hard to distract me."

"Are we back to that again?" He smoothed the fake goatee over his chin. "You're testing me, aren't you, because you don't trust me?"

"Why won't you tell me what happened to your marriage?" She refused to be diverted.

"I don't want to talk about it." He crossed his arms over his chest.

"Why not?"

"Because it's painful, is that what you want to hear?" His face turned all hard lines and jagged angles. "Do you want to know how much it hurt to have my wife run off and leave me? Not for another man, mind you, but for a damned assignment?   Everyone pretended to be so understanding, but I knew what they were really thinking. 'That poor fool. He wasn't man enough to keep his wife.' Is that what you want to hear?"

By the end of his speech, Mark's voice vibrated with anger, but beneath it Carla could hear his pain loud and clear. She studied him, noting his expression and the intonation of his voice. He had seemed just as sincere last night. Damn. Either he was a consummate liar, or he really had been honest about his feelings for her.

"So if she hurt you so badly, why were you having dinner with her the other night?"

"I thought she might have intel to help with our case."

"Really? I'm sure there were other people you could've contacted, so why her, why your ex-wife?" She couldn't imagine ever wanting to see her ex again, if she'd had one.

"She was in town on another case." He looked at her a long moment, his silver eyes darkening as he studied her. "My relationship with her was never like this." He took her hand in his and she felt the heat spark between them.

"Really." She pulled her hand back from him and clutched the magazine. It was too damned hard to think when he touched her.

"We started out colleagues. We worked well together and it seemed like we had a lot in common. I thought she'd be the perfect wife for me."

"So what happened?"

"A career-making assignment came up. She had to make a choice. She chose her job, so I divorced her." He shrugged and looked away.

"I'm sorry." She said the words, but she wasn't, not really.

"I realized something since then." He looked at her again.

"Yeah?"

"I must not have loved her that much, or I would've accepted her decision. And I could've waited for her to finish the assignment."

"But you didn't."

"No. I realized after the divorce and quitting my job that it had mainly been my pride she'd hurt. But it's kind of funny—"

"What?"

"I vowed after everything that happened with her that I'd never again get involved with someone I worked with." He looked meaningfully at her.

"Oh. Back to that." She closed the magazine and tucked it back in the seat pocket in front of her. "How exactly are we involved?" The question was out before she could stop it.

"You tell me," he said. "What did last night mean to you?" His gaze met hers and she felt her body instantly respond to the sensual message shimmering in his silver eyes.

"I was horny," she shrugged, trying to play it casual and lying through her teeth. There was no way she was going to let him know how much it'd meant to her.

"Just two people relieving stress, is that it?" He grinned. "If that's so," he continued, "you should know that all this talk about my ex has stressed me out. You're looking a little stressed, too. Maybe we can relieve some stress right now." He leaned close as if to kiss her.

She twisted her head aside and tried to redirect the conversation. "Tomorrow's going to be a big day, and what with this red eye flight, now is our only chance to get some sleep."

"We didn't sleep much last night," he said, his grin turning wolfish.

"Enough, *'Geoff!'*" She emphasized the alias and shakily pulled a pair of earplugs from her purse. They had to stop talking about sex!

"I don't know about you, but I'm going to try and get some sleep." She propped a pillow under her head and leaned against the side of the plane, putting some distance between them. She closed her eyes.

Sleep took its time in coming, her mind reeling from everything he'd said. Should she believe him? Her heart had gotten her into trouble with him time and time again, but her brain wasn't helping much at this point, either. Should she trust what her heart was telling her?

A while later, she covertly glanced at him. His head rested back against the airplane seat, the angle exposing the strong column of his neck, his eyes closed, that slight smile on his lips that she was quickly learning meant he was asleep.

Was she making a mistake, passing off what had happened between them as something simple? She wanted to believe last night meant something more to him than just sex, but she couldn't very well tell him the truth. It would give him way too much power over her. What was the truth?

Damn. She loved him. The realization slammed into her. Was she insane? The empirical evidence demanded that she not trust him. He was a rich, arrogant Lyons from the other side of town. That hadn't changed, not since their very first encounter. He'd driven her crazy as a kid, but she'd always been attracted to him.

And now? She felt her heart drawn to him, even as her brain warned her not be a fool. She'd never trusted instinct or emotion. She'd seen just how much hot water that could land people in. But here she was, in just such a pickle. Mark had been supportive and caring, but he'd also lied and hidden things from her to protect his brother. If he had to choose between Paul and her, who would he choose?

Mark's voice roused her from a deep, dreamless sleep.

"Good morning, sleepyhead." His hand caressed the sensitive nape of her neck.

She opened her eyes and found herself nestled against him, her arm clasped possessively across his chest.

"Oh, excuse me," she said, flustered.

She sat up hastily and removed the earplugs. Bright daylight streamed through the airplane windows as the plane taxied along the runway.

"No apologies needed." He smiled down at her.

"What time is it?" She looked at her watch, which was still on New York time.

"8 a.m. Zurich time."

"I hate traveling in this direction. Jet lag is such a killer."

"We'll pick up some coffee on the way." He stretched his arms wide above his head. She tried but failed to ignore the way his T-shirt rode up, revealing the taut skin of his stomach and little trail of hair disappearing into his jeans.

"Sounds good." She swallowed, forcing her eyes away from him and ignoring the little twist of pain gathering in the region of her heart.

CHAPTER 17

An hour later, they were cruising in a rental car through the scenic Swiss countryside toward Altstat, the small town nearest Chateau Falkenstein.   Under protest, she'd let Mark drive, but it did make it easier for her to call Tate. Her friend had left a terse message saying that the raid against the Illuminati had failed.

Carla checked her watch: 9 a.m., which meant it was just past 3 a.m. New York time. Tate wouldn't be happy about the late call, but there was no avoiding it. She had to know why the raid had failed. Tate picked up on the sixth ring.

"It's me," Carla said. "Sorry to wake you up, but what happened?"

"You must've got my message." Tate yawned. "The raid was a bust. We went in, but the place was empty. Someone must have tipped them off."

"Damn."

"You can say that again, but what I'd really like to know is who the informant was. You in Switzerland already?"

"Yep." Her eyes slid to Mark, dark thoughts running through her brain.   Was he the informant? Had he warned his brother?

"Be careful," Tate continued. "If someone really does have the inside scoop on our activities, they probably know where you're headed. Oh, and before I forget," Tate said sleepily, "Izzy located a witness who saw two people leaving the clinic yesterday that fit your sister and your mom's descriptions, so it doesn't look like your mom was abducted."

"Good, though I hope Gwen knows what she's doing," Carla murmured. "Thanks for the info and sorry I woke you up."

"No problem. Keep me posted."

Carla slid her cell phone back into her purse, her heart beating heavily in her chest.

"It didn't go well?" Mark's voice broke into her thoughts.

"The Illuminati never showed, including your brother." She looked pointedly at him.

She wanted to ask straight out if he was the informant, but she wasn't sure she could handle his answer, since she wouldn't know how to untangle the truth from his words—or from what she wanted to be true. She tore her eyes from him and looked out the window at the Swiss countryside sweeping by.

"I know you want to catch Paul." His voice broke into her painful thoughts. "But I have to be honest with you. I'm glad he wasn't caught. Maybe he had no idea what the Illuminati was planning. Maybe he's not as involved as you think."

"Maybe." Either Mark was outright lying to her, or he was in serious denial about his brother, and pointing that out to him wouldn't change a thing. He'd have to see for himself—and she would, too.

"I'm going to make arrangements for our arrival in Altstat." He turned on his phone.

As she listened to Mark speak with his colleague at the Phoenix, she was impressed by his professionalism and due diligence. She'd thought of him as a proud Lyons—a rich boy born with a silver spoon in his mouth—and as an annoyingly sexy man, and as an enemy, but she'd never thought of him in his professional capacity. She had to give it to him, he knew what he was doing.

"You're good," she said grudgingly when he finished.

"What do you mean?"

"You've covered all the bases. I can't think of anything else we need to do to prep for the mission."

"Is that a compliment, from you?" His silver eyes twinkled.

"Don't let it go to your head," she grimaced, but then found herself smiling.

The sun sparkled cheerfully on the melting early spring snow, the Alps towered majestically above them, and she was on assignment with Mark.

I'm probably an idiot, she told herself, but she couldn't help it. Friend or foe, the adrenaline rush she felt with him was thrilling. Life couldn't get much better.

When they arrived on the outskirts of the small Swiss town of Altstat, Mark pulled the car onto the shoulder. He leaned over the back seat and pulled a small leather pouch from his duffel bag.

"What're you doing?" she asked as he climbed out of the car, pouch in hand.

"This will just take a moment."

From the passenger's seat, she watched him walk up to the sign announcing the town, its population and its elevation. He withdrew what looked like a pen and quickly wrote something on the steel below the printed sign. He then extracted several items from the tan leather pouch. Curious, she got out of the car.

"Stay back." He gestured with his hand to stop.

"What're you doing?" she asked, but stopped where she was.

He didn't reply. She noticed he had some kind of black powder between his thumb and forefinger. He scattered the powder at the base of the sign and mumbled something she couldn't hear. Looking up, she tried to see what he'd written on the sign. The symbols were in dark red and looked very much like the symbols she'd seen written in blood both on her own doorstep and in the Magic Shop.

"What the hell are you doing, Mark?"

"You won't understand." He took her arm and tried to lead back to the car.

"Try me." She wrenched free of his grasp. "Are you warning the other Illuminati members that we're in town? Is that what those symbols mean?"

"No," he said tersely and strode quickly back to the car.

"Then tell me what they mean," she said as they got back into the rental.

"If I told you it was a protection spell, would you believe me?" He shot her quizzical glance as he stuck the key in the ignition.

"You're kidding, right?" she almost laughed. "You don't believe in all that magic hocus pocus, do you?"

"I told you, you wouldn't understand," he shrugged. "Believe me or not, it's your choice, but what you just saw me do was invoke a protection spell."

"What, to keep us safe while we take down a bunch of nuclear terrorists?" She couldn't keep the sarcasm from her voice. As if magic would have anything to do with their success! What they really needed was good intelligence, guns, and stealth.

"Yes." He started the car and put it in gear.

"You can't be serious. Are you telling me that you, Mark Lyons, believe in magic?"

Whatever she'd assumed about him, she'd never thought he actually believed in the occult. She stared at him incredulously.

"I love your absolute faith in factual reality," he said, glancing at her before refocusing on the road as he navigated the narrow streets into town. "I've never met such a devout believer in physical, empirical facts. Interesting..." he paused, then shot her another glance, a speculative look in his eye.

"What?" She continued to stare at him, but then realized she was focused on his hands. They were big and skillfully maneuvered the car. Memories of his hands on her working their magic skittered across her unruly mind. Her body pulsed in response.

Get your mind out of the gutter, girl! She forced her eyes back to his face.

"If I'm right, then last night must have meant a great deal more to you than just being horny," he said.

"Not that again." She rolled her eyes. There was no way she was going to let him know the truth. "Let's stay focused on the fact that you're a magician."

"A magician?" he chuckled. "I wouldn't go that far, Carla. All I'm saying is that reality is not always simply what meets the eye. Sometimes it's more complex, more multifaceted." He looked over at her a moment, a thoughtful expression on his face. "What about emotions? What about feelings?"

"What about them?"

"You love people, don't you, like your sister?"

"Of course."

"You can't see feelings, and yet you believe in them, don't you?"

"Believe in them? I wouldn't go that far," she paused, thinking. "I have feelings, and I'll admit they do affect my behavior."

"Like how you responded to me last night?"

She ignored him. "But I don't believe in them. Beliefs determine actions. I believe in using my brain and the power of reason to determine my course of action. I've always thought the world would be a better place if people relied more on logic than on their emotions. Think of all the wars and hatred that could be avoided."

"Whatever you say." His words dripped irony. His

voice deepened seductively. "I'm just glad your powers of deduction led you to sleep with me last night."

"Stop talking about it!" she snapped. "Boy do you have a one-track mind."

"My mind has nothing to do with it." His mouth kicked up in a lopsided grin.

Her eyes dropped to his lap before she could stop them. She tore them away, furious to feel the fire heating her cheeks.

"You're cute when you're embarrassed," he laughed. "We're here."

He parked the car outside one of the many town residences, a nondescript building in white plaster with a black slate roof. She followed him into the building, scowling, and still destabilized by their conversation.

She'd always assumed he approached reality like she did, like any other reasonable agent who valued empirical evidence over untrustworthy things like emotion and intuition and magic, but now she wondered.

Did he have more in common with her mother and her sister than she'd believed? A more disturbing thought crossed her mind. Had he guessed her feelings for him? But how could she love someone who might be her enemy?

A short, dark-haired man opened the door. They followed him into the living room.

"Albert, this is Carla. She's CIA. Carla, this is Albert Montague." Mark performed the introductions.

"Enchanté, mademoiselle." Albert shook her hand. "Mark speaks high praise of you." His dark eyes studied her with appreciation and curiosity.

"Does he?" Carla was surprised. It had never occurred to her that Mark might talk about her to others or that he might actually consider her a good operative.

Don't be naive, she told herself, but despite her brain's warning, the realization caused a warm glow to spread through her. She smiled up at Mark.

"Don't let it go to your head," he grinned, parroting her own words back to her, but then he reached over and gave her hand a gentle squeeze.

Albert led them into a rustic kitchen looking out into a walled garden with the snowy Alps standing tall in the distance.

"Let's have something to eat while we outline the details of the plan," Mark said. "We don't have much time."

#

Carla glanced at her watch and paced the tight confines of the small bedroom in the safe house at Alstat. She felt like a wild animal trapped in a cage, her body tense and her mind furiously impatient. Albert, Mark's Phoenix contact, had told them they needed to wait for backup before they risked infiltrating Chateau Falkenstein, but the backup wasn't going to arrive before nightfall. She'd been over the map and the floor plan of the small castle at least five times with Albert and Mark before retiring to this damned room.

She spun around for another lap across the small space, thinking about Mark and the strange ritual he'd performed on the side of the road. Had it really been a protection spell? The symbols he'd drawn looked almost identical to the ones outside her apartment and in Gwen's closet.

Wait a second! She stopped in the middle of the room as a realization hit her. She'd assumed Abaddon—or Paul— had drawn those symbols as a warning. But what if Mark had drawn them, instead?

She didn't believe in any of that hocus pocus stuff, but if they really were protection spells, maybe he'd been attempting to protect her and her sister.

Damn. Here I go again, she thought as she resumed pacing, *making excuses and looking for reasons to trust him.*

Maybe he'd drawn the symbols as a way to warn off the other Illuminati members. But with goat blood? Where had he gotten goat blood? And did he really believe in magic? She still had trouble believing that. It didn't seem consistent with his personality.

She glanced again at her watch. There were still more than two more hours of good light. Mark had told her to get some rest before nightfall, but it was only 3 p.m., and she'd slept plenty on the plane. Reviewing things on paper was nothing like verifying with one's own eyes. She stopped pacing, picked up her duffel bag and put it on the bed. She was not going to waste valuable time.

She pulled her black cat suit and a small backpack from the duffel. She checked inside the pack to make sure the 60 meter long dry rope, folding grappling hook, binoculars and headlight were still there. Once changed, she pulled on her winter coat and put her cell phone in the inside chest pocket. Digging through her duffel bag, she extracted her trusty Colt Defender, tucked it into her big pocket, and put on the backpack.

Everything was quiet in the hall outside the bedroom. She swung the door open just wide enough to squeeze through, cursing silently as the door creaked on old hinges. Albert had put Mark in the room adjacent to hers. Hopefully, Mark had taken his own advice and was sleeping. She cursed again as she walked down the hall. The old warped floorboards seemed to scream in the quiet house with each step of her boots.

Outside, the alpine air felt crisp and fresh. She inhaled deeply. It felt good to be doing something and not waiting around for someone else's orders. Alstat was quite small, and only a few pedestrians walked its medieval main street. Carla nodded politely as she passed the walkers and set off at a rapid pace up the narrow cobblestone street toward the chateau.

She looked up at the stone walls of Chateau Falkenstein looming on a rocky promontory less than a mile from Alstat. The fortifications weren't as beefy as a true castle, but the chateau did have several battlements with arrow slits and two wall towers that she could see from her vantage point.

Her plan was to circle the perimeter and check that the exits correlated with the layout Albert had shown them. Thoroughly knowing one's escape routes was essential on a mission like this. She also wanted to ascertain what she could of the manpower and firepower guarding the place, which might require scaling one of the chateau walls.

If she could see the chateau, then anyone up there could conceivably see her, so she hopped the low stone wall beside the road and ducked into the forest. She followed the old cobblestone road, which turned to asphalt at the end of town. Several delivery trucks and a few passenger cars cruised past as she walked through the forest, but none looked suspicious. She stopped at the intersection where the Alstat road met the alpine valley's main highway. As soon as the coast was clear, she dashed across and into the trees beside the narrow causeway leading up to the chateau.

Moments later, she heard the telltale crunching of snow behind her. Damn, someone was following her.

She circled behind a massive tree and waited, her hand steady on the gun in her pocket. She didn't plan on using it, but it was better to be safe than sorry.

A tall figure stepped into view.

"Mark, what are you doing?" She wasn't surprised to see him. Her getaway had hardly been silent.

"I had a feeling you weren't going to do what you were told."

"I didn't need a nap. I slept on the plane."

"Fatigue can dangerous. It can keep you from thinking clearly and lead you to make faulty decisions."

"I'm going to cross check our intel. There'll be plenty of time to sleep later."

"Maybe we should've taken a nap together." He took her gloved hand and pulled her into his arms. "Why don't we go back? We can wait where we'd be nice and warm, instead of out here in the cold." He grinned suggestively, his breath warm on her cheek. "Of course, we probably wouldn't get much sleep."

"You know as well as I do that it's all coming down tonight." She twisted out of his grasp.

"You don't know what you're walking into, Carla, " he said as she started to move away. "There will be armed guards on the lookout for intruders. Let's wait for tonight, OK?"

She turned and stared at him. "Armed guards? I'm so scared." She glinted hard green eyes at him. "Oh come on, Mark. I'm a spook, you're a spook. You know how it's done, simple in and out recon mission."

But a dark part of her brain niggled uncomfortably. Why was he trying so hard to dissuade her? Was it because he had an ulterior motive for not wanting her to see the chateau in daylight?

He read her expression and his face darkened. "Look, I trust you, so why can't you trust me?"

Damn, he was perceptive.

"Now is not the time to get into it," she scowled.

"Now's as good a time as any." Mark shot a glance around the empty forest and then looked back at her. "If we're going to work together successfully, we've got to trust each other."

"I'd trust you a whole lot more if you'd give me some real answers." Carla crossed her arms over her chest. "You said those symbols you drew on the sign outside Alstat were part of a protection spell, right?"

"Yes."

"So were you the one who drew the symbols on my apartment in D.C. a month ago?"

"Yes."

"Really?" She hadn't expected him to give her a straight answer. "Were they also protection spells?"

"Yes." He nodded.

"What about the symbols in Gwen's closet?"

"I drew them, too."

"So how exactly were they supposed to protect me and Gwen, huh?"

"You've made it very clear you don't believe in magic, so how can I explain in terms you'll accept?" He looked at her thoughtfully. "Let's just say that they served as warnings to the Illuminati."

"OK, I guess, but where the hell did you get the goat blood?"

"At a Mexican butcher shop in Santa Barbara. That's not important." He took her hand. His silver eyes were intent as he looked down at her. "I have never wanted to hurt you, or your sister. I've always done my best to protect you."

Heaven help her, but she almost believed he really was on her side. "Did you remove the symbols from Gwen's room?"

"No."

"Do you know who did?"

"I have to assume it was one of the Illuminati."

"You mean your brother, right? I overheard you talking to him yesterday." She looked at him accusingly.

"That explains it." His face tightened.

"Explains what?"

"Why you've turned cold on me all of a sudden."

"What do you take me for, an idiot?" It took a supreme effort to keep her voice quiet when what she really wanted to do was yell at him. "You betrayed me. I heard what you said about 'managing me'. What kind of game are you playing, Mark?"

"Can't you see past your own paranoia—" Mark's voice was drowned out by the rumble of a big diesel truck coming up the causeway.

Carla quickly unzipped her pack, pulled out her binoculars, and trained them on the truck as it rolled past.

Oh hell, she cursed silently as she identified the driver, *the Hulk,* or as she now knew, Garrett Oswald, Paul's evil muscleman.

"What do you see?" Mark wrapped his arms around her waist and snuggled against her.

"Garrett Oswald is driving that truck."

"Really? There was a passenger with him. Did you ID that guy, too?"

"I didn't have time." She fought the urge to squirm as his breath teased against her ear like a warm feather. "Pretty big truck, don't you think?"

Just then, a second truck came up the causeway. She scanned the driver and passenger, but didn't recognize either. The passenger was holding some kind of long barreled rifle.

"They look like cargo trucks," she whispered over her shoulder. "I doubt they're moving people in unheated cargo beds like that."

"I bet you're right." His deep voice vibrated through her.

She moved the binoculars to the chateau. The cobblestone causeway passed under a large gateway. Two gatehouse towers rose on either side. Connected to the towers and encircling the entire chateau stood the thirty-foot high curtain walls. The heavy iron portcullis was rising to admit the trucks. She counted eight men standing just inside the chateau's bailey, armed with Uzis and American-made M-16s.

"The guards are carrying a lot of firepower. That must be some really valuable cargo. Crud—" Carla caught sight of the next truck coming up the causeway. Unlike the other two, which had been standard issue, this next truck was bad news.

"That's got to be a rocket launcher. Let me go, Mark, I've gotta call Tate." She stepped free of his arms and moved out of sight behind the tree. She pulled out her cell. Tate answered on the first ring. She quickly cued her partner into the situation.

"Bottom line," she finished, "they've got a delivery mechanism for either rockets or missiles."

"But you don't know exactly which?"

"Not yet, but I'm going to find out, if I can."

"Nukes or no nukes, a rocket launcher spells trouble. I'll tell Frank. You be careful, Carla, you got me?"

"Will do." Carla snapped her phone shut. She stepped back around the tree and found Mark staring intently through his binoculars.

"They've closed the gate behind that last truck," he said. "I've spotted two men still visible, one in each guard tower. They're watching the causeway, but it looks like everyone else has moved inside the stronghold."

"Yep, and I don't see anyone on the ramparts, either." Carla double checked his surveillance through her binoculars. "We've got to find out what kind of armaments they've got and what our people will be walking into tonight."

She stowed her binoculars in her pack. "I'm going to get behind the chateau and climb the back wall. That should give me a good view of the bailey."

Mark checked his watch and nodded, his face grim. "We've still got time. I'm coming with you."

"What, no arguments? Don't you need a nap?" She waggled an eyebrow saucily at him, her adrenaline surging.

"Honey, you're like a cup of strong coffee." His expression lightened as he tucked his binoculars into his coat.

"Follow me, but do as I say."

"Sure thing, boss." He grabbed her and gave her a quick kiss.

"Hey, stay on track." Her green eyes met his. He was grinning. "Let's go, buddy," she said, but found herself grinning back at him. Missions were exciting, and so was he.

The forest thinned as they reached the chateau, but once they moved to the side away from the causeway, they were no longer within line of sight of the armed sentries, so as they hurried between trees, they felt fairly confident that they were undetected.

"This looks like our best bet," Carla said stopping and looking up at the wall tower.

Unlike the roofed ramparts with their narrow arrow slits and battlements, the wall tower had several windows that looked large enough to climb through. Each held a glass casement window The one closest to the ground stood about fifteen feet off the ground.

"Coast looks clear." Mark studied the arrow slits along the battlements and the windows of the wall tower.

"Easy, peasy," Carla said as she pulled the rope and grappling hook from her bag. She swung the hook and stuck the rope on her first try. She yanked on it to check its stability. It was solid. "Ready?" She looked at Mark.

"I'll spot you," he said.

She pulled the backpack on and quickly climbed the rope. When she reached the stone ledge outside the casement window, she propped herself in the opening and used her elbow to punch out the glass pane closest to the latch. She swung the window out and poked her head inside. Except for a bunch of spider webs and a few pieces of the broken window pane, the stairwell was empty.

She scanned the walls and ceiling of the tower.

Damn, a surveillance camera. She pulled her special issue flashlight from her coat pocket and switched on the laser beam and trained it on the camera. She climbed into the tower, making sure to keep the beam on the camera to blind it.

Mark landed lightly beside her on the small stone landing inside the window.

"Surveillance?" Mark said under his breath.

"Yeah. Can you get the rope?"

Mark wrapped up the rope, folded the grappling hook and slipped the into her pack.

"That make camera doesn't have audio, right?" she said, her mouth against his ear?

"We're good." Mark spoke a little louder. "Cool toy you've got there." He grinned.

"What, the Phoenix hasn't gotten you one, yet?" She grinned back.

They cautiously climbed the rest of the tower stairs. There were two more tower windows, and like the first, these also had cameras trained on them. At each interval, Carla zapped the camera view with her laser as they passed.

"We don't have much time," Carla said when they reached the roofed rampart. "If anyone's watching the security cameras, they'll know someone's gotten inside."

"Then let's move." Mark removed a semi-automatic from a shoulder holster he'd hidden under his jacket.

"Nice gun," she said when she saw what he packed.

"I always did like the Magnum," he said, a suggestive gleam in his eye.

"Figures." Amusement colored her voice. She had to hand it to the guy; he was one big walking innuendo.

She pulled her Colt from her coat pocket, but kept the flashlight handy in her other hand.

"There." Mark pointed to the ceiling further along the rampart.

Two security cameras were mounted facing either direction. Carla shot the laser at the closer one as they moved cautiously along rampart, lit by the narrow arrow slit windows on the external side of the chateau and several interior facing windows.

Fortunately, the first interior window was located directly below the two security cameras, so Carla and Mark were out of camera sight when they reached it. Carla switched off her flashlight and pocketed it.

The sound of engines and loud voices echoed off the stone walls. They carefully peeked through the window facing the castle's bailey, its inner courtyard.

"We've got trouble," she whispered in his ear.

His silver eyes widened in dismayed surprise.

Armed men stood guard as other men were busily unloading large metal crates from two of the waiting trucks. Each crate prominently displayed black and yellow radioactive warning symbols. Worse yet, other men were uncovering the device on the big third truck, a mobile rocket launcher.

"Oh hell," Carla cursed under her breath. "Frank was right. What better place than Switzerland, the center of Europe, to launch a terrorist attack? They don't even need long-range missiles."

Mark was already texting Albert.

"Good, I see you've brought her." Paul's voice caused them both to jump.

"Yes." Marks eyes flew to hers.

He palmed his phone, then closed his hand over her gun, hiding it from view. He winked as he tugged on it. Was she making a mistake? She let him have it, then looked past him. Paul was coming along the rampart, the Hulk silently looming behind him.

How had he known they were there? Maybe in the second or two before she'd zapped the first camera? And then they'd both been momentarily distracted by what was going on in the courtyard. Damn, they'd underestimated the extent of Paul's security vigilance.

"Where should I put her?" Mark sounded cold, detached.

Abruptly, she felt his gun—or was it hers—press lightly against her ribs. Had trusting him been a mistake?

"In the dungeon. Then I need to speak to you. The arrangements for tonight are almost complete."

Paul looked at Carla, his blue eyes icy. "You have caused enough trouble. But the time of the Offering is at hand. Do not think I will allow you to escape this time."

Her green eyes widened. He'd all but admitted he'd been the leader of the ritual at the farmhouse in Virginia. He and the Hulk disappeared back down the rampart.

As soon as they were alone, Carla turned to Mark.

"Now's our chance to get away. Let's go."

She started back toward the wall tower, but he blocked her path.

"What the hell are you doing? Get that thing off me." For a second, she considered fighting him, but then she looked at the gun. It was his gun, the Magnum, and it was big and deadly looking. She scowled. Her Green Dragon skills wouldn't work against that.

"I'm sorry, honey, but I can't. We're going to have to play this thing out, but don't worry. Backup will be here tonight."

"Can't you just let me go? There's no one around right now." But then the red blinking light on the security camera caught her eye, and she knew escape would be impossible at this point.

"Great," she said sarcastically. "I've got to wait around for backup when I could be sacrificed at any moment by your crazy brother."

"I won't let that happen," he said, his voice sharp. "Let's go." He gestured with the gun.

They walked along the rampart to a set of stairs that descended past the inner courtyard and kept descending. They arrived at a long hallway. An armed guard opened a heavy oak door at the far end of the hall that led to a steep stairwell.

They descended into the dungeon. It was dark, dank, and a cold breeze wafted through the cavernous space.

"There aren't any cameras here, so you could let me go now. Please?" She was starting to feel a little desperate. There was something mortally final about the dungeon. How many people had died and rotted down here?

He took a coil of rope off an iron hook in the wall and gestured for her to sit down on the hard stone floor.

"I know you don't trust me, but I'm going to ask you to try, OK? I won't let anything bad happen to you, I promise." He bound her hands and feet, then took her chin in his hand and gazed intently into her eyes. "You mean everything to me, Carla. I'll die before I let anyone hurt you." He kissed her hard on the mouth and then stood up.

"Great. Are you just going to leave me down here?" She tried to keep the panic out of her voice, but the dungeon was cold and dark, very dark.

"I'm sorry, but I have to." He struck a match and a large torch hanging from the wall blazed to life. "It won't be for long."

She leaned back against the cold stone wall and listened to his retreating steps as he climbed up the stone stairwell.

Damn it! He'd asked her to trust him, but could she? Was he just playing along with his brother for the moment? Or was he actually setting her up?

She peered through the poorly lit darkness. From what she could see, the dungeon consisted of an enormous room with smaller cells attached to it, though she couldn't see all the way across the space in the darkness.

She set to work trying to free herself from the rope. Twisting her hands, she was able to use her fingers to lightly graze the rope. It felt like nylon kernmantle rope.

Suddenly, something caught her eye. She stopped wrestling with the rope and stared across the dungeon, trying to see what was there, but there was only blackness, complete and total, somehow unnatural, horrible. She shivered.

Oh hell, was her mind playing tricks on her again, as it had at that farmhouse in Virginia? She forced herself to ignore the hair rising on the back of her neck and focus on the rope.

Just then, the dungeon door creaked open. The Hulk came lumbering down the stone stairs.

"What do you want, you big lug?" she shouted, her voice echoing in the cavernous dungeon, but he remained eerily silent. "Get away from me!" She tried to wriggle away from him, but she was helpless to stop him from plunging the syringe into the side of her neck.

CHAPTER 18

The next thing she knew, Carla found herself bound spread-eagle to iron rings above a black pit.

Oh hell, not this again, she scowled, her mouth dry around the cloth gag.

Numerous torches lit the dungeon. Eight crimson-robed men circled the pit beneath her, the leader chanting in Latin. Was Mark among them? Their faces were masked in black, their eyes visible only through slits.

She tested the strength of the rope binding her hands and feet. What was this?

Her left hand was fisted around something. She rotated the object carefully to keep from dropping it. An automatic stiletto! Mark must have put it there. He'd known she was left-handed.

So he hadn't been lying, after all.

Using her thumb, she pressed the button to eject the blade and set to work cutting through the mantle, the protective outer sheath of the rope binding her left hand.

The leader, whose voice she now recognized as Paul's, continued his incantation in Latin.

"We now submit to you, oh Lord, our Gift. We hope that by your accepting the Offering you will shed a measure of your power upon us, upon the Illuminati. Our strength is nothing without your power. May the light within reflect the light outside."

The eight other men repeated Paul's chant as they circled the pit. She glanced up at her left hand and the rope. The stiletto was sharp, but the rope's mantle was strong.

Damn. From what she could see, she was only partially through the rope's protective sheath.

"Sonneillon, we grant you the privilege and responsibility to release the Offering to our Lord."

Paul handed the long black twisting knife to the biggest man in the group, probably the Hulk. The huge man took the long knife and stepped to the edge of the pit. Carla carefully palmed the stiletto, thankful he didn't see it as he reached up to cut the rope binding her left foot. His eyes glinted malevolently behind the slits of his mask.

"Wait!" A man standing directly behind and beneath her called out. It was Mark. She couldn't see him, but his voice was unmistakable. He spoke in English.

"The ritual must proceed," Paul said, also in English. "Continue," he ordered the Hulk, who sawed steadily through the rope. The other men watched expectantly.

The rope tore free. Gravity jerked Carla's left foot violently downward and she almost dropped the knife. Biting hard on the gag and using every ounce of strength in her lower body, she managed to swing her foot up and hook it through the iron ring attached to the ceiling.

"Stop!" Mark stepped into view. He spoke quickly, urgently. "We are not ready to make the Offering, not yet. Two times we have tried to raise Him, but two times we have failed."

"We will not fail tonight," Paul said angrily.

"No, Abaddon, we will not fail. But that is because we will not sacrifice the Offering hastily, not until we are truly ready. Look around." Mark gestured with his cloaked arm at the group. "We are only nine. Eleven is the magic number. You know this, Abaddon. Without the eleven, we will not succeed."

The other cloaked men looked at Paul.

"Seven and nine are powerful magickal numbers in their own right, Lucifer," Paul said haughtily. "As you well know, or why would you not mention the magickal eleven on the other occasions? Our Lord must not be kept waiting. Continue, Sonneillon." He pointed at the Hulk, who circled around the pit on the opposite side from Mark. He began to saw the rope binding Carla's right foot.

Oh hell, was Mark going to be able to stall Paul long enough for Albert and the Phoenix back up to get there?

Carla glanced down at her right foot and the Hulk. He'd severed the rope's mantle and had severed more than half the core fibers.

"Stop, Sonneillon. Now." Mark's voice dropped low, commanding, threatening. "Give me the knife."

Carla twisted her head sideways and saw the dusky glint of the Magnum's big muzzle peeking out from under Mark's crimson robe. He pointed it at the Hulk. The Hulk stopped cutting the rope and held the long knife up. He looked across the pit at Paul. Carla exhaled slowly around the gag. Maybe Mark would succeed after all. She resumed cutting the rope binding her left hand with the small stiletto.

"I was mistaken about the correct number we need to make the Offering, Abaddon." Mark extended his unarmed hand toward the Hulk, reaching for the knife and talking quickly. "Obviously, we were all mistaken about how much power it would take to raise Him. With the requisite magickal eleven, we will have enough power. I beg of you to await the arrival of the final two."

"Final two? What final two, *Lucifer?*" Paul spat the name disdainfully. He threw back his hooded head and laughed contemptuously. "There are no 'final two.' I am no fool. This ploy of yours to delay the Offering will not work."

"It is no ploy." Mark glanced up at Carla, the urgency in his voice betrayed the confidence of his words. "I swear it."

"You are not truly loyal to the cause. You have become emotionally involved with her." Paul reached inside his robe. "I suspected as much."

Damn, he'd pulled a gun and was now pointing it at Mark. Carla sawed hard and fast on the rope. Only a few tenacious threads remained and then she'd be free.

"Brother, please. I am loyal. I do speak the truth. We cannot raise Him, not without the power of the eleven."

"You lie," Paul sneered. He turned to the others. "The world must be cleansed once and for all of its filth and corruption. There is no time to wait. The Illuminati must initiate the ultimate purification. Only then may the reign of Light begin."

"Paul, please," Mark spoke hastily, desperately, breaking anonymity. "Ahriman and Sorat will be here any minute. Their magick is a hundredfold stronger than our own, you know that, and with them, we will achieve the magick eleven. Then, truly, we will be able to raise our Lord."

"Ahriman and Sorat coming here?" Paul laughed dismissively. "They are too busy with their own affairs. You are either deluded, or you are lying." His voice dropped, becoming both intimate and deadly. His ice blue eyes glinted behind the mask. "Or is it treachery that drives you to interfere and delay the Offering? I'm sorry, brother, for what you are forcing me to do, but no more delays."

"But Father and Jon—"

A blinding light ripped through the dungeon and the resounding report echoed around and around the stone walls.

Mark! Carla wanted to scream, her teeth clamping the gag in fear and fury. Paul had shot his own brother!

She twisted her neck in every direction, trying to see

where Mark had fallen, but all she could see was one booted foot. He'd collapsed onto the stone floor on the far side of the pit, but there was no way to tell if he was still alive.

Damn it, she wasn't going to lose him! She had to get to him and make sure he was OK. And then she'd make Paul pay, even if it was the last thing she did.

She ripped through the final fiber with the stiletto and freed her left hand at last. She swung her arm up and grabbed the iron ring with her left hand. She had to drop the knife to get a good grip on the ring. The stiletto disappeared soundlessly into the black pit.

"Get him out of the way," Paul ordered, and several men dragged Mark away and out of Carla's line of sight.

"Proceed," Paul gestured to the Hulk, who approached her with the knife once more.

In minutes, he severed the rope holding her right foot. She tried to lift it high enough to hook it into the iron ring as she had her left, but she just wasn't strong enough. Her right leg dangled uselessly, pulling the rest of her body downward.

She reached up with her left hand and yanked the gag from her mouth, thinking hard and fast. What had Mark said, something about a magic eleven?

"Paul is wrong!" she shouted at the other Illuminati members, her voice shrill in the darkness. "You need the magic eleven to perform the offering."

"Sonneillon, finish the task," Paul ignored her. "Sacrifice the Offering, now!"

Was this the end? It couldn't be!

"No, stop! Listen to me. You have to stop Paul, Abaddon. He's going to fail. Didn't you hear what Lucifer said, it won't work without the right number?" She had no idea what she was talking about, but she tried to sound convincing.

"The Offering knows nothing. Continue, Sonneillon."

The Hulk approached Carla's right side and reached up

to cut through the rope binding her right hand.

"I know you're wrong, Paul."

She swung sideways and lashed at the Hulk with her free left hand, trying to knock the knife from his meaty fist.

"No you don't," he growled and twisted the knife abruptly, stabbing at her hand.

She yanked away, but not quickly enough. He opened up a three inch gash on the side of her hand. The blood started running down her arm to the bend in her elbow and dripping into the pit. She tried to grab the ring again, but the blood made her hand too slippery. Only her bound right hand and left foot hooked through the ring kept her aloft. She ignored the pain and her body's growing fatigue and tried to stay focused.

"Don't you guys realize he's crazy?" She shouted, desperate. "He killed his brother. He could just as easily kill any of you. You can stop him from committing another murder. Right now. Stop him!"

Her words had no effect. The men stood transfixed, watching the Hulk cut through the binding on her right hand. The rope cut loose and she plunged downward.

She screamed as she fell, but her left foot remained hooked in the iron ring and stopped her fall into the pit. Her ankle torqued violently sideways, brutally twisted by the iron ring and the full weight of her body pulling her down. The pain was excruciating and black spots hovered in her vision as she started to lose consciousness. The bottomless black pit yawned beneath her.

Suddenly, a burst of wind swept through the chamber and extinguished the torches. The dungeon pitched into total darkness.

What was happening? Carla blinked blindly, fighting to remain conscious. She had to get free. She strained upwards, grappling in the darkness, trying to reach the ring holding her left foot captive.

"There will be no death in this place tonight." A

woman's voice pierced the darkness.

Carla paused in her efforts to reach the ring. Who was that? She knew that voice.

"Darkness be gone!" the voice commanded.

Abruptly, candles lit on all sides of the dungeon. Everything looked bizarre from her upside down vantage point. Women holding candles stood in a ring around the walls of the dungeon. Gwen and Moon Ray were there. Circe had come to the rescue!

The Illuminati spun around to face the witches. Paul was holding the gun again, but now he was pointing it at her.

"You can't stop us from sacrificing the Offering," he said, addressing the woman who stood beyond Carla's line of sight. "If you try, I'll shoot her."

"Satan holds no power here." The woman's voice vibrated with power.

Paul's gun clattered to the floor. Carla sensed more than saw the other Illuminati members jump in surprise.

"Who are you?" Paul stared across the pit at the woman.

"The Circle is broken no longer. Circe is complete and the power restored. The forces of true light illuminate you for what you are. Abaddon, Sonneillon, Lucifer, all the sons of Satan, I cast you out."

What the hell? Carla's eyes widened in surprise as the Illuminati collapsed into crimson heaps on the stone floor.

"Hold it, right there!" a man shouted in German. It was Albert from the Phoenix.

Brilliant electric lights flooded the dungeon and the sound of men running echoed off the stone walls. Men in combat gear swarmed into the underground chamber, guns in hand. Albert repeated his command in English. Chaos ensued as everyone milled about.

"Help!" Carla shouted, but no one heard. She couldn't stay suspended a moment longer. Black spots were again swimming in front of her eyes.

She made a final, extraordinary effort, willing her body to defy gravity. She twisted sideways, engaging the strength of her lats so she could reach her left foot with her left hand. Then she pulled herself up and gripped the iron ring with both hands to wriggle her foot clear. She was free! Swinging her body, she gained enough momentum to leap clear of the pit.

She landed on solid ground, but then the black curtain of unconsciousness descended and she staggered backwards. She felt the edge of the pit under her feet, her left ankle buckled, and she lost her balance and began to fall into the void.

Strong hands grabbed her by the shoulders and stopped her fall. They pulled her upright and steadied her.

"You are brave, my child," a deep male voice said.

Carla forced her eyes to focus past the swimming black spots. She looked up at a tall Illuminati member in a crimson cloak. He was staring down at her through the slits in his black mask. His eyes were black, hypnotic, and weirdly familiar.

"Who are you?" She tried to reach up and grab at his hood, but he smoothly moved aside.

"I am glad you are not seriously harmed, my dear. Now I must go." He reached out and brushed a strand of hair from her face, then turned and disappeared into the melee.

Carla ignored the people fighting around her. One thought filled her mind.

Mark! Was he still alive?

She ignored the horrible throbbing in her ankle and the bleeding gash in her hand and hobbled to the back of the dungeon. His crumpled form lay by the back wall. There was an Illuminati member bending over him. What was that man doing?

"Get away from him!" she shouted and hobbled faster.

The Illuminati member turned, saw her coming, and hurried away. She rushed to Mark's side. Someone had removed his hood and mask and positioned the bundled material under his head. His eyes were closed, his face deathly still.

"You can't be dead, do you hear me?" she whispered, laying a shaking finger against his carotid artery.

His pulse beat strong and sure against her finger and his neck was warm. Her knees went weak with relief. She sank down onto the floor beside him. Slipping an arm under his shoulders, she hoisted him up and against her.

"Can you hear me? Mark?" She shook him slightly.

"My shoulder," he groaned, reaching up and placing a hand over hers.

"Oh, sorry." She pulled her hand back. In her panic, she hadn't noticed where the bullet had torn a hole through the left shoulder of his heavy coat. The wool had soaked up most of the blood.

"I thought I'd lost you." She held him as close as she could, uncaring that tears were falling freely down her face.

"It's OK, honey. It's just a flesh wound." He grimaced as he shifted himself to sit up. He ran his fingers tentatively through his hair to the back of his head and winced. "I must have hit my head when I fell. Don't cry. I'll be OK." He cupped her face with his right hand and used his thumb to brush away the tears.

"It's not OK, don't you understand?" She stared at him, drinking in his dear features and his masculine beauty. "I almost lost you. I can't lose you. Don't you get it? I love you." She kissed him gently on the side of his mouth.

He moved back slightly. His eyes met hers and darkened with emotion.

"I love you, too." His hand snaked up and into her hair, pulling her closer. "God help me, but I've always loved you, Carla. I've loved you from the first day I met you and I'll love you to the day I die." He kissed her full on the mouth.

He must not be too injured if he can kiss like that, she thought as relief and love flooded through her. She happily returned the kiss.

"Will you introduce me to your beloved?"

Carla jerked back from Mark and looked up at the woman standing above them.

"Mom? Mom!" She launched herself up and into Madeline deVille's arms. "What are you doing here? Are you OK?"

"I have you to thank, my dear," her mother said cryptically. She turned to Mark, who was getting slowly and carefully to his feet. "Are you going to introduce me?"

"Of course," Carla said, flustered. "This is Mark Lyons. Mark, this is my mom, Madeline deVille."

"Pleased to meet you, ma'am." He reached out and shook Madeline's hand. "I guess we have you to thank for helping us get out of this mess."

"And your friends," she said as Albert approached with another man, who was carrying a first aid kit.

"Hey buddy, glad you could finally make it." Mark grinned.

"Let's take care of that wound," Albert said.

"Carla, shall we give them some privacy?" Madeline began moving away from the two men.

"I don't want to leave you." Carla gripped Mark's hand, but she was torn because she also wanted to talk to her mother.

"It's OK, honey." He gave her hand a gentle squeeze and smiled. "I'll be fine, and don't worry, I don't plan on going anywhere. You go with your mom. I'm sure you have a lot of catching up to do."

"You take good care of him." Carla glared at Albert, her green eyes flashing.

"Oh I will," Albert laughed, then looked down at her bleeding left hand. "You'll need some of this." He retrieved a roll of gauze and a container of antiseptic and handed the items to her mother.

"I don't know about you," Madeline smiled at her

daughter, "but I'd like to get out of this musty old dungeon."

"Sounds good to me." Carla said. Her mother gripped her arm and helped her climb the stairs.

#

A light snow fell in the castle courtyard when Carla and her mother emerged from the dungeon. Bright beams of light illuminated the night as an assortment of Swiss and NATO military personnel worked to remove the nuclear arsenal from Chateau Falkenstein. They crossed over to the temporary barracks erected against the opposite side of the castle courtyard, stopping periodically for Carla to rest her injured ankle. Gwen hurried toward them.

"Carly, I'm so glad you're safe." She hugged Carla.

"I could say the same about you, sis," Carla grinned. "I can't believe you showed up here. How on earth did you work it? And Mom, I just can't believe it!"

The two sisters wrapped their mother between them in a group hug, joy filling their hearts

"I have both of you to thank," Madeline whispered.

"Let's get something hot to drink," Gwen said when they broke apart.

Minutes later, they sat on makeshift benches inside the barracks.

"I just can't believe you're you again." Carla watched Madeline clean the blood from her hand and bandage it. Tears filled her eyes and she swiped at them in embarrassment.

"It's OK to cry, my dear. You and Gwen have suffered for so long. I'm so sorry I couldn't be there for you all those years." Madeline's voice broke as she finished taping Carla's hand. She took both her daughters good hands in hers. "You have carried such a burden, haven't you? But I am so proud of you. You have both grown into remarkable, beautiful women."

"But I don't understand," Carla said after a moment. "How did you get better?"

"Gwen took me from that clinic and returned me to Circe, to my circle of power."

"But that wasn't enough," Gwen interrupted. "You did something none of us were able to do, Carly."

"I did?"

"You broke the spell that was binding Mom."

"What?"

"It's true. If you hadn't broken the spell, I wouldn't be here tonight," Madeline said, sipping her cup of tea.

"I don't understand." Carla looked back and forth at the both of them. "What spell? What are you talking about?"

"Do you know why the Illuminati was after you and me?" Gwen asked.

Carla shook her head.

"They were after us because we were Mom's daughters." Gwen looked at their mother.

"Yes, I'm afraid that's true. That's also why Circe was in danger. I'm sorry I put you all at risk."

"What?" Carla was more confused than ever. She stared at her mother. "You had a mental breakdown and spent the last twelve years institutionalized. Why would the Illuminati care about you? How did they even know about you?"

"Hey, I didn't think of that. That's a good question, Mom?"

Both daughters looked expectantly at their mother.

"It's a long story, and not very pretty, I'm afraid. I don't suppose you'd let it go if I told you it really doesn't matter much now that the Illuminati has been stopped?"

"How can you say that? You've spent the last twelve years in the loony bin and now you want us to just drop it? No way." Carla scowled.

"It was the Illuminati who originally put the binding spell on you, wasn't it?" Gwen asked.

"Not exactly." Madeline looked at her two daughters, a look of indecision on her face. She closed her eyes for a moment and then let out a deep breath. She put the unfinished cup of tea on the bench beside her. "There was a reason I never told you about your father."

"What?" Carla and Gwen exclaimed simultaneously.

"Your father is a man of tremendous power."

"He was High Priest of Circe, wasn't he?" Carla said.

"How did you know that?" Madeline looked at her in surprise.

"Emily Trent told me."

"Yes, Moon Ray knew him. That was so long ago." Madeline smiled faintly. "He was so handsome, so smart. He was such a good man, back then."

"What happened?" Carla asked.

"Power is a dangerous thing, my dears. It can be used for good, or for evil, but it can also possess you. It can, it does, change you. Once you open certain doors, there can be no turning back." Madeline sighed.

"What do you mean?" Carla asked.

"Your father sought to possess power, but it began to possess him. I saw what a dangerous force he was becoming and I determined to stop him." Madeline shrugged. "But he stopped me, at least for a while."

"Where is he now?" Carla drained her cup of tea.

"What's his name?" Gwen asked.

"You have seen him twice, my dear, in the last two days." Madeline smiled at Carla.

"What?" Carla stared at her mother incredulously; Gwen stared at them both.

"Yes, you saw him in New York yesterday, when you broke the spell binding me."

Carla's mind raced over the course of the last two days. Memories of smashing crystal skittered across her mind.

"Jonathan Carter?" She shook her head incredulously. "Jonathan Carter is our father?"

"Who's Jonathan Carter?" Gwen asked, confused.

"He's an eccentric Wall Street financier," Carla said impatiently. She turned on her mom. "You're telling me that weirdo I met in New York is our father?"

"Weirdo, what are you talking about?" Gwen interrupted.

"I met this guy yesterday, his place was full of occult stuff, and he was a real weirdo."

"You say such things only because you don't understand them. You don't understand him." Madeline broke in. "When you saw him yesterday, did you break something of his?"

"I did." Carla nodded. "There was this strange crystal sculpture of a woman he had in his office. I knocked it over by accident and it smashed on the floor. He totally freaked out."

"You broke the binding spell." Gwen looked at Carla in surprised wonder.

Carla's mind was racing. She'd seen him eating dinner with Richard and Paul Lyons. His stationery had been in Harrington's safe. She'd seen Paul leaving his offices in New York.

"Is he a member of the Illuminati?" she asked.

"Yes," Madeline nodded. "He joined the secret sect just a few months after you were born." She turned to Gwen. "It was one of the main reasons I kicked him out."

"He didn't abandon us?" Gwen looked shell shocked.

"No, he never would have left willingly." Madeline shook her head. "His association with the Illuminati and his other forays into the occult were becoming too dangerous, too dark. There was no way I was going to risk your safety or that of my sisters in the coven by letting him stay in our home."

"How does he know Richard Lyons?" Carla was still trying to piece together the bigger puzzles of the case.

"They've been friends for years, my dear."

"So Richard is a member of the Illuminati, too?"

"I would assume."

Carla frowned, remembering something. "What did you mean when you said I've seen him twice in the last day?"

"He was here tonight."

"What?" Carla and Gwen stared at her in shock, but then Carla remembered those hypnotic black eyes behind the Illuminati mask, strong steady hands on her shoulders, a deep voice speaking her name.

"He saved my life," she said in wonder. "He stopped me from falling into the pit. Why would he help me if he's a member of the Illuminati?" She looked at her mother, puzzled. "And when I went to see him in New York, he warned me the Illuminati was stockpiling nuclear weapons. Why? It doesn't make sense."

"Only because you do not know what drives your father. You must understand that the Illuminati has only ever been one of his many interests. And you must never forget that he is your father, and in his own way, he loves you. If either of you were in true danger, I am sure he'd do his best to keep you from harm. As he did tonight."

"He said I looked just like you. He said you were beautiful." Carla remembered her strange interchange with him in his weird, occult office.

"Did he? I wonder what he looks like now." A secret smile crept up Madeline's face.

"But didn't you see him here tonight?" Carla asked.

"No, I did not, but I felt his power."

"You still love him." Gwen's blue eyes widened.

"How could you, after what he did to you, to all of us?" Carla scowled angrily.

"You must remember that none of us is perfect." Madeline smiled gently. "Your father has always had trouble distinguishing between love and possessiveness, and in that, he has sometimes been weak." She embraced both her daughters "Do not close your hearts off with hate, my dear, dear girls. True love is a power of inestimable force. It transcends all bounds."

Albert approached them. "Ladies, it's time to move."

"Where's Mark?" Carla looked at Albert with concern.

"We've transported him back down to the safe house in Alstat. He needed a transfusion."

"I've got to go to him. Mom, Gwen, will you be OK?"

"Of course, my dear. Go find your love." Madeline smiled warmly.

Gwen took Carla aside and spoke softly. "We're going to throw a birthday party for mom at the Magic Shop tomorrow night. Could you come? There's so much to celebrate."

"I'll to my best." Carla gave her sister a quick hug.

CHAPTER 19

"I've finally got you to myself." Mark closed and locked the door to the apartment safe house in New York.

It was way past midnight and the apartment was dark. He flipped on the lights, took Carla's duffel bag, and dropped it on the entryway floor next to his own. "I've been looking forward to this moment since forever." He wrapped her in his arms.

"Me, too." Carla returned the embrace, reveling in his solid strength, happiness and fatigue washing over her in equal amounts. Except for a fitful hour-long nap on the flight back from Switzerland, she hadn't slept in over twenty-four hours. She sighed in exhaustion. "I am so ready for bed."

"I like the sound of that." Mark's laughter rumbled through her body as he hugged her. He tipped up her chin and studied her face. His eyes twinkled. "You don't mean just sleep, right?"

"Sleep first?" She leaned heavily against him.

"As you wish." He swung her up into his arms and strode down the hall to the bedroom.

"Doesn't your shoulder hurt?"

"It'll hurt more if I can't get you into bed."

"Has anyone told you that you have a one track mind?" she laughed.

Had it really been just yesterday morning that they'd last been together in that bed? Sensual memories swept through her. The huge bed was very comfortable, she knew. He laid her gently on it, but not before she saw him wince.

"Take that off." She pointed at his black T shirt.

"Your wish is my command." He chuckled, but then winced again as he tried to lever the shirt over his head.

"Let me help." She straddled his waist and took hold of the T-shirt. She lifted it gently off him.

"I like playing doctor," he grinned, his hands dropping to her hips. He stroked her thighs through the form fitting material of her yoga pants. "Can I take your temperature?"

"Enough with the innuendo!" She giggled, but the laughter died in her throat as she felt him raised, hard and ready, pushing intimately against her.

"First things first, buster." She climbed off him and headed to the bathroom. "Let's make sure you didn't just bust open your stitches." She found a first aid kit in one of the cabinets and brought it back to the bedroom.

"My shoulder's fine, honey. Believe me, I am just fine."

He leaned back against the pillows, his muscles flexing deliciously in his torso as he stretched. Carla tore her eyes from the broad expanse of his chest and forced herself to focus on the bandage taped across his shoulder. She carefully peeled it back and checked the sutures. They were still in place.

"I can't believe Paul got away." She scowled as she taped him back up, her mind processing the events of the past twenty four hours.

"Albert was stretched pretty thin taking control of the Chateau. I'm just glad he got to us in time."

She put the first aid kid on the bedside table and lay back against the pillows next to him. It felt absolutely marvelous to be horizontal.

"Don't worry about my brother. There's not much Paul can do, now that he's lost his financial base and his following. I just wish I'd known how unbalanced he'd become. What a waste of a genius mind."

"Unbalanced? Genius? Is that how you put it? Believing in the occult is crazy!"

"You're putting too much emphasis on sanity. We're all crazy to some extent. Like how I feel about you." He leaned over and nuzzled the side of her neck. "Paul knew we had a history together. He wanted me to use it against you."

"You mean as Lucifer, the 'Great Seducer'?" She giggled and waggled an eyebrow at him.

"I succeeded, didn't I?" He reached under her black tank top and unhooked her bra. He cupped her breast and tested its weight, his thumb lightly brushing over its tip. His silver eyes fixed on her green ones and watched her reaction.

Carla sat up and took his hand in her good one, her expression serious. "I'm sorry I didn't listen to you."

"About what?"

"When you told me to wait for backup before going to the Chateau. I should've kept to the plan you and Albert laid out."

"You had your reasons."

"I didn't trust you, Mark, and because of that, you got shot." Her eyes drifted to his bandaged shoulder.

"It's all over, honey. I'm OK. In fact, I'm better than OK. I'm with you." He used their joined hands to pull her down on top of him.

"There's something I still don't understand." She studied his nose.

"What's that?" His eyes were starting to gleam as his free hand swept down her back to her hip.

"I could've sworn I broke your nose that night we sparred at the farmhouse in Virginia. And yet when I saw you the next night in Gwen's room at the Magic Shop, you were completely fine. You didn't have a mark on you."

"I faked it."

"You what?" She rolled off him and stared at his nose.

"I made it look like you succeeded, so you could get away without blowing my cover."

"You didn't have a bloody nose?"

"Nope."

"Wow, your Green Dragon style is pretty good," she said reluctantly, not wanting the praise to go to his head. He had enough pride as it was.

"Better than yours?" he challenged, a wolfish grin lighting his face.

"We'll have to schedule a sparring match sometime."

"I'd rather schedule another kind of match." He braced himself on his good side and looked down at her. An unholy light glittered in his eyes.

"Scheduling is overrated," she laughed and pulled the bra and tank top off over her head. She leaned into him and reveled in the delicious sensation of her bare breasts brushing the warm hard wall of his chest.

"My sentiments exactly." He dipped his head to hers. Their lips touched.

Her cell phone rang.

"Impeccable timing," he whispered against her mouth, one hand sneaking up and cupping her breast. "Don't answer it."

"It's probably Tate." She pulled far enough away to grab her cell and check the ID. "I gotta get it." She hadn't had an update from her partner since leaving Switzerland. She flipped it open.

"Hey, Tate. Anything new on the Illuminati?"

"Not much." Tate sounded glum. "I just finished filing the report. The case is pretty much dead."

"What?" Carla swung her legs off the bed and sat up, rubbing her tired eyes.

"You heard me. We got the henchmen and bit players,

but none of the Illuminati. We haven't been able to trace them since they implemented that intricate escape plan we hadn't anticipated. As it stands, all we've got is hearsay and circumstantial evidence against Harrington. Practicing the occult is not a crime. I'm guessing he'll walk."

"Damn it," Carla frowned. "What about Paul Lyons? Do you have anything on him?"

"He's gone underground. Both Interpol and the Department of Homeland Security have added him to their terrorist watch lists, but unless he resurfaces and causes more trouble, he's less of a concern right now than the religious terrorists in the Middle East."

"What about Jonathan Carter and Richard Lyons? Are you going to tell me they're free to go about their business?"

"That's the way it goes sometimes, Carla." Tate expelled a long, tired breath. "You know it as well as I do. Sometimes the bad people get away."

"So our mission was a failure."

"I wouldn't say that. We managed to stop one nuclear terrorist incident. That's something, right?"

"Right." Carla hung up and angrily tossed the phone on the bed. The Illuminati was still out there, unstopped.

Mark looked at her curiously. "Why did you ask Tate about my dad?

"He was a member of the Illuminati, wasn't he?"

"What makes you say that?"

"I saw him in Montecito having dinner with your brother and Carter, both deeply involved with the Illuminati, and he was business partners with Carter." She lay back against the pillows and looked at the ceiling. It still felt really weird to think of Jonathan Carter as her father.

"That's a bit of a stretch, isn't it? I can't imagine my dad getting involved in something as unusual as the occult. He's more the country club type." But then Mark looked at her, a perplexed expression crossing his face.

"What is it?"

"I just remembered something. When I was lying on the floor of the dungeon after I'd been shot, someone helped me. He was wearing the Illuminati robes and mask. He took off my mask and hood and put them under my head."

"I saw the same guy. It was smoky and dark in the dungeon, so I couldn't really see what he was doing, but I thought he was going to hurt you, so I chased him off."

"He said something. I was barely conscious, and I wasn't sure I heard him correctly."

"What did he say?"

"He said, 'You'll be all right, son.'" Mark sat up in surprise. "I think that man was my dad. If that's true, that means he was one of the Final Two. He must be either Sorat or Ahriman."

"I'm pretty sure Jonathan Carter was the other guy."

"Why do you think that?"

"Long story, but the real kicker is that he's my father."

"He's your what?" Mark stared at her.

"Jonathan Carter is my father." The words didn't come easily. "He was there last night, too. He saved me from falling into the pit after you got shot. I don't know how he made it in or out of the dungeon unseen by anyone else, but he did."

"Are you sure?"

"My mom told me after Albert took you away. I'm still having trouble believing it." Carla shook her head, remembering the strange man and his hypnotic eyes. Why couldn't her father be someone normal, instead of another occult weirdo?

"I can't believe it, your dad and mine are Sorat and Ahriman!" Mark ran his hands through his hair, making his curls even more tousled.

"So how did you know they were going to show up last night?"

"Someone called and left me an anonymous voicemail

from a restricted phone number. It was a man's voice I didn't recognize."

"It was probably Carter, I mean my father." The word stuck on her tongue. "But why tell you they were coming and not your brother?"

They fell silent, thinking. After a few minutes, Mark looked up thoughtfully.

"My dad's no fool, and neither is the Jonathan Carter I've read about in the press. I bet they discovered what Paul was up to and wanted to stop him. What better way than by warning us, right? That way, they could let Paul hang himself while keeping their hands clean."

Carla considered his theory. It would explain why Carter had warned her about Paul's plans. It was also consistent with what she knew of their characters. Both Richard and Jonathan were savvy and extremely adept in the world of high finance. Neither struck her as foolhardy or crazy enough to stoop to terrorism in their quest for world power.

"I think you're right," she said finally. "They were able to stop Paul and do it without revealing their identities, at least not publicly. Except for our own personal encounters with them in the dungeon, we don't have any concrete proof connecting them to the Illuminati, do we?"

"No, and I'm pretty sure we won't find any, either."

"So then who warned Paul about the raid in New York? We could have caught him then, but someone told him and the others they'd be walking into a trap." She stared accusingly at him.

"You caught me." He held up his hands in mock surrender.

"You're admitting you were the informant?"

"You suspected as much, right?" He put his hands down and leaned back against the pillows. "When you got the intel from Carter about the nukes being in Switzerland, we knew we'd have to let the thing play out. We—"

"When you say 'we' you mean the Phoenix, right?"

Carla interrupted.

"Right," Mark continued. "We had to make sure we'd get possession of the nuclear weaponry and dismantle Paul's arsenal. The only way to ensure we'd be able to do all that was to allow Paul and the rest of the Illuminati to go to Switzerland for the final Offering."

"Why didn't you tell me your plan? I thought we were supposed to be working together as partners." She was too tired to try and keep the hurt from her voice.

"The situation was complicated, really complicated." Mark expelled a deep breath and ran a hand through his hair. "I probably could have handled it better. I'm sorry."

Carla stared up at the ceiling, thinking how Mark's loyalties must have been torn, between his duties to the Phoenix, his love of his brother, and his assignment to partner with her and the CIA—not to mention their own tangled romantic history. Everything was finally becoming clear about him, and she felt a wonderful sense of relief as her doubt melted away.

"Apology accepted." She rolled onto her side and made to drop a light kiss on his cheek.

He anticipated her move, turning and catching her mouth with his own. His free hand wandered up over her bare back and pulled her close to deepen the kiss, but one last thing was still niggling at her. She put a hand on his chest and pushed, breaking off the kiss.

"So who are 'Sorat' and 'Ahriman', the 'Final Two'?"

"Can't we talk about that later?" His eyes were on her bare breasts.

"Now, please," she grinned.

"I don't want to bore you with the finer points of esoteric occultism."

"Try me."

"Ahriman and Sorat play key roles in the cosmology of power developed by a nineteenth century Austrian philosopher named Rudolph Steiner. The current manifestation of the Illuminati adopted many tenets of

Steiner's thoughts about power and evil."

"Do you really believe in all that black magic crap?"

"What is magic, anyway?" He brushed the hair back from her face, caressing her lower lip with his thumb in the process. "Casting spells, performing rituals, holding ceremonies, all to produce desired effects. All of us believe in things we can't see."

His silver eyes dropped to her breasts again, a smile tugging at his lips. "Like the things we can feel. Close your eyes."

She looked at him warily but did as he said.

"Like this?" He whispered his lips over the smooth skin of her breast.

"Like heaven," she writhed in sensual pleasure as his mouth closed over her nipple. She forgot how tired she was and pulled him close.

\#

"This isn't the way to the Magic Shop," Carla noticed as Mark took a right turn out of the small Santa Barbara airport parking lot and headed for the beach. The sun hung low in the late afternoon sky.

"Just a brief detour." Mark smiled mysteriously at her.

They drove the short distance and parked at the far end of the parking lot. Palm trees rustled in the wind and the breeze chopped up white caps on the ocean. The Channel Islands rose in the distance above the marine mist.

Mark took Carla's right hand in his and walked with her onto the sand. "I wanted somewhere that I could talk to you in private."

Goleta in mid-March was not a tourist destination, and except for a distant jogger and another couple strolling further down the beach, they had the place to themselves.

"We had plenty of privacy last night," Carla said.

"We were kind of busy, remember?" He grinned and took her in his arms. "And we were so tired it was hard to think straight."

"I still didn't get enough sleep." She nestled into the

warmth of his arms. The stiff wind off the ocean blew her hair across her face.

"Neither did I," he chuckled, remembering their hours of loving.

They'd had to leave at the crack of dawn to make their flight, and their last minute travel plans had sent them through three different cities with three plane changes to get to Santa Barbara in time for Madeline's birthday party.

"I got a call while you were in the shower this morning." He brushed the hair out of her face. "Honey, I've got to leave tonight after the party and head back to D.C. I've been assigned to a new case."

"What?" She felt the earth plummet out from under her.

"You want to join me? We'd make an awesome team, don't you think?"

She looked up at him. "But you vowed never to become involved with an agent again."

"You're not just any agent."

The love in his eyes made her heart ratchet up a notch. Things had been so crazy she hadn't had time to think about what would come next in their relationship. All she knew was she didn't want him to leave.

"I suggested it to Stan Petersen when he called this morning. He's my boss at the Phoenix. I persuaded him to give us a chance to work together." Mark cupped her face and leaned close. He gazed earnestly into her green eyes. "I can't think of anything better than having you by my side, both day and night, in disguise and out."

"That sounds like heaven," she sighed against him, her heart swelling with joy.

After a moment, he pulled back, his expression serious. "There's something else I've been wanting to ask you, but I have a feeling you'll run the other way, what with our parents' lousy track records."

"What are you talking about?"

"Marriage."

"What?" She pulled away from him, the cold March wind instantly chilling her. "Are you proposing to me?"

The sun was sinking into the ocean. Mark's hair blew wildly around his head. He took her hand in his.

"I love you, Carla. Will you marry me?"

"Oh, yes!"

She wrapped her arms around him and pulled him close again, his body radiating heat and strength and love. They stood together and watched the sun disappear.

"I've got something for you," Mark said several minutes later.

He pulled a small black velvet box from the inner pocket of his leather jacket. He carefully opened it and removed a delicate antique ring, set with a large ruby and several diamonds. "This was my grandmother's. Hard to believe, but she and my grandfather were happily married for over fifty years. Would you like it?"

"It's beautiful." Carla admired the antique as he tried it on her ring finger, but it was too small. She took it from him and slid it onto her pinky. "This works for now."

She stepped back into his arms. She couldn't remember ever being so happy, but she still owed him the truth.

"You've been so honest with me, laying your feelings on the line, Mark. I've got a confession to make."

"Yes?"

"You asked me a while back how I used to feel about you when we knew each other in high school. I didn't want you to know the truth then, because I didn't trust you. I was afraid you'd use my feelings against me."

"What do you mean?"

"I'd never met anyone like you, not then. And I never have since. You were—you are—the most compelling, the most attractive man, I've ever met. I used to hate how much I wanted you."

"What about now?"

"I love you," she said baldly, but then shot him a tart

glance. "Just don't let it go to your head."

"Impossible," he grinned wickedly and kissed her quick and hard. "Now, let's get to that party. We don't have much time."

#

The party was in full swing by the time they entered the brightly lit Magic Shop. All of Circe was there, as well as their husbands and children. Madeline stood against one wall speaking with Moon Ray. The three McCormick sisters were there with Gwen.

"Carla's here!" Tate announced to the crowd. She came forward and hugged Carla. "Hey, the Cota Club is reunited again! I think this calls for a toast."

"Here you go," Izzy said, coming forward and handing Tate and Carla glasses of champagne.

Gwen and Kristi joined them in the middle of the room.

"To the best of friends," Tate toasted.

They all tapped glasses and exchanged hugs, laughing and giggling. It had been years since they'd all been in the same room together. In the mayhem, Carla spilled some of her champagne.

"I guess I'm so happy my cup runneth over," she hooted.

When the hilarity died down, Carla took Tate aside.

"There's something I need to tell you." She spoke quietly to her friend.

"What?"

"It's about Mark and me."

"Oh." Tate's eyes followed Carla's. Mark was at the back of the shop, talking to Madeline. "Wow, I forgot how good-looking he is. You two an item, right?"

"That's just it," Carla said. "He's asked me to join him at the Phoenix."

"Really? That's great," Tate said sincerely.

"You don't mind?"

"Hey, I got stuck behind the desk for most of this

assignment. Maybe when you're off kicking ass for the Phoenix, Frank'll give me the chance to get my hands dirty."

"What's this about getting your hands dirty?" Mark came over.

"Tate, you remember Mark Lyons?" Carla made the introductions.

"How could I forget?" Tate said. "I hear you're stealing my partner."

"I hope that doesn't cause any hard feelings."

"Not at all, but keep an eye on her. She has a tendency to go off half-cocked sometimes," she smiled.

"Half-cocked? We wouldn't want that," he returned her smile with a devilish grin of his own.

Wrapping a hand around Carla's waist, he held her close. "Your mom gave me her approval," he said and dropped a brief kiss on the side of her neck.

"Excellent," she gasped and arched into the kiss, reveling in how good it felt to be with him and to be surrounded by all those she loved.

"Folks, I'd like to make an announcement," Mark spoke to the crowd as he picked up a glass of champagne. He took Carla's free hand in his. "Carla and I are going to get married."

Wild exclamations of joy filled the room.

"My congratulations to you both." Madeline approached. She joined their hands and placed hers on top. "You have my blessing and the blessing of Circe. We will work to keep the both of you safe."

"Thanks, Mom."

What the hell, she thought as she returned her mother's embrace. She may not believe in magic, but blessings of good will couldn't hurt.

"We're going to have to postpone the wedding until after our next assignment," Mark said.

"Just as long as you invite all of us to the wedding," Izzy piped up.

"Of course," Carla laughed. "We wouldn't have it any other way."

"If you need a space for the event, you could use the Magic Shop, right Mom?" Gwen said.

"Just name the date, my dear," Madeline smiled.

"Thanks. Happy birthday, Mom." Carla gave her mom another hug.

Mark touched her on the shoulder. "We've gotta get going. Do you mind?" he asked softly so no one else would hear.

"No, not really. It's just so great to see everyone having such a great time. It'd be fun to hang out a while longer, but if I get any happier than I am at this moment, I'll probably explode," she laughed.

They said their goodbyes on the way to the door.

In the rental car on the way to the airport, she turned to him. "Where are we headed?"

"Tangiers. Tonight."

"But I still gotta call Frank and tell him I'm quitting. I'll also need to be debriefed and hand in my CIA-issued equipment."

"Don't worry about that. You can handle the paperwork later. Stan'll talk to Frank. In the meantime, we need to get our butts to Morocco. A private jet's waiting for us at the airport."

"Why Tangiers?"

"I'll tell you when we're on the plane." He pulled into the small Santa Barbara airport parking lot.

"I can't wait." Her green eyes glittered in the dark.

THE END

ACKNOWLEDGMENTS

Many thanks to Rebecca Douglass and Emily Cooke for their many hours reading, editing and talking over the details of my writing, while enjoying lots of coffee and devouring delicious treats at our favorite cafes. Rebecca's edits in the final read through were invaluable in helping me clean up loose plot threads and tighten the ending. Thank-you, Donna Calia and Stella Kister for encouraging me to resurrect *The Offering* and bring it from hard drive darkness into published light. Stella's photography made my author photo look that much more professional. Annie Kaskade and Karina Fitch kept me sane with lots of hiking and great feedback on the cover. None of my work would be possible without the love and support of my man, my other half, Kurt—whose own offering to me, his kidney, has kept me alive and feeling great as the years roll by.

ABOUT THE AUTHOR

Lisa Frieden grew up in California and spent a few unforgettable years in Santa Barbara. She's read everything from William Shakespeare to Linda Howard and has developed a passion for romantic suspense, in which she finds the perfect blend of love, mystery and suspense to shape her own storytelling. She lives, loves, dreams and writes in the Bay Area. www.lisafrieden.com

LISA FRIEDEN

www.ingramcontent.com/pod-product-compliance
Lightning Source LLC
Chambersburg PA
CBHW031223120726

47905CB00002B/447